William Sloane Kennedy, Samuel Francis Smith

John Greenleaf Whittier

his life, genius, and writings

William Sloane Kennedy, Samuel Francis Smith

John Greenleaf Whittier
his life, genius, and writings

ISBN/EAN: 9783743324336

Manufactured in Europe, USA, Canada, Australia, Japa

Cover: Foto ©Raphael Reischuk / pixelio.de

Manufactured and distributed by brebook publishing software
(www.brebook.com)

William Sloane Kennedy, Samuel Francis Smith

John Greenleaf Whittier

JOHN GREENLEAF WHITTIER

His Life, Genius, and Writings

BY

W. SLOANE KENNEDY

Author of a "Life of Henry Wadsworth Longfellow," Etc.

REVISED AND ENLARGED

INTRODUCTION BY REV. S. F. SMITH, D.D.
Author of Hymn "America"

Such music as the woods and streams
Sang in his ear, he sang aloud
The Tent on the Beach

For all his quiet life flowed on,
As meadow streamlets flow,
Where fresher green reveals alo
The noiseless ways they go
The Friend's Burial

CHICAGO NEW YORK.
THE WERNER COMPANY

INTRODUCTION.

WHO does not admire and love John Greenleaf Whittier? And who does not delight to do him honor? He was a man raised up by Providence to meet an exigency in human history, and an exigency in the experiences of the United States. And he met the exigency with distinguished success. He was a true exponent of New England life and the New England spirit. He drew his inspiration from the soil where he was born, from the necessities of the times, from the demands of human rights, from the love of God and of man. He was a unique man. We knew not his like before him. We shall see no other like him after him. He was the product of his age; and the age in which he lived belonged to him, and he to and In it. He was a unique literary man. He was so meek and retiring; he was so keenly sensitive to the wrongs done by man to man; he was so devoid of self-seeking; so pure and exalted in motive, and so sturdy a defender of the rights of the oppressed; he was so full of trust in God that we seem never to have seen his equal among men. His beautiful gentleness of character and his inflexible and fearless advocacy of the cause of righteousness — even when such advocacy involved persecution and personal harm and loss, a rare combination of qualities — remind us of the sentiment of Oliver Wendell Holmes,

" The gentle are the strong."

If ever in modern days the character of the apostle John has been reproduced among men it was in John G. Whittier. See with what sweetness and meekness the shy and loving Quaker moved through the ranks of society in times of peace and prosperity, and with what an adamantine boldness and bravery he stood up before the mob in Philadelphia when his types and manuscripts were scattered, his printing office burned and himself threatened with personal violence by the foes of human equality and freedom. Did he quail before the storm? Not he. Did he abandon his principles and retire from the arena? Oh, no; no more than did the apostle John — the apostle of love — forsake his Christian faith when the persecutors immersed him in boiling oil and exiled him to a desert island in the Ægean Sea.

The poetry of Mr. Whittier is a complete autobiography. It is a reflection, as in a polished mirror, of himself. We miss only the accidents of dates and places, which are of merely external importance; but we find in his works, amply displayed, the portraiture of the man; even as the architect records himself and his thoughts in his plans, and builds his own soul into his edifices. Read the poetry of Mr. Whittier, and you have no need to ask what kind of man produced it. Behold the portrait: a thorough New England man, a son of its soil and a legitimate product of its institutions; a fruit of the simple education which was open to the people in the times of his youth and manhood;

a philanthropist, loving all righteousness and all men, and scorning all oppression, injustice and iniquity; a stern advocate of human freedom, prepared to fight for it even "to the bitter end;" a bachelor, but having always a sweet and tender side for women; petted by society, but never tempted to swerve from the straight line of his principles; holding the faith of his fathers as a birthright and the result of his honest convictions, but with sympathies as broad as the universe and an appreciation of the privilege of private judgment on religious matters as the right and duty of all men; animated by a patriotism which took in his whole country, but a yearning for his own New England, its people, its scenery, its institutions and its honor; warmly attached to the friends whom he met along the pilgrimage of this life, but preserving to the last the memory and the love of the survivors whom he knew in his school days in the Haverhill Academy; living very much apart from his fellowmen, as he did in his latter days, on account of the increasing infirmities of his age, and absorbed in the world of his own thoughts, yet ever most affable, and as accessible as a most warm-hearted and cordial associate; every inch a man, as in stature, so also in soul, but exhibiting also the simplicity and the loving and confiding spirit of a child ("of such is the kingdom of heaven"); conscious of his human weakness and dependence on a higher Power, as he approached the goal of life, but relying on that higher Power with a sublime courage and a firm faith. How the man stands forth, like an orator on the stage, in the presence of throngs of admiring and reverent spectators! Unconsciously he sets forth in his works, whether they be prose or poetry, an

example of the beauty of righteousness, the charm
of philanthropy, the power and attractiveness of the
broadest charity, the fervor of patriotism and the con-
trolling force of love. The century which is about
to close has been honored and made better, as well as
gladder, by his presence in it. He has enriched its literature. He has elevated its ethics. He has breathed
a divine life into its inspirations. He has warmed its
heart.

Mr. Whittier, like another Wordsworth, glorifies the
scenes of common life, and hallows the landscapes of
his New England homes. His verses speak in the
dialect of the people, and deal with themes with which
they are familiar. He lifts toil above its drudgery,
and sanctifies, as with a sacred glow, the things with
which men in common spheres chiefly have to do. He
admired nature as he saw in it the landscapes which
surrounded his several homes, the rolling green hills
of Haverhill and Bradford, the mighty trees of Oak
Knoll, the flowing stream and graceful curves of the
Merrimack; the sober and quiet graces of Amesbury;
and with his pen he stamped upon them immortality.

The sun has set, but no night follows. The singer
is gone, but his songs remain, and will long be a power
among men far beyond the places adorned and honored
by his personal presence. We love his poems which
on account of their helpfulness the grateful world will
long continue to read. How little he wrote — did he
ever write anything — " which, dying, he could wish
to blot?" and his life was a poem. The seal of Death
is on his virtues, and the seal of universal approval is
on his works.

S. F. SMITH.

CONTENTS.

Identifies Himself with the Anti-Slavery Movement. Publication of his *Brochure*, "Justice and Expediency." Social Martyrdom. Prudence Crandall and her Battle with the Philistinism of Canterbury, Conn. Tailor Woolman and Saddler Lundy. Account of the Philadelphia Convention for the Formation of the American Anti-Slavery Society. Whittier's Account of the Convention. William Lloyd Garrison draws up the Famous Declaration of Principles. Samuel J. May Mobbed at East Haverhill. Whittier and George Thompson Mobbed at Concord, N. H. Story of the Landlord and the Flight by Night. The Poet's Account of the Mobbing of William Lloyd Garrison. Letters of John Quincy Adams. Harriet Martineau on Slavery. Attitude of Whittier toward the Quakers on the Slavery Question.

Removal to Amesbury. Description of the Town and of the Poet's Residence. The Study. Whittier Corresponding Editor of the *National Era*. Various Works Written, including "Stranger in Lowell," " Supernaturalism of New England," " Songs of Labor," "Child-Life," " Child-Life in Prose," "Introduction" to Woolman's Journal, and "Songs of Three Centuries " (Edited). Whittier College Established.

Danvers. Oak Knoll. Summerings of the Poet at the Isles of Shoals and the Bearcamp House. *The Literary World* Tribute, and the Whittier Banquet at the Hotel Brunswick. The Whittier Club. Various Volumes of Poetry Published.

Whittier's Personal Appearance Described by Frederika Bremer, Geo. W. Bungay, David A. Wasson, and others. Incident of his Kind-heartedness to a Stranger. Dom Pedro II. and Whittier at Mrs. John T. Sargent's Reception. Letter to Mrs. Sargent. Humor. Love of Children. Offices of Dignity and Honor.

Part II.

ANALYSIS OF HIS GENIUS AND WRITINGS.

The Moral in Whittier Predominates over the Æsthetic. Love of Freedom the Central Element of his Character. Freedom, Democracy, and Quakerism, links in one Chain. Quakerism Described; Freedom and the Inner Light; Quakerism is Pure Democracy or Christianity, and Pure Individualism, or Philosophical Idealism; it Resembles Transcendentalism; the Details of the Quaker Religion Considered; Quotations from William Penn, Mary Brook, and A. M. Powell; Objections to Quakerism; Beautiful Lives of the Quakers; Whittier's Attitude Toward the Religion of his Fathers. His Religious Development, Doubt, and Trust. Patriotism. Has Blood Militant in his Veins. A Representative American Poet. Summing Up.

Little or no *Technique*. More Fancy than Imagination. The Artistic Quality of his Mind a Fusion of that of Wordsworth and Byron. His Bookish Lore. The Beauty and Melody of his Finest Ballads. His Strength and Nervous Energy. Culmination of his Genius. His Three Crazes. Letters to the *Nation*, and to the American Anti-Slavery Society. Illustrations of the Predominance of the Moral in his Nature. Taine Quoted. Pope-Night. His Over-religiousness. Love of Consecutive Rhymes. Minor Mannerisms. Originality.

Mr. David A. Wasson's Classification of Epochs in the Poet's Development. The Author's Classification. Four Periods: 1st, *Introductory;* 2d, *Storm and Stress;* 3d, *Transition;* 4th, *Religious and Artistic Repose.* General Review of Earlier Productions. The Indian Poems. "Songs of Labor." The Ballad Decade. "Prophecy of Samuel Sewall." John Chadwick on "Skipper Ireson's Ride." The "Barbara Frietchie" Controversy. The Romance of the "Countess." Winter in Poetry. "Snow-Bound." "The Tent on the Beach." Various Poems.

Part III.

TWILIGHT AND EVENING BELL.

APPENDIX.

Part I.

LIFE.

JOHN GREENLEAF WHITTIER.

CHAPTER I.

ANCESTRY.

THE Hermit of Amesbury, the Woodthrush of Essex, the Martial Quaker, the Poet of Freedom, the Poet of the Moral Sentiment, — such are some of the titles bestowed upon Whittier by his admirers. Let us call him the Preacher-Poet, for he has written scarcely a poem or an essay that does not breathe a moral sentiment or a religious aspiration. What effect this predetermination of character has had upon his artistic development shall be discussed in another place.

The present chapter — which may be called the propylæum or vestibule of the biographical structure that follows — will deal with the poet's ancestry, and the information afforded by it, and the two chapters that succeed will afford unmistakable evidence of the truth that a poet, no less than a solar system or a loaf of bread, is the logical resultant of a line of antecedent forces and circumstances. The fine but infrangible threads of our destiny are spun and woven out of atom-fibres indelibly stamped with the previous owners' names. Their characters immingle in our own,—the affluence or the indigence of their intellects, the sugar or the nitre of their wit, the shifting sand or the unwedgeable iron of their moral natures.

The name Whittier is spelled in thirty-two different ways in the old records: a list of these different spellings is given in Daniel Bodwell Whittier's genealogy of the family. The common ancestor of the Whittiers is Thomas Whittier, who in the year 1638 came from Southampton, England, to New England, in the ship "Confidence," of London, John Dobson, master. It is recorded of Thomas Whittier, says his descendant, the poet, in a half facetious way, that the only noteworthy circumstance connected with his coming was that he brought with him a hive of bees. He was born in 1620. His mother was probably a sister of

John and Henry Rolfe, with the former of whom he came to America. His name at that time was spelled "Whittle." He married Ruth Green, and lived at first in Salisbury, Mass. He seems afterward to have lived in Newbury. In 1650 he removed to Haverhill, where he was admitted freeman, May 23, 1666.

It was customary in those days, says the historian of Haverhill, for the nearest neighbors to sleep in the garrisons at night, but Thomas Whittier refused to take shelter there with his family. " Relying upon the weapons of his faith, he left his own house unguarded, and unprotected with palisades, and carried with him no weapons of war. The Indians frequently visited him, and the family often heard them, in the stillness of the evening, whispering beneath the windows, and sometimes saw them peep in upon the little group of practical ' non-resistants.' Friend Whittier always treated them civilly and hospitably, and they ever retired without molesting him."* Thomas Whittier

---

* "The History of Haverhill, Mass.; from its first settlement in 1640 to the year 1860. By George Wingate Chase, Haverhill. Published by the author, 1861."

2

died in Haverhill, November 28, 1696. His autograph appears in the probate records of Salem, Mass., as witness to a will of Samuel Gild.   His widow died in July, 1710, and her eldest son John was appointed administrator of her estate. Thomas had ten children, of whom John became the ancestor of the most numerous branch of the Whittiers. Joseph, the brother of John, became the head of another branch of the family, and is the great-grandfather of our poet. Joseph married Mary, daughter of Joseph Peasley, of Haverhill, by whom he had nine children, among them Joseph, 2d, the grandfather of the poet. Joseph, 2d, married Sarah Greenleaf of Newbury, by whom he had eleven children. The tenth child, John (the father of the poet), married Abigail Hussey, who was a daughter of Joseph Hussey, of Somersworth,—now Rollinsford,—N. H., a town on the Piscataqua River, which forms the southern part of the boundary line between New Hampshire and Maine. The mother of Abigail Hussey (the poet's mother) was Mercy Evans, of Berwick, Me. John Whittier, the father of the poet, died in Haverhill, June 30, 1830. His children were four in number :   (1) **Mary**, born September 3, 1806, married Jacob Caldwell, of Haverhill, and died January 7, 1860; (2) John Greenleaf, the poet, born December 17, 1807, in Haverhill; (3) Matthew Franklin, born July 18, 1812, married Jane E. Vaughan; (4) Elizabeth Hussey, born December 7, 1815, died September 3, 1864.   From this statement it will be seen that Matthew is the only surviving member of the family, besides the poet himself.   Matthew resides in Boston, and has sons, daughters, and grandchildren.*

The name Whittier constantly appears in important documents signed by the chief citizens of Haverhill.   The family was evidently respected and honored by the community.   In 1669 a Whittier was chosen town-constable.   It is recorded that in 1711 Thomas Whittier — probably a son of Thomas (1st) — was one of a militia company provided with snow-shoes in order the

---

* The foregoing statements are taken from the Whittier genealogy.   But the author finds that there are a few slight discrepancies of date between this book and the inscriptions on the family tombstones in Amesbury.   The tombstones say that John Whittier died "11th of 6m.o., 1831," and that Mary died "1st mo. 7, 1861."

better to repel an anticipated attack of the Indians. But, in spite of civil honors, it is well known that, down to comparatively recent times, the family suffered considerable social persecution and slight on account of their religious belief. For example, when the citizens built a new meeting-house, in 1699, they peremptorily refused to allow the Quakers to worship in it, although petitioned to do so by Joseph Peasley and others, and although they were taxed for its support. It was not until 1774 that an act was passed by the State exempting dissenters from taxation for the support of what we may call the State religion. It is important to bear this in mind, if we would know all the influences that went to form the character of the poet.

The poet's paternal grandmother was Sarah Greenleaf, of Newbury. The genealogist of the Greenleafs says: "From all that can be gathered it is believed that the ancestors of the Greenleaf family were Huguenots, who left France on account of their religious principles some time in the course of the sixteenth century, and settled in England. The name was probably translated from the French *Feuillevert*.* Edmund Greenleaf, the ancestor of the American Greenleafs, was born in the parish of Brixham, and county of Devonshire, near Torbay, in England, about the year 1600." He came to Newbury, Mass., in 1635. He was by trade a silk-dyer. Respecting the family coat-of-arms the genealogist gives, on page 116, the following interesting statement: —

"The Hon. William Greenleaf, once of Boston, and then of New Bedford, being in London about the year 1760, obtained from an office of heraldry a device, said to be the arms of the family, which he had painted, and the painting is now in the possession of his grand-daughter, Mrs. Ritchie, of Roxbury, Mass. The field is white (argent), bearing a chevron between three leaves (vert). The crest is a dove standing on a wreath of green and white, holding in its mouth three green leaves. The helmet is that of a warrior (visor down); a garter below, but no motto."

---

* Whittier has thus alluded to this surmise: —
" The name the Gallic exile bore,
St. Malo! from thy ancient mart,
Became upon our Western shore
Greenleaf for Feuillevert."

What more appropriate emblazonment for the escutcheon of our Martial Quaker poet than a warrior's helmet, and a dove holding in its mouth the emblem of peace!

Jonathan Greenleaf, born in Newbury, in 1723, is described as possessing a remarkably kind and conciliatory disposition. "Even the tones of his voice were gentle and persuasive, and he was very frequently resorted to as a peacemaker between contending parties. His dress was remarkably uniform, usually in his later years being deep blue or drab. He seldom walked fast, his gait being a measured and moderate step. His manners were plain, unassuming, but very polite. He was very religious, and a strict Calvinist. Nothing but absolute necessity kept him from public worship on the Sabbath, and he was scarce ever known to omit regular morning and evening worship."

Of Professor Simon Greenleaf, the Harvard Law Professor (1833–1845), the family genealogist says: - "For the last thirty years of his life he was one of the most spiritually-minded of men, evidently intent on walking humbly with God, and doing good to the bodies and souls of his fellow-men; scarce ever writing a letter of friendship even, without breathing in it a prayer, or delivering in it some good message." Professor Greenleaf published some dozen works, both legal and religious. It is a curious fact that his son James married Mary Longfellow, a sister of the Cambridge poet, thus making Whittier and Longfellow distant kinsmen.*

Another English Greenleaf—contemporary with Edmund, being a silk-dyer as well as he, and in all probability a near kinsman—was a lieutenant under Oliver Cromwell, and served also under Richard Cromwell, and was in the army of the Protector under General Monk, at the time of the restoration of Charles II.

It is hardly necessary to call the reader's attention to the significant fact, elicited by the foregoing researches, that, in tracing down two hereditary lines of the poet's

* It may be added that the ancestral home of the Longfellows is still standing in Byfield, about five miles distant from the Whittier homestead in Haverhill. (See the author's Life of Henry Wadsworth Longfellow, p. 15.)

paternal ancestors, we discover that for many generations those ancestors suffered religious persecution for loyalty to their religious convictions, and that many of them were remarkable for their sensitive piety.

Turn we now to the maternal ancestry of Whittier.

In 1873 the poet wrote to Mr. D. B. Whittier, of Boston, as follows: —

"My mother was a descendant of Christopher Hussey, of Hampton, N. H., who married a daughter of Rev. Stephen Bachelor, the first minister of that town.

"Daniel Webster traces his ancestry to the same pair, so Joshua Coffin informed me. Colonel W. B. Greene, of Boston, is of the same family."*

In the light of the preceding note, the following letter of Col. W. B. Greene explains itself: —

"JAMAICA PLAIN, MASS., Sept. 24, 1873.
"Mr. D. B. WHITTIER, Danville, Vt.

"DEAR SIR,— Yours of September 20 is just received, and I reply to it at once.

---

* The name of Daniel Webster's paterna. grandmother was Susannah Bachelor, or Batchelder.

My grandfather, on my mother's side, was the Rev. William Batchelder, of Haverhill, Mass. In the year 1838 I had a conversation, on a matter of military business, with the Hon. Daniel Webster; and, to my astonishment, Mr. Webster treated me as a kinsman. My mother afterwards explained his conduct by telling me that one of Mr. W.'s female ancestors was a Batchelder. In 1838 or 1839, or thereabouts, I met schoolmaster [Joshua] Coffin on a Mississippi steamboat, near Baton Rouge. The captain of the boat told me, confidentially, that Coffin was engaged in a dangerous mission respecting some slaves, and inquired whether my aid and countenance could be counted on in favor of Coffin, in case violence should be offered him. This he did because I was on the boat as a military man, and in uniform. When Coffin found he could count on me, he came and talked with me, and finally told me he had [once] been hired by Daniel Webster *to go to Ipswich*, and there look up Mr. W.'s ancestry. He spoke of Rev. Stephen Batchelder, of New Hampshire, and said that Daniel Webster, John G. Whittier, and myself were related by Batchelder blood. I did not feel at all ashamed of my relatives. In 1841 or 1842 Mrs. Crosby, of Hallowell, Me., who had charge of my grandfather when he was a boy, and knew all about the family, told me that Daniel Webster was a Batchelder, that she had known his father intimately, and knew Daniel when he was a boy. At the time of my conversation with her, Aunt Crosby might have been anywhere from seventy-five to eighty-five years of age. When I was a boy, at (say) about the year 1827 or 1828, I used to go often to the house of J. G. Whittier's father, a little out of the village (now city) of Haverhill, Mass. There was a Mrs. Hussey in the family, who baked the best squash pies I ever ate, and knew how to make the pine floors shine like a looking-glass.

"This is, I think, all the information, in answer to your request, that I am competent to give you.

"Yours respectfully,

"WILLIAM BATCHELDER GREENE."

In a note addressed to the New England Historical and Genealogical Society, the poet says: "On my mother's side **my** grandfather was Joseph Hussey, of Somersworth, N. H.; married Mercy Evans, of Berwick, Me."

Some of the genealogical links connecting the Husseys of Somersworth with those of Hampton have not yet been recovered. But this much is known of the family,* that in 1630 Christopher Hussey came from Dorking, Surrey, England, to Lynn, Mass. He had married, in Holland, Theodate, the daughter of the Rev. Stephen Bachiler, a Puritan minister, who had fled to that country to avoid persecution in England. The author was told by a local antiquary in Hampton, N. H., that there is a tradition in the town that Stephen Bachiler would not let his daughter marry young Hussey unless he embraced the Puritan faith. His love was so great that he consented, and came with his bride to America, where two years later his father-in-law followed him. Stephen Bachiler came to Lynn in 1632, with six persons, his relatives and friends, who had belonged to his church in Holland, and with them he established a little inde-

* See histories of Lynn and Newbury, *passim.*

pendent church in Lynn. The progenitive
faculty of this worthy divine must have
been highly developed: he was married
four times, and was dismissed from his
church at Lynn on account of charges twice
preferred against him by women of his congregation. The recorded dates show that
both he and his son-in-law, Hussey, came
to Hampton in the year 1639. The Hampton authorities had the previous year made
Mr. Bachiler and Mr. Hussey each a grant
of three hundred acres of land, to induce
them to settle there. When and how the
Husseys became Quakers is not known to
the author. But in Savage's Genealogical
Dictionary, II. 507, it is recorded that as
early as 1688 a certain John Hussey of
Hampton was a preacher to the Quakers in
Newcastle, Del. The mother of the poet
was a devoted disciple of the Society of
Friends. That she was a person of deep
and tender religious nature is evident to
one looking at the excellent oil-portrait of
her which hangs in the little parlor at Amesbury. The head is inclined graciously to
one side, and the face wears that expression
of ineffable tranquillity which is always a

witness to generations of Quaker ancestry. In the picture, her garments are of smooth and immaculate drab. The poet once remarked to the writer that one of the reasons why his mother removed to Amesbury, in 1840, was that she might be near the little Friends' "Meeting" in that town.

Thus among the maternal as well as the paternal progenitors of our Quaker poet we find the religious nature predominant.

CHAPTER II.

THE VALLEY OF THE MERRIMACK.

IN the valley of the Merrimack John Greenleaf Whittier was born (December 17, 1807), and in the same region he has passed nearly his entire life, first in the town of Haverhill, and then in Amesbury, some nine miles distant. To strangers, the hilly old county of Essex wears a somewhat bleak and Scotian look; but it is fertile in poetical resources, and the tillers of its glebe are passionately attached to its blue hills and sunken dales, its silver rivers and winding roads, umbrageous towns and thrifty homes. Like Burns and Cowper, Whittier is distinctively a rustic poet, and he and Whitman are the most indigenous and patriotic of our singers. His idyllic poetry savors of the soil and is full of local allusions. It is, therefore, essential to the full enjoyment of his writings that one should get, at the outset, as vivid an idea as possible both of the Essex landscape and the Essex farmer.

Whittier was born some three miles northeast of what is now the thriving little city of Haverhill. It was settled in 1640 by twelve men from Newbury and Ipswich. Its Indian name was Pentucket,— the appellation of a tribe once dwelling on its site, a tribe under the jurisdiction of Passaconaway, chief of the Pennacooks. The city is built partly on the river-terrace of the northern shore, and partly on the adjoining hills. It is celebrated in colonial history for the heroic exploit of Hannah Duston, who, when taken captive by a party of twenty savages at the time of the Haverhill massacre, killed and scalped them all, with the aid of her companion (also a woman), and returned in safety to the settlement. A handsome monument has recently been erected to her memory in the city square; it is a granite structure, with bronze bas-reliefs, and surmounted by a bronze statue of the heroine. In the public library of the city (founded in 1873) may be seen a fine bust of Whittier, by Powers. On February 17 and 18, 1882, almost the entire business portion of the city was destroyed by fire; eight acres were burned over, and $2,000,000 worth of property destroyed. Haverhill is eighteen miles east of Lowell, thirty-two miles northwest of Boston, and six miles northeast of Lawrence. The manufacture of boots and shoes gives employment to 6,000 men. The population in 1870 was 13,092.

Down to the sea, some seventeen miles away, winds the beautiful Merrimack, with the deep-shaded old town of Newburyport seated at its mouth. A little more than half way down lies Amesbury, just where the winding Powwow joins the Merrimack, but not before its nixies and river-horses have been compelled to put their shoulders to the wheels of several huge cotton mills that lift their forbidding bulk out of the very centre of the village. A horse-railroad connects Amesbury with Newburyport, six miles distant. At about half that distance the road crosses the Merrimack by way of Deer Island and connecting bridges. The sole house on this wild, rough island is the home of the Spoffords.

As you near Newburyport, coming down

from Amesbury, you see the river widened into an estuary, and bordered by wide and intensely green salt-meadows. Numerous large vessels lie at the wharves, a "gundelow," with lateen sail, creeps slowly down the current; the draw of the railroad bridge is perhaps opening for the passage of a tug, and out at sea athwart the river's mouth —

> " Long and low, with dwarf trees crowned,
> Plum Island lies, like a whale aground,
> A stone's toss over the narrow sound."
> *Prophecy of Samuel Sewall.*

Far off to the left lie Salisbury and Hampton beaches, celebrated by Whittier in his poems "Hampton Beach," "Snow-Bound," and "The Tent on the Beach":—

> " Where Salisbury's level marshes spread
> Mile-wide as flies the laden bee ;
> Where merry mowers, hale and strong,
> Swept, scythe on scythe, their swaths along
> The low green prairies of the sea."
> *Snow-Bound.*

Standing on the sand-ridge by the beach, you have before you the washing surf, and miles on miles of level sand, rimmed with creeping, silver water-lace, overhung here and there by thinnest powdery mist. Out

3

at sea the waves are tossing their salt-threaded manes, or flinging the sunlight from their supple coats — (æonian roar; white-haired, demoniac shapes)— while at evening you see far away to the northeast the revolving light of the Isles of Shoals.

> "Quail and sandpiper and swallow and sparrow are here;
>   Sweet sound their manifold notes, high and low, far
>   and near;
>   Chorus of musical waters, the rush of the breeze,
>   Steady and strong from the south, — what glad voices
>   are these!"

So sings the poet of the Isles of Shoals, Celia Thaxter, who, it is said, was discovered and introduced to the world by Whittier,— her rocky home being still one of his favorite summer resorts.

Landward, your gaze sweeps the beautiful salt-meadows and rests on the woods beyond, or reaches still farther to the steeples of Newburyport rising sculpturesquely in the pellucid atmosphere, and often at evening filling the air with faint silver hymns that chime with the liquid undertone of the pouring surf.

The valley of the Merrimack with the surrounding region, is, or was until recently, full of legends of the marvellous and the supernatural, which, in this remote and isolated corner of the State, have come down in unbroken tradition from earlier times. One of the distinguishing peculiarities of Whittier's genius is his story-telling power, and since he has not only written many poems about the legends of his native province, but also published in his youth two small collections of those legends in prose form, it will be proper to give the reader a taste of them, both here and elsewhere in the volume, and thus assist him to an understanding of our poet's early environment.

.The following extracts from his " Supernaturalism of New England," published in the year 1847, are germane to the subject in hand : —

"One of my earliest recollections," he says, " is that of an old woman residing at Rocks Village, in Haverhill, about two miles from the place of my nativity, who for many years had borne the unenviable reputation of a witch. She certainly had the look of one,— a combination of form, voice,

and features, which would have made the
fortune of an English witch-finder in the
days of Matthew Paris or the Sir John Pod-
gers of Dickens, and insured her speedy
conviction in King James' High Court of
Justiciary. She was accused of divers ill-
doings, such as preventing the cream in her
neighbor's churn from becoming butter, and
snuffing out candles at huskings and quilt-
ing parties. The poor old woman was at
length so sadly annoyed by her unfortunate
reputation, that she took the trouble to go
before a Justice of the Peace, and made a
solemn oath that she was a Christian woman
and no witch."

"Some forty years ago, on the banks of
the pleasant little creek separating Berwick,
in Maine, from Somersworth, in New Hampshire, within sight of my mother's home,
dwelt a plain, sedate member of the Society
of Friends, named Bantum. He passed,
throughout a circle of several miles, as a
conjurer and skilful adept in the art of
magic. To him resorted farmers who had
lost their cattle, matrons whose household
gear, silver spoons, and table-linen had been

stolen, and young maidens whose lovers were absent; and the quiet, meek-spirited old man received them all kindly, put on his huge, iron-rimmed spectacles, opened his 'conjuring book,' which my mother describes as a large clasped volume, in strange language and black-letter type, and after due reflection and consideration gave the required answers without money and without price. The curious old volume is still in possession of the conjurer's family. Apparently inconsistent as was this practice of the Black Art with the simplicity and truthfulness of his religious profession, I have not been able to learn that he was ever subjected to censure on account of it."

This incident reminds one of some verses in a poem of Whittier's entitled " Flowers in Winter": —

"A wizard of the Merrimack—
    So old ancestral legends say —
Could call green leaf and blossom back
    To frosted stem and spray.

The dry logs of the cottage wall,
    Beneath his touch, put out their leaves;
The clay-bound swallow, at his call,
    Played round the icy eaves.

> The settler saw his oaken flail
>   Take bud, and bloom before his eyes;
> From frozen pools he saw the pale,
>   Sweet summer lilies rise.
>
> .   .   .   .
>
> The beechen platter sprouted wild,
>   The pipkin wore its old-time green;
> The cradle o'er the sleeping child
>   Became a leafy screen."

In chapter second of the "Supernaturalism" we have a whimsical story about a certain "Aunt Morse," who lived in a town adjoining Amesbury: —

"After the death of Aunt Morse no will was found, though it was understood before her decease that such a document was in the hands of Squire S., one of her neighbors. One cold winter evening, some weeks after her departure, Squire S. sat in his parlor, looking over his papers, when, hearing some one cough in a familiar way, he looked up, and saw before him a little crooked old woman, in an oil-nut colored woollen frock, blue and white tow and linen apron, and striped blanket, leaning her sharp, pinched face on one hand, while the other supported a short black tobacco pipe, at which she was puffing in the most vehement and spiteful manner conceivable.

"The squire was a man of some nerve; but his first thought was to attempt an escape, from which he was deterred only by the consideration that any effort to that effect would necessarily bring him nearer to his unwelcome visitor.

"'Aunt Morse,' he said at length, 'for the Lord's sake, get right back to the burying-ground! What on earth are you here for?'

"The apparition took her pipe deliberately from her mouth, and informed him that she came to see justice done with her will; and that nobody need think of cheating her, dead or alive. Concluding her remark with a shrill emphasis, she replaced her pipe, and puffed away with renewed vigor. Upon the squire's promising to obey her request, she refilled her pipe, which she asked him to light, and then took her departure."

"Elderly people in this region," says our author, "yet tell marvellous stories of General M., of Hampton, N. H., especially of his league with the devil, who used to visit him occasionally in the shape of a small man in a leathern dress. The general's house was once burned, in revenge, as it is said, by the fiend, whom the former had outwitted. He had agreed, it seems, to furnish the general with a boot full of gold and silver poured annually down the chimney. The shrewd Yankee cut off, on one occasion, the foot of the boot, and the devil kept pouring down the coin from the chimney's top, in a vain attempt to fill it, until the room was literally packed with the precious metal. When the general died, he was laid out, and put in a coffin, as usual; but, on the day of the funeral, it was whispered about that his body was missing; and the neighbors came to the charitable conclusion that the enemy had got his own at last."

It should be understood that the state of society which produced such superstitions and legends as the foregoing lingers now only in secluded corners of New England. The railroad, the newspaper, and the influx of foreign population, have combined to frighten away ghost, conjurer, and witch, or to drive them up into the mountainous districts. There are still plenty of quaint and picturesque old Puritan farmers; and their

mythology is antique and rusty enough, to
be sure. But the folk-lore of the early days,
—where is it? Let the shriek of the steam-
demon answer, or that powerful magician,
the " Spirit of the Age," who, ten thousand
times divided, and slyly hidden in plethoric
leathern mail bags, daily rushes into the remotest nooks and corners of the land, there
to enter into the nooks and corners of the
mind of man. The " Spirit of the Age " has
exorcised the spirits of the ingle and the
forest.

CHAPTER III.

BOYHOOD.

THE birthplace and early home of Whittier is a lonely farm-house situated at a distance of three miles northeast of the city of Haverhill, Mass. The winding road leading to it is the one described in "Snow-Bound." A drive or a walk of one mile brings you to sweet Kenoza Lake, with the castellated stone residence of Dr. J. R. Nichols crowning the summit of the high hill that overlooks it. From the hill the eye sweeps the horizon in every direction to a distance of fifty or a hundred miles. Far to the northwest rise bluely the three peaks of Monadnock. Nearer at hand, in the same direction, the towns of Atkinson and Strafford whiten the hillsides, while southward, through a clove in the hills, one catches a glimpse of the smoky city of Lawrence.

Two other lakes besides Kenoza lie

WHITTIER'S BIRTHPLACE, NEAR HAVERHILL, MASS.

in the immediate vicinity: namely, Round Lake and Lake Saltonstall. Kenoza is the lake in which Whittier used to fish and boat. It was he who gave to it its present name (meaning pickerel): he wrote a very pretty poem for the day of the rechristening, in 1859. The lake lies in a bowl-shaped depression. The country thereabouts seems entirely made up of huge earth-bowls, here open to the sky, and there turned bottom-upwards to make hills.

No prettier, quieter, lovelier lake than Kenoza exists, — a pure and spotless mirror, reflecting in its cool, translucent depths the rosy clouds of morning and of evening, the silver-azure tent of day, the gliding boat, the green meadow-grasses, and the massy foliage of the terraced pines and cedars that sweep upward from its waters in stately pomp, rank over rank, to meet the sky. Here, in one quarter of the lake, the surface is only wrinkled by the tiniest wavelets or crinkles; yonder, near another portion of its irregularly picturesque shore, a thousand white sun-butterflies seem dancing on the surface, and the loveliest wind-dapples curve and gleam. Along the shore are sweet wild roses interpleached, and flower-de-luce, and yellow water-lilies. In such a circular earth-bowl the faintest sounds are easily heard across the water. Far off you hear the cheery cackle of a hen; in the meadows the singing of insects, the chattering of blackbirds, and the cry of the peewee; and the ring of the woodman's axe floats in rippling echoes over the water.

In one of his earlier essays Mr. Whittier tells the following romantic story: "Whoever has seen Great Pond, in the East Parish of Haverhill, has seen one of the very loveliest of the thousand little lakes or ponds of New England. With its soft slopes of greenest verdure — its white and sparkling sand-rim — its southern hem of pine and maple, mirrored with spray and leaf in the glassy water — its graceful hill-sentinels round about, white with the orchard-bloom of spring, or tasselled with the corn of autumn — its long sweep of blue waters, broken here and there by picturesque headlands, — it would seem a spot, of all others, where spirits of evil must shrink, rebuked and abashed, from the presence of the beautiful. Yet here, too, has the shadow of the supernatural fallen. A lady of my acquaintance, a staid, unimaginative church-member, states that a few years ago she was standing in the angle formed by two roads, one of which traverses the pond-shore, the other leading over the hill which rises abruptly from the water. It was a warm summer evening, just at sunset. She was startled by the appearance of a horse and cart of the kind used a century ago in New England, driving rapidly down the steep hillside, and crossing the wall a few yards before her, without noise or displacing of a stone. The driver sat sternly erect, with a fierce countenance; grasping the reins tightly, and looking neither to the right nor the left. Behind the cart, and apparently lashed to it, was a woman of gigantic size, her countenance convulsed with a blended expression of rage and agony, writhing and struggling, like Laocoön in the folds of the serpent." The mysterious cart moved across the street, and disappeared at the margin of the pond.

The two miles of road that separate Kenoza from the old Whittier homestead form a lonely stretch, passing between high hills rolled back on either side in wolds that show against the sky. The homestead is situated at the junction of the main road to Amesbury and a cross-road to Plaistow. It is as wild and lonely a place as Craigen-puttock, — the hills shutting down all around, so that there is absolutely no prospect in any direction, and no other house visible. But so much the better for meditation. "The Children of the Light" need only their own souls to commune with. The expression that rose continually to the author's lips on visiting this place was a line from "Snow-Bound,"—

> "A universe of sky and snow."

Not that the time was winter, but that the locality explained the line so vividly,—better than any commentary could do. Locality exercises a great influence on a poet's genius. Whitman, for example, has always lived by the sea, and he is the poet of the infinite. Whittier was born, and passed his boyhood and youth, in a green, sunken pocket of the inland hills, and he became the poet of the heart and the home. The one poet wrestled with the waves of the sea and the waves of humanity in great cities; the other lived the simple, quiet life of a farmer, loving his mother, his sister, his Quaker sect, freedom, and his own hearth. Both are as lowly in origin as Carlyle or Burns.

Between the front door of the old homestead and the road rises a grassy, wooded bank, at the foot of which flows a little amber-colored brook. The brook is mentioned in " Snow-Bound ": —

> "We minded that the sharpest ear
> The buried brooklet could not hear,
> The music of whose liquid lip
> Had been to us companionship,
> And, in our lonely life, had grown
> To have an almost human tone."

Across the road is the barn. The house is very plain, and not very large. Entering the front door you are in a small entry with a steep, quaint, little staircase. On the right is the parlor where Whittier wrote. In the tiny, low-studded room on the left, he was born, and in the same room his father and "Uncle Moses" died. The room is about fourteen by fourteen feet, is partly wainscoted, has a fireplace and three windows.

All the windows in the house have small panes, nine in the upper and six in the lower sash. The building is supposed to be two hundred and twelve years old. The kitchen is, of course, the great attraction. Let us suppose that it is winter, and that we are all cosily seated around the blazing fireplace. Now, let us talk over together the old days and scenes. The best picture of the inner life of the Quaker farmer's family can of course be had in " Snow-Bound,"— a little idyl as delicate, spontaneous, and true to nature in its limnings as a minute frost-picture on a pane of glass, or the fairy landscape richly mirrored in the film of a water-bubble. After such a picture, painted by the poet himself, it only remains for the writer to give a few supplementary touches here and there. The old kitchen, although diminished in size by a dividing partition, is otherwise almost unchanged. It is a cosey old room, with its fireplace, and huge breadth of chimney with inset cupboards and oven and mantelpiece. Above

the mantel is the nail where hung the old
bull's-eye watch. Set into one side of the
kitchen is the cupboard where the pewter
plates and platters were ranged; and here
upon the wall is the circle worn by the "old
brass warming-pan, which formerly shone
like a setting moon against the wall of the
kitchen": —

"Shut in from all the world without,
We sat the clean-winged hearth about,
Content to let the north-wind roar
In baffled rage at pane and door,
While the red logs before us beat
The frost-line back with tropic heat;
And ever, when a louder blast
Shook beam and rafter as it passed,
The merrier up its roaring draught
The great throat of the chimney laughed,
The house-dog on his paws outspread,
Laid to the fire his drowsy head,
The cat's dark silhouette on the wall
A couchant tiger's seemed to fall;
And, for the winter fireside meet,
Between the andirons' straddling feet,
The mug of cider simmered slow,
The apples sputtered in a row,
And, close at hand, the basket stood
With nuts from brown October's wood."

Snow-Bound.

John Whittier, the father of the poet, is described by citizens of Haverhill as being a rough but good, kind-hearted man. He went by the soubriquet of "Quaker Whycher." In "Snow-Bound," we learn something of his *Wanderjahre,*—how he ate moose and samp in trapper's hut and Indian camp on Memphremagog's wooded side, and danced beneath St. François' hemlock-trees, and ate chowder and hake-broil at the Isle of Shoals. He was a sturdy, decisive man, and deeply religious. Although there was no Friends' church in Haverhill, yet on "First-Days" Quaker Whycher's "one-hoss shay" could be seen wending toward the old brown meeting-house in Amesbury, six miles away.

The mother has been alluded to in Chapter I. p. 12. Hers was a deeply emotional and religious nature, pure, chastened, and sweet, lovable, and kind-hearted to a fault. In "Snow-Bound," she tells incidents of her girlhood in Somersworth on the Piscataqua, and retells stories from Quaker Sewell's "ancient tome," and old sea-saint Chalkley's Journal. An incident in Mr.

KITCHEN IN THE WHITTIER HOMESTEAD, HAVERHILL.

"Our own warm hearth seemed blazing free." —SNOW BOUND.

Whittier's "Yankee Gypsies" (Prose Works, II. p. 326,) will afford an indication of her kind-heartedness: —

"On one occasion," says the poet, "a few years ago, on my return from the field at evening, I was told that a foreigner had asked for lodgings during the night, but that, influenced by his dark, repulsive appearance, my mother had very reluctantly refused his request. I found her by no means satisfied with her decision. 'What if a son of mine was in a strange land?' she inquired, self-reproachfully. Greatly to her relief, I volunteered to go in pursuit of the wanderer, and, taking a cross-path over the fields, soon overtook him. He had just been rejected at the house of our nearest neighbor, and was standing in a state of dubious perplexity in the street. His looks quite justified my mother's suspicions. He was an olive-complexioned, black-bearded Italian, with an eye like a live coal, such a face as perchance looks out on the traveller in the passes of the Abruzzi,— one of those bandit-visages which Salvator has painted. With some difficulty, I gave him to understand my errand, when he

overwhelmed me with thanks, and joyfully
followed me back.   He took his seat with us
at the supper-table; and when we were all
gathered around the hearth that cold au-
tumnal evening, he told us, partly by words,
and partly by gestures, the story of his life
and misfortunes, amused us with descriptions
of the grape-gatherings and festivals of his
sunny clime, edified my mother with a
recipe for making bread of chestnuts; and
in the morning when, after breakfast, his
dark sullen face lighted up and his fierce eye
moistened with grateful emotion as in his
own silvery Tuscan accent he poured out
his thanks, we marvelled at the fears which
had so nearly closed our doors against him;
and, as he departed, we all felt that he had
left with us the blessing of the poor.

"It was not often that, as in the above instance, my mother's prudence got the better
of her charity.   The regular 'old stragglers' regarded her as an unfailing friend;
and the sight of her plain cap was to them
an assurance of forthcoming creature comforts."

In "Snow-Bound," too, we learn that the

good mother often stayed her step to express
a warm word of gratitude for their own comforts, and to hope that the unfortunate might
be cared for also. It is a facetious saying in
Philadelphia that beggars are shipped to that
city from all parts of the country that they
may share the never-failing bounty of the
Quakers. However this may be, it is evident that benevolence was the predominant
trait in the character of our poet's mother.

Other members of the household in Whittier's boyhood were his elder sister Mary,
who died in 1861; Uncle Moses Whittier,
who in 1824 received fatal injuries from the
falling of a tree which he was cutting down;
the poet's younger brother Matthew, who
was born in 1812, and has been for many
years a resident of Boston,— himself a versifier, and a contributor to the newspapers
of humorous dialect articles, signed " Ethan
Spike, from Hornby "; and finally the aunt,
Mercy E. Hussey, the younger sister Elizabeth, and occasionally the " half-welcome "
eccentric guest, Harriet Livermore.

Elizabeth Hussey Whittier—the younger
sister and intimate literary companion of her

brother, the poet — was a person of rare and saintly nature. In the little parlor of the Amesbury home there hangs a crayon sketch of her. The face wears a smile of unfailing sweetness and patience. That her literary and poetical accomplishments were of an unusually high order is shown by the poems of hers appended to Mr. Whittier's "Hazel Blossoms," published after her death. Her poem, "Dr. Kane in Cuba," would do honor to any poet. In the piece entitled the "Wedding Veil," we have a hint of an early love transformed by the death of its object into a spiritual worship and hope, nourished in the still fane of the heart. In the prefatory note to "Hazel Blossoms," Mr. Whittier says: "I have ventured, in compliance with the desire of dear friends of my beloved sister, Elizabeth H. Whittier, to add to this little volume the few poetical pieces which she left behind her. As she was very distrustful of her own powers, and altogether without ambition for literary distinction, she shunned everything like publicity, and found far greater happiness in generous appreciation of the gifts of her friends than in the cultivation of her own.

Yet it has always seemed to me that, had her health, sense of duty and fitness, and her extreme self-distrust permitted, she might have taken a high place among lyrical singers. These poems, with perhaps two or three exceptions, afford but slight indications of the inward life of the writer, who had an almost morbid dread of spiritual and intellectual egotism, or of her tenderness of sympathy, chastened mirthfulness, and pleasant play of thought and fancy, when her shy, beautiful soul opened like a flower in the warmth of social communion. In the lines on Dr. Kane, her friends will see something of her fine individuality,— the rare mingling of delicacy and intensity of feeling which made her dear to them. This little poem reached Cuba while the great explorer lay on his death-bed, and we are told that he listened with grateful tears while it was read to him by his mother.

"I am tempted to say more, but I write as under the eye of her who, while with us, shrank with painful deprecation from the praise or mention of performances which seemed so far below her ideal of excellence. To those who best knew her, the beloved circle of her intimate friends, I dedicate this slight memorial."

Many readers of "Snow-Bound" have doubtless often wondered who the beautiful and mysterious young woman is who is sketched in such vigorous portraiture,— "the not unfeared, half-welcome guest," half saint and half shrew. She is no other than the religious enthusiast and fanatical "pilgrim preacher," Harriet Livermore,* the same who startled

> "On her desert throne
> The crazy Queen of Lebanon
> With claims fantastic as her own."

By the "Queen of Lebanon" is meant Lady Hester Stanhope. Harriet Livermore was the grand-daughter of Hon. Samuel Livermore, of Portsmouth, N. H., and the daughter of Hon. Edward St. Loe Livermore, of Lowell. She was born April 14, 1788, at Concord, N. H. Her misfortune was her temper, inherited from her father. When Whittier was a little boy, she taught needlework, embroidery, and the common school

---

* For many items of information concerning this strange woman we are indebted to the sketch of her published by Miss Rebecca I. Davis, of East Haverhill.

branches, in the little old brown school-house in East Haverhill, and was a frequent guest at Farmer Whittier's. The poet thus characterizes her: —

> " A certain pard-like, treacherous grace
>   Swayed the lithe limbs and dropped the lash,
>   Lent the white teeth their dazzling flash ;
>   And under low brows, black with night,
>   Rayed out at times a dangerous light ; ·
>   The sharp heat-lightnings of her face
>   Presaging ill to him whom Fate
>   Condemned to share her love or hate.
>   A woman tropical, intense
>   In thought and act, in soul and sense."

When a mere girl, she fell in love with a young gentleman of East Haverhill, but the parents of both families opposed the match, and were not to be moved by her honeyed words of persuasion or by her little gifts. The poet says she often visited at his father's home, " and had at one time an idea of becoming a member of the Society of Friends; but an unlucky outburst of rage, resulting in a blow, at a Friend's house in Amesbury, did not encourage us to seek her membership." She embraced the Methodist Perfectionist doctrine, and one day strenuously maintained that she was incapable of sinning.

But a few minutes afterward she burst out into a violent passion about something or other. Her opponent could only say to her, "Christian, thou hast lost thy roll." She became an itinerant preacher, and spoke in the meetings of various sects in different parts of the country. She made three voyages to Jerusalem. Says one: "At one time we find her in Egypt, giving our late consul, Mr. Thayer, a world of trouble from her peculiar notions. At another we see her amid the gray olive slopes of Jerusalem, demanding, not begging, money for the Great King [God]. And once when an American, fresh from home, during the late rebellion, offered her a handful of greenbacks, she threw them away with disdain, saying, 'The Great King will only have gold.' She once climbed the sides of Mt. Libanus, and visited Lady Stanhope,— that eccentric sister of the younger Pitt, who married a sheik of the mountains,— and thus had a fine opportunity of securing the finest steeds of the Orient. Going to the stable one day, Lady Hester pointed out to Harriet Livermore two very fine horses, with peculiar marks, but differing in color. 'That one,' said Lady Hester, 'the Great King when he comes will ride, and the other I will ride in company with him.' Thereupon Miss Livermore gave a most emphatic 'no!' declaring with foreknowledge and *aplomb* that 'the Great King will ride this horse, and it is I, as his bride, who will ride upon the other at his second coming.' It is said she carried her point with Lady Hester, overpowering her with her fluency and assertion."

To pass now to the boy-poet himself. An old friend and schoolmate of his, in Haverhill, told the author that Whittier, instead of doing sums on his slate at school, was always writing verses, even when a little lad. His first schoolmaster was Joshua Coffin, afterward the historian of Newbury. Another master of his was named Emerson. To Coffin, Whittier has written a poetical epistle, in which he says:—

> "I, the urchin unto whom,
>   In that smoked and dingy room,
>   Where the district gave thee rule
>   O'er its ragged winter school,
>   Thou didst teach the mysteries
>   Of those weary A, B, C's,—

> Where, to fill the every pause
> Of thy wise and learned saws,
> Through the cracked and crazy wall
> Came the cradle-rock and squall,
> And the goodman's voice, at strife
> With his shrill and tipsy wife, —
> Luring us by stories old,
> With a comic unction told,
> More than by the eloquence
> Of terse birchen arguments
> (Doubtful gain, I fear), to look
> With complacence on a book! —
>
> I, — the man of middle years,
> In whose sable locks appears
> Many a warning fleck of gray, —
> Looking back to that far day,
> And thy primal lessons, feel
> Grateful smiles my lips unseal," etc.

In "School Days" he gives us another and a pleasanter picture:—

> "Still sits the school-house by the road,*
>   A ragged beggar sunning;
> Around it still the sumachs grow,
>   And blackberry-vines are running.
>
> Within, the master's desk is seen,
>   Deep scarred by raps official;
> The warping floor, the battered seats,
>   The jack-knife's carved initial;

* The old brown school-house is now no more, having been removed to make room for a reservoir.

THE OLD SCHOOLHOUSE, HAVERHILL, MASS.

The charcoal frescos on its wall;
　Its door's worn sill, betraying
The feet that, creeping slow to school
　Went storming out to playing !

Long years ago a winter sun
　Shone over it at setting;
Lit up its western window-panes,
　And low eaves' icy fretting.

It touched the tangled golden curls,
　And brown eyes full of grieving,
Of one who still her steps delayed
　When all the school were leaving.

For near her stood the little boy
　Her childish favor singled :
His cap pulled low upon a face
　Where pride and shame were mingled.

Pushing with restless feet the snow
　To right and left, he lingered; —
As restlessly her tiny hands
　The blue-checked apron fingered.

He saw her lift her eyes; he felt
　The soft hand's light caressing,
And heard the tremble of her voice,
　As if a fault confessing.

'I 'm sorry that I spelt the word:
　I hate to go above you,
Because,' — the brown eyes lower fell, —
　'Because, you see, I love you !'"

It is probable that "My Playmate" is in memory of this same sweet little lady: —

"O playmate in the golden time!
Our mossy seat is green,
Its fringing violets blossom yet,
The old trees o'er it lean.

The winds so sweet with birch and fern
A sweeter memory blow;
And there in spring the veeries sing
The song of long ago.

And still the pines of Ramoth Wood
Are moaning like the sea, —
The moaning of the sea of change
Between myself and thee!"

Elsewhere in the poem we are told that the little maiden went away forever to the South: —

"She lives where all the golden year
Her summer roses blow;
The dusky children of the sun
Before her come and go.

There haply with her jewelled hands
She smooths her silken gown, —
No more the homespun lap wherein
I shook the walnuts down."

We also learn from the poem that he was the boy "who fed her father's kine." What

a pretty little romance!—and, let us hope,
not too sad a one. Shall we have one more
stanza about this lovely little school-idyl?
It is from "Memories":—

> "I hear again thy low replies,
>   I feel thy arm within my own,
>   And timidly again uprise
>   The fringèd lids of hazel eyes,
>   With soft brown tresses overblown.
>   Ah! memories of sweet summer eves,
>   Of moonlit wave and willowy way,
>   Of stars and flowers, and dewy leaves,
>   And smiles and tones more dear than they!"

The reading material that found its way
to Farmer Whittier's house consisted of the
almanac, the weekly village paper, and
"scarce a score" of books and pamphlets,
among them Lindley Murray's "Reader":—

> "One harmless novel, mostly hid
>   From younger eyes, a book forbid,
>   And poetry (or good or bad,
>   A single book was all we had),
>   Where Ellwood's meek, drab-skirted Muse,
>   A stranger to the heathen Nine,
>   Sang, with a somewhat nasal whine,
>   The wars of David and the Jews."

Knowing, as we do, the great influence
exerted upon our mental development by

the books we read as children, and knowing that a rural life, such as Whittier's has been, is especially conducive to tenacity of early customs, it becomes important to know what the books were that first formed his style and colored his thought. It seems that Ellwood's "Davideis; or the Life of David, King of Israel," was one of these. The book was published in 1711, and had a sale of five or more editions. Ellwood, born in 1639, early adopted the then new doctrines of George Fox. He has written a quaint and pictorial autobiography, somewhat like that of Bunyan or that of Fox. In 1662 he was for six weeks reader to Milton, who was then blind, and living in London, in Jewin Street. It was he who first suggested to Milton that he should write "Paradise Regained." *

* This was in 1665, when Milton was living at Giles-Chalfont. Ellwood says: "After some common discourse had passed between us, he called for a manuscript of his, which he delivered to me, bidding me take it home with me and read it at my leisure; and, when I had done so, return it to him with my judgment thereon." It was "Paradise Lost." When Ellwood returned it, and was asked his opinion, he gave it, and added: "'Thou hast said much here of "Paradise Lost," but what hast thou to say of "Paradise Found"?' He made no answer, but sat some time in a muse."

An idea of the execrable nature of his versification may be obtained from a few specimens. Upon the passing of a severe law against Quakers, he relieves his mind in this wise: —

> "Awake, awake, O arm o' th' Lord, awake!
>   Thy sword up take;
> Cast what would thine forgetful of thee make,
>   Into the lake.
> Awake, I pray, O mighty Jah! awake,
> Make all the world before thy presence quake,
> Not only earth, but heaven also shake."

Another poem, entitled "A Song of the Mercies and Deliverances of the Lord," begins thus: —

> "Had not the Lord been on our side,
>   May Israel now say,
> We were not able to abide
>   The trials of that day:
>
> When men did up against us rise,
>   With fury, rage, and spite,
> Hoping to catch us by surprise,
>   Or run us down by night."

An opponent's poetry is lashed by Ellwood in such beautiful stanzas as the following: —

> "So *flat*, so *dull*, so *rough*, so *void of grace*,
> Where *symphony* and *cadence* have no place;
> So full of *chasmes* stuck with *prosie pegs*,
> Whereon his *tired* Muse might rest her legs,
> (Not having wings) and take new breath, that then
> She might with much adoe hop on again."

A striking peculiarity of Whittier's poetry is the exceedingly small range of his rhymes and metres. He is especially fond of the four-foot iambic line, and likes to rhyme successive or alternate lines in a wofully monotonous and see-saw manner. These are the characteristics of much of the lyric poetry of a hundred years ago, and especially distinguish the verses of Burns and Ellwood, —the first poets the boy Whittier read. Burns, especially, he learned by heart, and there can be no doubt that the Ayrshire ploughman gave to the mind of his brother-ploughman of Essex its life-direction and coloring,— as respects the swing of rhythm and rhyme at least. Indeed, we shall presently find him contributing to the *Haverhill Gazette* verses in the Scotch dialect. His introduction to the poetry of Burns was in this wise: He was one afternoon gathering in hay on the farm, when by good hap a wandering peddler stopped and took from his pack a copy of Burns, which was eagerly purchased by the poetical Quaker boy. Alluding to the circumstance afterward in his poem, "Burns," he says:—

> "How oft that day, with fond delay,
>   I sought the maple's shadow,
> And sang with Burns the hours away,
>   Forgetful of the meadow!
>
> Bees hummed, birds twittered, overhead
>   I heard the squirrels leaping,
> The good dog listened while I read,
>   And wagged his tail in keeping."

By the reading of Burns his eyes were opened, he says, to the beauty in homely things. In familiar and humble things he found the "tender idyls of the heart." But the wanton and the ribald lines of the Scotch poet found no entrance to his pure mind.*

He had other relishing tastes of the rich dialect of heather poetry. In "Yankee Gypsies" he says: "One day we had a call from a 'pawky auld carle' of a wandering Scotchman. To him I owe my first introduction to the songs of Burns. After eating

* See Appendix II.

his bread and cheese and drinking his mug of cider, he gave us Bonny Doon, Highland Mary, and Auld Lang Syne. He had a rich full voice, and entered heartily into the spirit of his lyrics. I have since listened to the same melodies from the lips of Dempster (than whom the Scottish bard has had no sweeter or truer interpreter); but the skilful performance of the artist lacked the novel charm of the gaberlunzie's singing in the old farm-house kitchen."

A page or two of these personal recollections of the poet will serve to fill out the picture of his boyhood life; and, at the same time, give the reader a taste of his often charming prose pieces:—

"The advent of wandering beggars, or 'old stragglers,' as we were wont to call them, was an event of no ordinary interest in the generally monotonous quietude of our farm life. Many of them were well known; they had their periodical revolutions and transits; we could calculate them like eclipses or new moons. Some were sturdy knaves, fat and saucy; and whenever they ascertained that the 'men-folks' were absent would order provisions and cider like men who expected to pay for them, seating themselves at the hearth or table with the air of Falstaff,—'Shall I not take mine ease in mine own inn?' Others poor, pale, patient, like Sterne's monk, came creeping up to the door, hat in hand, standing there in their gray wretchedness, with a look of heart-break and forlornness which was never without its effect on our juvenile sensibilities. At times, however, we experienced a slight revulsion of feeling when even these humblest children of sorrow somewhat petulantly rejected our proffered bread and cheese, and demanded instead a glass of cider.

.　　.　　.　　.　　.

"One — I think I see him now, grim, gaunt, and ghastly, working his way up to our door — used to gather herbs by the wayside, and call himself doctor. He was bearded like a he-goat, and used to counterfeit lameness, yet when he supposed himself alone would travel on lustily, as if walking for a wager. At length, as if in punishment for his deceit, he met with an accident in his rambles, and became lame in earnest, hobbling ever after with difficulty on his gnarled crutches. Another used to go stooping, like Bunyan's pilgrim, under a pack made of an old bed-sacking, stuffed out into most plethoric dimensions, tottering on a pair of small, meagre legs, and peering out with his wild, hairy face from under his burden, like a big-bodied spider. That 'man with the pack' always inspired me with awe and reverence. Huge, almost sublime in its tense rotundity, the father of all packs, never laid aside and never opened, what might there not be within it! With what flesh-creeping curiosity I used to walk round about it at a safe distance, half expecting to see its striped covering stirred by the motions of a mysterious life, or that some evil monster would leap out of it, like robbers from Ali Baba's jars, or armed men from the Trojan horse!"

.　　.　　.　　.　　.

"Twice a year, usually in the spring and autumn, we were honored with a call from Jonathan Plummer, maker of verses, peddler and poet, physician and parson,— a Yankee Troubadour,— first and last minstrel of the valley of the Merrimack, encircled to my wondering eyes with the very nimbus of immortality. He brought with him pins, needles, tape, and cotton thread for my mother; jack-knives, razors, and soap for my father; and verses of his own composing, coarsely printed and illustrated with rude woodcuts, for the delectation of the younger branches of the family. No love-sick youth could drown himself, no deserted maiden bewail the moon, no rogue mount the gallows, without fitting memorial in Plummer's verses. Earthquakes, fires, fevers and shipwrecks he regarded as personal favors from Providence, furnishing the raw material of song and ballad. Welcome to us in our country seclusion as Autolycus to the clown in Winter's Tale, we listened with infinite satisfaction to his readings of his own verses, or to his ready improvisation upon some domestic incident or topic suggested by his auditors. When once fairly over the difficulties at the outset of a new subject, his rhymes flowed freely, ' as if he had eaten ballads, and all men's ears grew to his tunes.' His productions answered, as nearly as I can remember, to Shakespeare's description of a proper ballad,

—'doleful matter merrily set down, or a very pleasant theme sung lamentably.'   He was scrupulously conscientious, devout, inclined to theological disquisitions, and withal mighty in Scripture.   He was thoroughly independent; flattered nobody, cared for nobody, trusted nobody.   When invited to sit down at our dinner-table, he invariably took the precaution to place his basket of valuables between his legs for safe-keeping. 'Never mind thy basket, Jonathan,' said my father, 'we shan't steal thy verses.'   'I'm not sure of that,' returned the suspicious guest.   'It is written, Trust ye not in any brother.' "

"Thou, too, O Parson B.,— with thy pale student's brow and thy rubicund nose, with thy rusty and tattered black coat, overswept by white flowing locks, with thy professional white neckcloth scrupulously preserved, when even a shirt to thy back was problematical,— art by no means to be overlooked in the muster-roll of vagrant gentlemen possessing the *entrée* of our farm-house.   Well do we remember with what grave and dignified courtesy he used to step over its threshold, saluting its inmates with the same air of gracious condescension and patronage with which in better days he had delighted the hearts of his parishioners. Poor old man! He had once been the admired and almost worshipped minister of the largest church in the town, where he afterwards found support in the winter season as a pauper. He had early fallen into intemperate habits, and at the age of threescore and ten, when I remember him, he was only sober when he lacked the means of being otherwise."

Among the books read by Whittier when a boy we must number the "Pilgrim's Progress" of Bunyan.

In his "Supernaturalism of New England" the poet says: "How hardly effaced are the impressions of childhood! Even at this day, at the mention of the Evil Angel, an image rises before me like that with which I used especially to horrify myself in an old copy of 'Pilgrim's Progress.' Horned, hoofed, scaly, and fire-breathing, his caudal extremity twisted tight with rage, I remember him illustrating the tremendous encounter of

Christian in the valley where 'Apollyon straddled over the whole breadth of the way.' There was another print of the enemy which made no slight impression upon me; it was the frontispiece of an old, smoked, snuff-stained pamphlet (the property of an elderly lady, who had a fine collection of similar wonders, wherewith she was kind enough to edify her young visitors), containing a solemn account of the fate of a wicked dancing party in New Jersey, whose irreverent declaration that they would have a fiddler, if they had to send to the lower regions after him, called up the fiend himself, who forthwith commenced playing, while the company danced to the music incessantly, without the power to suspend their exercise until their feet and legs were worn off to the knees! The rude woodcut represented the Demon Fiddler and his agonized companions literally *stumping* it up and down in 'cotillions, jigs, strathspeys, and reels.'"

. So grew up the Quaker farmer's son, drinking eagerly in such knowledge as he could, and receiving those impressions of

nature and home-life which he was afterward to embody in his popular lyrics and
idyls. Above all, his home education saturated his mind with religious and moral
earnestness. In the second part of this volume will be given some remarks on Quaker
life in America, and an analysis of the
blended influence of Quakerism and Puri-
tanism upon the development of Whittier's
genius. Enough has been said to show that
the surroundings of his early life were of
the plainest and simplest character, and not
different from those of a thousand other
secluded New England farms of the period.

We are now to follow the shy young poet
out into the world. He is nineteen years of
age. The circle of his experiences begins
to widen outward; manhood is dawning;
the village paper has taught him that there
are men beyond the mountains. He thirsts
for individuality,— to know his powers, to
cast the horoscope of his future, and see if
the consciousness within him of unusual gifts
be a trustworthy one. To begin with, he
will write a poem for "our weekly paper."
Accordingly one day in 1826 the following
poem, written in blue ink on coarse paper,

6

was slipped by the postman under the door of the office of the *Free Press*, in Newburyport,— a short-lived paper, then recently started by young William Lloyd Garrison, and subscribed for by Farmer Whittier.

The poem is the first ever published by the poet, and is his earliest known production.* The manuscript of it is now in the possession of Whittier's kinsman, Mr. S. T. Pickard, associate editor of the *Portland Transcript*, in which journal it was republished November 27, 1880:—

THE DEITY.

The Prophet stood
On the high mount and saw the tempest-cloud
Pour the fierce whirlwind from its reservoir
Of congregated gloom.   The mountain oak
Torn from the earth heaved high its roots where once
Its branches waved.   The fir-tree's shapely form
Smote by the tempest lashed the mountain side ;
Yet, calm in conscious purity, the seer
Beheld the awful devastation, for
The Eternal Spirit moved not in the storm.

The tempest ceased.   The caverned earthquake burst
Forth from its prison, and the mountain rocked
Even to its base : The topmost crags were thrown
With fearful crashing down its shuddering slopes.
Unawed the Prophet saw and heard : He felt
Not in the earthquake moved the God of Heaven.

* See note on p. 301.

The murmur died away, and from the height,
Torn by the storm and shattered by the shock,
Rose far and clear a pyramid of flame,
Mighty and vast! The startled mountain deer
Shrank from its glare and cowered beneath the shade:
The wild fowl shrieked; yet even then the seer
Untrembling stood and marked the fearful glow —
For Israel's God came not within the flame.

The fiery beacon sank. A still small voice
Now caught the Prophet's ear. Its awful tone,
Unlike to human sound, at once conveyed
Deep awe and reverence to his pious heart.
Then bowed the holy man; his face he veiled
Within his mantle, and in meekness owned
The presence of his God, discovered not in
The storm, the earthquake, or the mighty flame,
But in the still small whisper to his soul.

It is characteristic of the man that his
first poem should be of a religious nature.
There is grandeur and majesty in the poem.
The rhetoric is juvenile, but the diction is
strong, nervous, and intense, and the general
impression made upon the mind is one of harmony and solemn stateliness, not unlike that
of "Thanatopsis," composed by Bryant when
he was about the same age as was Whittier
when he wrote "The Deity." It was probably owing to its anonymity that the first
impulse of the editor was to throw it into

the waste-basket. But as he glanced over the sheet his attention was caught: he read it, and some weeks afterward published it in the poet's corner. But in the interval of waiting the boy's heart sank within him. Every writer knows what he suffered. Did we not all expect that first precious production of ours to fairly set the editor wild with enthusiasm, so that nothing short of death or apoplexy could prevent him from assigning it the most conspicuous position in the *very next issue* of his paper?

But one day, as our boy-poet was mending a stone fence along the highway, in company with Uncle Moses, along came the postman on horseback, with his leathern bag of mail, like a magician with a Fortunatus' purse; and, to save the trouble of calling at the house, he tossed a paper to young Whittier. He opened it with eager fingers, and behold! his poem in the place of honor. He says that he was so dumfounded and dazed by the event that he could not read a word, but stood there staring at the paper until his uncle chided him for loitering, and so recalled him to his senses. Elated by his success, he of course sent other poems to the *Free Press.* They attracted the attention of Garrison so strongly that he inquired of the postman who it was that was sending him contributions from East Haverhill. The postman said that it was a "farmer's son named Whittier." Garrison decided to ride over on horseback, a distance of fifteen miles, and see his contributor. When he reached the farm, Whittier was at work in the field, and when told that there was a gentleman at the house who wanted to see him, he felt very much like "breaking for the brush," no one having ever called on him in that way before. However, he slipped in at the back door, made his toilet, and met his visitor, who told him that he had power as a writer, and urged him to improve his talents. The father came in during the conversation, and asked young Garrison not to put such ideas into the mind of his son, as they would only unfit him for his home duties. But, fortunately, it was too late: the spark of ambition had been fanned into a flame. Years afterward, in an introduction to Oliver Johnson's "William Lloyd Garrison and his Times," Mr. Whittier said: " My acquaintance with him

[Garrison] commenced in boyhood. My father was a subscriber to his first paper, the *Free Press*, and the humanitarian tone of his editorials awakened a deep interest in our little household, which was increased by a visit he made us. When he afterwards edited the *Journal of the Times*, at Bennington, Vt., I ventured to write him a letter of encouragement and sympathy, urging him to continue his labors against slavery, and assuring him that he could do great things." Indeed, the acquaintance thus begun ripened into the most intimate friendship and mutual respect. Mr. Whittier told the writer that when he went to Boston, in the winter of 1828–29, he and Garrison roomed and boarded at the same house. Mr. Whittier frequently contributed to the *Liberator*, and was for a quarter of a century associated with Garrison in anti-slavery labors.

Before we pass with our young Quaker from the farm to the world at large, let us correct an erroneous statement that has been made about him. It has been said that he worked at the trade of shoemaking when a boy. The truth is that almost every farmer in those days was accustomed to do a little cobbling of his own, and what shoemaker's work Whittier performed was done by him solely as an amateur in his father's house.

In the year of his *début* as a poet (1826), he being then nineteen years of age, Whittier began attending the Haverhill Academy, or Latin School. Whether his parents were influenced to take this step for his advantage by the visit of the editor Garrison, and by his evident taste for learning, is not positively known, but it is quite possible that such was the case. In 1827 he read an original ode at the dedication of the new Academy. The building is still standing on Winter Street. While at the Academy he read history very thoroughly, and his writings show that it has always been a favorite study with him. He also contributed poems at this time to the *Haverhill Gazette*. Many of them were in the Scotch dialect: it would be interesting to see a few of these; but unfortunately no file of the *Gazette* for those years can be found. A friendly rival in the writing of Scotch poems was good Robert Dinsmore, the "Farmer Poet of Windham," as Whittier calls him. A few specimens of Farmer Dinsmore's verse have been preserved. Take this on "The Sparrow" : —

> "Poor innocent and hapless Sparrow!
>   Why should my moul-board gie thee sorrow?
>   This day thou'll chirp, and mourn the morrow
>   Wi' anxious breast;
>   The plough has turned the mould'ring furrow
>   Deep o'er thy nest!
>
> Just i' the middle o' the hill
> Thy nest was placed wi' curious skill,
> There I espied thy little bill
>   Beneath the shade.
> In that sweet bower, secure frae ill,
>   Thine eggs were laid.
>
> Five corns o' maize had there been drappit,
> An' through the stalks thy head was pappit,
> The drawing nowt could na be stappit
>   I quickly foun',
> Syne frae thy cozie nest thou happit,
>   Wild fluttering roun'.
>
> The sklentin stane beguiled the sheer,
> In vain I tried the plough to steer,
> A wee bit stumpie i' the rear
>   Cam 'tween my legs,
> An' to the jee-side gart me veer
>   An' crush thine eggs."

.   .   .   .

The following elegiac stanza, written by honest Robert on the occasion of the death of his wife, is irresistibly ludicrous:—

> "No more may I the Spring Brook trace,
>   No more with sorrow view the place
>   Where Mary's wash-tub stood;
>   No more may wander there alone,
>   And lean upon the mossy stone,
>   Where once she piled her wood.
> 'T was there she bleached her linen cloth,
>   By yonder bass-wood tree;
> From that sweet stream she made her broth,
>   Her pudding and her tea."

Mr. Whittier says that the last time he saw Robert, "Threescore years and ten, to use his own words,

> 'Hung o'er his back,
> And bent him like a muckle pack,'

yet he still stood stoutly and sturdily in his thick shoes of cowhide, like one accustomed to tread independently the soil of his own acres,— his broad, honest face seamed by care and darkened by exposure to all the 'airts that blow,' and his white hair flowing in patriarchal glory beneath his felt hat. A genial, jovial, large-hearted old man, simple as a child, and betraying neither in look nor manner that he was accustomed to

> 'Feed on thoughts which voluntary move
> Harmonious numbers.'"

CHAPTER IV.

EDITOR AND AUTHOR: FIRST VENTURES.

THE winter of 1828–29 was passed by Whittier in Boston. He once with characteristic modesty told the writer that he drifted into journalism that winter, as editor of the *American Manufacturer*, in the following way: He had gone to Boston to study and read. He undertook the writing for the *Manufacturer* not because he had much liking for questions of tariff and finance, but because his own finances would thereby be improved. Mr. Whittier's chief personal trait is extreme shyness and distrust of himself, and he deprecated the idea that he had any special power as a writer at the time of which we are speaking, saying that he had to study up his subjects before writing. But undoubtedly he must have wielded a vigorous pen, and been known to possess a cool and careful

head, or he would not have been invited to
assume the editorship of such a paper. He
himself admitted,. in the course of the conversation, that at that time he had political
ambitions, and made a study of political
economy and civil politics.

In 1830 we find Whittier at Haverhill
again. In March of that year he was occu-
pying the position of editor of the *Essex
Gazette*, and " issued proposals to publish a
' History of Haverhill,' in one volume of
two hundred pages, duodecimo, price
eighty-seven and one-half cents per copy.
' If the material swelled the volume
above two hundred pages, the price
was to be one dollar per copy.'" But
the limited encouragement offered, and the
amount of work required to compile the
volume, led the young editor to abandon the
project. Whittier was editor of this *Gazette* for six months,—from January 1 to
July 10, 1830. On May 4, 1836, after he
had returned from Philadelphia, he resumed
the editorship of the journal, retaining the
position until December 17 of the same year.

He left the *Gazette* at the time of his
first connection with it, to go to Hartford

for the purpose of editing the *New England Weekly Review* of that city. His
first acquaintance with this Connecticut
periodical had been made while attending the
Academy at Haverhill. While there he
happened to see a copy of the *Review*, then
edited by George D. Prentice. He was
pleased with its sprightly and breezy tone,
and sent it several articles. Great was his
astonishment on finding that they were
accepted and published with editorial com-
mendation. He sent numerous other contributions during the same year.

One day in 1830, he was at work in the
field, when a letter was brought to him from
the publishers of the Hartford paper, in
which they said that they had been asked
by Mr. Prentice to request him to edit the
paper during the absence of Mr. Prentice
in Kentucky, whither he had gone to write
a campaign life of Henry Clay. "I could
not have been more utterly astonished," said
Mr. Whittier once, "if I had been told that
I was appointed prime minister to the great
Khan of Tartary."

Mr. Whittier was at this time a member

of the National Republican party. He afterward belonged to the anti-slavery Liberty party, a faction of the Abolitionists which had separated from the Garrison band. In 1855 Mr. Whittier acted with the Free Democratic party. In the conversation alluded to a moment ago, the poet laughingly remarked that the proprietors of the paper had never seen him when he went to Hartford in 1830 to take charge of their periodical. They were much surprised at his youth. But at the first meeting he discreetly kept silence, letting them do most of the talking. Here most assuredly, if never again, his Quaker doctrine of silence stood him in good stead; since, if we may believe him, he was most wofully deficient in a knowledge of the intricacies of the political situation of the time.

Whittier was twenty-four years old when he published his first volume. It is a thin little book entitled "Legends of New England" (Hartford: Hanmer and Phelps, 1831), and is a medley of prose and verse. The style is juvenile and extravagantly rhetorical, and the subject-matter is far from being massive with thought. The libretto has been suppressed by its author, and it would be ungracious as well as unjust to criticise it at any length, or quote more than a single morsel of its verses, which are inferior to the prose. But one may be pardoned for giving two or three specimens of the prose stories, for they are intrinsically interesting. In the preface we have a striking passage, which may be commended to those who accuse Whittier of hatred of the Puritan fathers, and undue partiality toward the Quakers. He says: "I have in many instances alluded to the superstition and bigotry of our ancestors, the rare and bold race who laid the foundation of this republic; but no one can accuse me of having done injustice to their memories. A son of New England, and proud of my birthplace, I would not willingly cast dishonor upon its founders. My feelings in this respect have already been expressed in language which I shall be pardoned, I trust, for introducing in this place: —

> Oh! — never may a son of thine,
> Where'er his wandering steps incline,
> Forget the sky which bent above
> His childhood like a dream of love,

> The stream beneath the green hill flowing,
> The broad-armed tree above it growing,
> The clear breeze through the foliage blowing:
> Or hear unmoved the taunt of scorn,
> Breathed o'er the brave New England born;
> Or mark the stranger's jaguar hand
>   Disturb the ashes of thy dead —
> The buried glory of a land
>   Whose soil with noble blood is red,
>   And sanctified in every part,
> Nor feel resentment, like a brand,
>   Unsheathing from his fiery heart!"

The flow of language in these prose pieces is smooth and easy, and the narratives are in the same vein and style as the "Twice Told Tales," or Irving's stories, only they are very much weaker than these, and more extravagant and melodramatic in tone. "The Midnight Attack" describes the adventure of Captain Harmon and thirty Eastern rangers on the banks of the Kennebec River in June, 1722. A party of sleeping Indians are surprised by them and all shot dead by one volley of balls. An idea of the style of the piece will be obtained from the following paragraphs. The men are waiting for the signal of Harmon:—

"'Fire!' he at length exclaimed, as the sight of his piece interposed full and distinct between his eye and the wild scalp-lock of the Indian. 'Fire, and rush on!'

"The sharp voice of thirty rifles thrilled through the heart of the forest. There was a groan—a smothered cry—a wild and convulsive movement among the sleeping Indians; and all again was silent.

"The rangers sprang forward with their clubbed muskets and hunting knives; but their work was done. The red men had gone to their audit before the Great Spirit; and no sound was heard among them save the gurgling of the hot blood from their lifeless bosoms."

It was one of the superstitions of the New England colonists that the rattlesnake had the power of charming or fascinating human beings. Whittier's story, "The Rattlesnake Hunter," is based upon this fact. An old man with meagre and wasted form is represented as devoting his life to the extermination of the reptiles among the hills and mountains of Vermont, the inspiring motive of his action being the death of his young and beautiful wife, many years previously, from the bite of a rattle-snake.

"The Human Sacrifice" relates the escape of a young white girl from the hands of the Matchit-Moodus, an Indian tribe formerly dwelling where East Haddam now stands. The Indians are frightened from their purpose of sacrificing the girl by a rumbling noise proceeding from a high hill near by. In his note on the story Mr. Whittier says: "There is a story prevalent in the neighborhood, that a man from England, a kind of astrologer or necromancer, undertook to rid the place of the troublesome noises. He told them that the sound proceeded from a carbuncle — a precious gem, *growing in the bowels of the rock.* He hired an old blacksmith shop, and worked for some time with closed doors, and at night. All at once the necromancer departed, and the strange noises ceased. It was supposed he had found the precious gem, and had fled with it to his native land." This story of the carbuncle reminds us of Hawthorne's story on the same subject.

The following remarks are prefixed to the poem, "The Unquiet Sleeper": "Some fifty or sixty years since an inhabitant of ——, N. H., was found dead at a little distance from his dwelling, which he left in the morning in perfect health. There is a story prevalent among the people of the neighborhood that, on the evening of the day on which he was found dead, strange cries are annually heard to issue from his grave! I have conversed with some who really supposed they had heard them in the dead of the night, rising fearfully on the autumn wind. They represented the sounds to be of a most appalling and unearthly nature."

"The Spectre Ship" is the versification of a legend related in Mather's "Magnalia Christi." A ship sailed from Salem, having on board "a young man of strange and wild appearance, and a girl still younger, and of surpassing beauty. She was deadly pale, and trembled even while she leaned on the arm of her companion." They were supposed by some to be demons. The vessel was lost, and of course soon reappeared as a spectre-ship.

Mr. Whittier's next work was the editing, in 1832, of the "Remains" of his gifted friend, J. G. C. Brainard. Students of Whittier's poems know that for many years the genius and writings of Brainard exercised a potent influence on his mind. Brainard undoubtedly possessed genius. He was at one time editor of the *Connecticut Mirror.* He died young, and his work can be considered as hardly more than a promise of future excellence. Whittier, in his Introduction to the "Remains," shows a nice sense of justice, and a delicate reserve in his eulogistic estimate of his dead brother-poet and friend. That he did not falsely attribute to him a rare genius will be evident to those who read the following portion of Brainard's spirited ballad of "The Black Fox": —

> " ' How cold, how beautiful, how bright
>   The cloudless heaven above us shines ;
> But 'tis a howling winter's night,—
>   'Twould freeze the very forest pines.
>
> ' The winds are up while mortals sleep ;
>   The stars look forth while eyes are shut ;
> The bolted snow lies drifted deep
>   Around our poor and lonely hut.

'With silent step and listening ear,
  With bow and arrow, dog and gun,
We'll mark his track, for his prowl we hear,
  Now is our time — come on, come on.'

O'er many a fence, through many a wood,
  Following the dog's bewildered scent,
In anxious haste and earnest mood,
  The Indian and the white man went.

The gun is cock'd, the bow is bent,
  The dog stands with uplifted paw;
And ball and arrow swift are sent,
  Aim'd at the prowler's very jaw.

— The ball, to kill that fox, is run
  Not in a mould by mortals made!
The arrow which that fox should shun
  Was never shap'd from earthly reed!

The Indian Druids of the wood
  Know where the fatal arrows grow —
They spring not by the summer flood,
  They pierce not through the winter snow!"*

---

* Mr. Whittier quotes this fine ballad in Vol. II. p. 243 of his prose works, but with numerous changes of punctuation and phrase. The differences between the poem as it there appears and as it is given in his own edition of Brainard. published in 1832, seem to show that he has amended the ballad and punctuated it to suit himself, or else has quoted it from memory, or at third or fourth remove. It must be admitted that the changes are all improvements, however they were made. The ballad is quoted above, however, as it appears in Brainard's Poems.

Whittier's Introduction to Brainard's poems reveals a mind matured by much reading and thought. We hardly recognize in the author and editor of Hartford the shy girlish boy we so recently left on the farm at Haverhill. There has evidently been a good deal of midnight oil burned since then.

The following sentiments respecting the resources and the proper field of the American poet show that thus early had Whittier taken the manly and patriotic resolution to find in his native land the chief sources of poetic inspiration: "It has been often said that the New World is deficient in the elements of poetry and romance; that its bards must of necessity linger over the classic ruins of other lands; and draw their sketches of character from foreign sources, and paint Nature under the soft beauty of an Eastern sky. On the contrary, New England is full of romance; and her writers would do well to follow the example of Brainard. The great forest which our fathers penetrated, the red men, their struggle and their disappearance, the powwow and the war-dance, the savage inroad and the English sally, the tale of superstition and the scenes of witchcraft,— all these are rich materials of poetry. We have, indeed, no classic vale of Tempe, no haunted Parnassus, no temple gray with years, and hallowed by the gorgeous pageantry of idol worship, no towers and castles over whose moonlight ruins gathers the green pall of the ivy; but we have mountains pillaring a sky as blue as that which bends over classic Olympus, streams as bright and beautiful as those of Greece and Italy, and forests richer and nobler than those which of old were haunted by sylph and dryad."

It is easy to see here a foreshadowing of "Mogg Megone," "The Bridal of Pennacook," the "Supernaturalism of New England," and a hundred poems and ballads of Whittier's founded on native themes. The sentiments in the quotation just made remind one of Emerson's "Nature," the preface of Whitman to his first portentous quarto, "Leaves of Grass," and Wordsworth's essay on the nature of the poetic art. But however laudable was the Quaker poet's resolve to choose indigenous subjects, it cannot be said that either he or Bryant attained to more than an indigeneity of theme. In form and style they are imitative.   Emerson and Whitman are our only purely original poets.

Whittier was editor of the *New England Weekly Review* for about eighteen months, at the end of which time he returned to the farm at Haverhill, and engaged in agricultural pursuits for the next five or six years.   In 1831 or 1832 he published "Moll Pitcher," a tale of the Witch of Nahant. This youthful poem seems to have completely disappeared, and Mr. Whittier will no doubt be devoutly thankful that the writer has been unable to procure a copy.

CHAPTER V.

WHITTIER THE REFORMER.

*" God said: ' Break thou these yokes ; **undo***
These heavy burdens.   I ordain
A work to last thy whole life through,
A ministry of strife and pain.

' Forego thy dreams of 'cttered ease,
Put thou the scholar's promise by,
The rights of man are more than these.'
He heard, and answered: 'Here am I!'"
WHITTIER, *Sumner.*

ON New Year's day of 1831 William Lloyd Garrison issued the first number of the *Liberator* from his little attic room, No. 6 Merchants' Hall, Boston. Its clear bugle-notes sounded the onset of reform and the death-knell of slavery. It called for the buckling on of moral armor. Its words were the touchstone of wills, the shibboleth of souls. Cowards and time-servers quickly ranged themselves on one side, and heroes on the other. Before young Whittier,—editor, *littérateur,* and poet,— a career full of brilliant promise had opened up at Hartford. But through the high chambers of his soul the voice of duty rang in solemn and imperative tones. He heard and obeyed. The cost was counted, and his resolution taken. Upon his brow he placed the lustrous fire-wreath of the martyr, well assured of his power to endure unflinchingly to the end its sharpest pains. It was the most momentous act of his life; it formed the keystone in the arch of his destinies.

The first decided anti-slavery step taken by him was the publication of his fiery philippic, "Justice and Expediency." About this time also he began the writing of his stirring anti-slavery poems, many of them full of pathos, fierce invective, cutting irony and satire, — stirring the blood like a trumpet-call, giving impulse and enthusiasm to the despised and half-despairing Abolitionists of that day, and becoming a part of the very religion of thousands of households throughout the land.

It is almost impossible for those who were not participants in the anti-slavery conflict, or who have not read histories and memoirs of the struggle, to realize the deep opprobrium that attached to the word "Abolitionist." To avow one's self such meant in many cases suspicion, ostracism, hunger, blows, and sometimes death. It meant, in short, self-renunciation and social martyrdom. All this Whittier gladly took upon himself; and he knew that it was a long struggle upon which he was entering. As he says in one of his poems, he was

> "Called from dream and song,
> Thank God! so early to a strife so long,
> That, ere it closed, the black, abundant hair
> Of boyhood rested silver-sown and spare
> On manhood's temples."

That the martyrdom was a severe one to all who took up the cross goes without saying. Mr. Whittier remarked to the writer that it was at some sacrifice of his ambition and plans for the future that he decided to throw in his lot with the opponents of slavery. He knew that it meant the annihilation of his hopes of literary preferment, and the exclusion of his articles from the pages of magazines and newspapers. "For twenty years," said he, "my name would have injured the circulation of any of the literary or political journals of the country."

When Whittier joined the ranks of the despised faction, Garrison had been imprisoned and fined in Baltimore for his arraignment of the slave traffic; Benjamin Lundy had been driven from the same city by threats of imprisonment and personal outrage; Prudence Crandall was waging her battle with the Philistinism of Canterbury, Conn.; and the Legislature of Georgia had offered a reward of five thousand dollars for "the arrest, prosecution, and trial to conviction under the laws of the State, of the editor or publisher of a certain paper called *The Liberator*, published in the town of Boston, and State of Massachusetts."

But it is not within the province of this biography to give an exhaustive *résumé* of the anti-slavery conflict, but only to speak of such of its episodes as were especially participated in by Mr. Whittier. How tailor John Woolman became a life-long itinerant preacher of his mild Quaker gospel of freedom; how honest saddler Lundy left his leather hammering, and walked his ten thousand miles, carrying his types and column-rules with him, and printing his "Genius of Universal Emancipation" as he went; in what way and to what extent the labors and writings of Lucretia Mott, Samuel J. May, Lydia Maria Child, George Thompson, James G. Birney, and Gerrit Smith helped on the noble cause,—to all these things only allusion can be made. For a full account of those perilous times one must go to the pages of Henry Wilson's "History of the Rise and Fall of the Slave Power," and to the fascinating "Recollections" of Samuel J. May. Let us now return to Whittier and consider his own writings, labors, and adventures in the service of the cause.

It was in the spring of 1833 that he published at his own expense "Justice and Expediency; or, Slavery Considered with a view to its Rightful and Effectual Remedy, Abolition." [Haverhill: C. P. Thayer and Co.] It is a polemical paper, full of exclamation points and italicized and capitalized sentences. The hyperbole speaks well for the author's heart, but betrays his juvenility. He shrieks like a temperance lecturer or a stump politician. The pamphlet, however, shows diligent and systematic study of the entire literature of the subject. Every statement is fortified by quotation or reference. He enumerates six reasons why the African Colonization Society's schemes were unworthy of good men's support, and buttresses up his theses by citations from the official literature of his opponents. A thorough familiarity with slavery in other lands and times is also manifested. As a specimen of the style of the book the following will serve:—

"But, it may be said that the miserable victims of the System have our sympathies.

"Sympathy!—the sympathy of the Priest and the Levite, looking on, and acknowledging, but holding itself aloof from mortal suffering. Can such hollow sympathy reach the broken of heart, and does the blessing of those who are ready to perish answer it? Does it hold back the lash from the slave, or sweeten his bitter bread?

"Oh, my heart is sick — my very soul is weary of this sympathy — this heartless mockery of feeling. . . .

"No — let the TRUTH on this subject — undisguised, naked, terrible as it is, stand out before us. Let us no longer seek to cover it — let us no longer strive to forget it — let us no more dare to palliate it."

In his sketch of Nathaniel P. Rogers, the anti-slavery editor, Whittier remarks incidentally that the voice of Rogers was one of the few which greeted him with words of encouragement and sympathy at the time of the publication of his "Justice and Expediency."*

On the fourth day of December, 1833, the Philadelphia Convention for the formation of the American Anti-slavery Society held its first sitting; Beriah Green, President, Lewis Tappan and John G. Whittier, Secretaries. This assembly, if not so famous as that which framed the Declaration of Independence in the same city some two generations previously, was at any rate as worthy of fame and respect as its illustrious prede-

* "He gave us a kind word of approval," says Whittier, "and invited us to his mountain home, on the banks of the Pemigewasset, an invitation which, two years afterwards, we accepted."

cessor. A deep solemnity and high consecration filled the heart of every man and
woman in that little band. Heart answered
unto heart in glowing sympathy. They did
their work like men inspired. Perfect una-
nimity prevailed. They were too eagerly
engaged to adjourn for dinner, and "baskets
of crackers and pitchers of cold water sup-
plied all the bodily refreshment." Among
those who were present and spoke was
Lucretia Mott, "a beautiful and graceful woman," says Whittier, "in the prime of life,
with a face beneath her plain cap as finely
intellectual as that of Madame Roland."
She "offered some wise and valuable suggestions, in a clear sweet voice, the charm
of which I have never forgotten."

A committee, of which Whittier was a
member, with William Lloyd Garrison as
chairman, was appointed to draw up a Declaration of Principles. Garrison sat up all
night, in the small attic of a colored man,
to draft this Declaration. The two other
members of the committee, calling in the
gray dawn of a December day, found him
putting the last touches to this famous

JOHN GREENLEAF WHITTIER AT MIDDLE LIFE.

paper, while his lamp burned on unheeded into the daylight. His draft was accepted almost without amendment by the Convention, and, after it had been engrossed on parchment, was signed by the sixty-two members present.*

In the *Atlantic Monthly* for February, 1874, Mr. Whittier has given an interesting account of the Convention. Some of his pictures are so graphic that they shall here be given in his own words: —

"In the gray twilight of a chill day of late November, forty years ago, a dear friend of mine residing in Boston, made his appearance at the old farm-house in East Haverhill. He had been deputed by the Abolitionists of the city, William L. Garrison, Samuel E. Sewall, and others, to inform me of my appointment as a delegate to the Convention about to be held in Philadelphia for the formation of an American Anti-slavery Society; and to urge upon me the necessity of my attendance.

* Twenty-one of these persons were Quakers, as Mr. Whittier and the writer proved by actual count of the names on Mr. Whittier's fac-simile copy of the Declaration.

"Few words of persuasion, however, were needed. I was unused to travelling; my life had been spent on a secluded farm; and the journey, mostly by stage-coach, at that time was really a formidable one. Moreover the few abolitionists were everywhere spoken against, their persons threatened, and, in some instances, a price set on their heads by Southern legislators. Pennsylvania was on the borders of slavery, and it needed small effort of imagination to picture to oneself the breaking up of the Convention and maltreatment of its members. This latter consideration I do not think weighed much with me, although I was better prepared for serious danger than for anything like personal indignity. I had read Governor Trumbull's description of the tarring and feathering of his hero Mac-Fingal, when after the application of the melted tar, the feather-bed was ripped open and shaken over him, until

> Not Maia's son with wings for ears,
> Such plumes about his visage wears,
> Nor Milton's six-winged angel gathers
> Such superfluity of feathers,'

and I confess I was quite unwilling to undergo a martyrdom which my best friends could scarcely refrain from laughing at. But a summons like that of Garrison's bugle-blast could scarcely be unheeded by one who, from birth and education, held fast the traditions of that earlier abolitionism which, under the lead of Benezet and Woolman, had effaced from the Society of Friends every vestige of slaveholding. I had thrown myself, with a young man's fervid enthusiasm, into a movement which commended itself to my reason and conscience, to my love of country, and my sense of duty to God and my fellow-men. My first venture in authorship was the publication, at my own expense, in the spring of 1833, of a pamphlet entitled 'Justice and Expediency,' * on the moral and political evils of slavery, and the duty of emancipation. Under such circumstances, I could not hesitate, but prepared at once for my journey. It was necessary that I should start on the morrow, and the intervening

---

* Mr. Whittier here made a slip of memory. His first work was "Legends of New England," as he himself testifies, in his own handwriting, in a memorandum sent to the New England Historic-Genealogical Society.

time, with a small allowance for sleep, was spent in providing for the care of the farm and homestead during my absence."

Mr. Whittier proceeds to tell of his journey to the Quaker City, and of the organization and work of the Convention. The following pen-portraits are too valuable to be omitted: —

"Looking over the assembly, I noticed that it was mainly composed of comparatively young men, some in middle age, and a few beyond that period. They were nearly all plainly dressed, with a view to comfort rather than elegance. Many of the faces turned toward me wore a look of expectancy and suppressed enthusiasm; all had the earnestness which might be expected of men engaged in an enterprise beset with difficulty, and perhaps with peril. The fine intellectual head of Garrison, prematurely bald, was conspicuous; the sunny-faced young man at his side, in whom all the beatitudes seemed to find expression, was Samuel J. May, mingling in his veins the best blood of the Sewalls and Quincys;

a man so exceptionally pure and large-hearted, so genial, tender, and loving, that he could be faithful to truth and duty without making an enemy.

> The de'il wad look into his face,
> And swear he could na wrang him.'

That tall, gaunt, swarthy man, erect, eagle-faced, upon whose somewhat martial figure the Quaker coat seemed a little out of place, was Lindley Coates, known in all Eastern Pennsylvania as a stern enemy of slavery; that slight, eager man, intensely alive in every feature and gesture, was Thomas Shipley, who for thirty years had been the protector of the free colored people of Philadelphia, and whose name was whispered reverently in the slave cabins of Maryland as the friend of the black man,— one of a class peculiar to old Quakerism, who, in doing what they felt to be duty, and walking as the Light within guided them, knew no fear and shrank from no sacrifice. Braver men the world has not known. Beside him, differing in creed but united with him in works of love and charity, sat Thomas Whitson, of the Hicksite school of Friends, fresh from his farm in Lancaster County, dressed in plainest homespun, his tall form surmounted by a shock of unkempt hair, the odd obliquity of his vision contrasting strongly with the clearness and directness of his spiritual insight. Elizur Wright, the young professor of a Western college, who had lost his place by his bold advocacy of freedom, with a look of sharp concentration, in keeping with an intellect keen as a Damascus blade, closely watched the proceedings through his spectacles, opening his mouth only to speak directly to the purpose. . . . . In front of me, awakening pleasant associations of the old homestead in Merrimack valley, sat my first school-teacher, Joshua Coffin, the learned and worthy antiquarian and historian of Newbury. A few spectators, mostly of the Hicksite division of Friends, were present in broad-brims and plain bonnets, among them Esther Moore and Lucretia Mott."

The year 1834 was passed by Whittier quietly on the farm at East Haverhill. In April of this year the first anti-slavery society was organized in Haverhill, with John

G. Whittier as corresponding secretary. Not long after a female anti-slavery society was organized in the same town. The pro-slavery feeling in Haverhill was as bitter as in other places.

One Sabbath afternoon in August, 1835, the Rev. Samuel J. May occupied the pulpit of the First Parish Society in Haverhill, and in the evening attempted to give an anti-slavery lecture in the Christian Union Chapel, having been invited to do so by Mr. Whittier. In his "Recollections of the Anti-Slavery Conflict" (p. 152), Mr. May says: —

"I had spoken about fifteen minutes when the most hideous outcries and yells, from a crowd of men who had surrounded the house, startled us, and then came heavy missiles against the doors and blinds of the windows. I persisted in speaking for a few minutes, hoping the blinds and doors were strong enough to stand the siege. But presently a heavy stone broke through one of the blinds, shattered a pane of glass, and fell upon the head of a lady sitting near the centre of the hall. She uttered a shriek, and fell bleeding into the arms of her sister.

The panic-stricken audience rose *en masse,*
and began a rush for the doors."

Mr. May succeeded in quieting the fears
of the audience, and himself escaped through
the crowd of infuriated ruffians without by
walking between two ladies, one of them
the sister of Mr. Whittier and the other the
daughter of a wealthy and determined citizen of the place, who, it was well known,
would take summary vengeance for any
disrespect shown to his daughter. It was
well that the audience dispersed when it
did, since a loaded cannon was being drawn
to the spot by the furious mob.

This year, 1835, was a year of mobs. On
the very same evening that Mr. May was
mobbed in Haverhill, Mr. Whittier and his
English friend, the orator George Thompson, were treated in a similar manner in
Concord, N. H. Whether an account of
the Concord mob has been elsewhere published or not the author cannot say, but the
story given here is as he had it from the lips
of Mr. Whittier himself.

"Oh! we had a dreadful night of it," he
said. The inhabitants had heard that an
Abolition meeting was to be held in the

town, and that the arch anarchist, George Thompson, was to speak. So on that Sabbath evening they were on the alert, an angry mob some five hundred strong. Mr. Whittier, knowing nothing of their state of mind, started down the street with a friend: the mob surrounded them, thinking that he was Thompson. His friend explained to them that he was Mr. Whittier. "Oh!" they exclaimed, "so you are the one who is with Thompson, are you?" and forthwith they began to assail the two men with sticks and stones. Mr. Whittier said that both he and his friend were hurt, but escaped with their lives by taking refuge in the house of a friend named Kent, who was not an Abolitionist himself, but was a man of honor and bravery. He barred his door, and told the mob that they should have Whittier only over his dead body.

In the course of the evening Mr. Whittier learned that the house in which Thompson was staying was surrounded by the mob. Becoming anxious, he borrowed a hat, sallied out among the crowd, and succeeded in reaching his friend. The noise and violence of the mob increased; a cannon was brought, and at one time the little band in the house feared they might suffer violence. "We did not much fear death," said Mr. Whittier, "but we did dread gross personal indignities."

It was fortunately a bright moonlight night, suitable for travelling, and about one o'clock the two friends escaped by driving off rapidly in their horse and buggy. They did not know the road to Haverhill, but were directed by their friends with all possible minuteness. Three miles away, also, there was the house of an anti-slavery man, and they obtained further directions there. Some time after sunrise they stopped at a wayside inn to bait their horse, and get a bite of breakfast for themselves. While they were at table the landlord said,—

"They've been having a h—l of a time down at Haverhill."

"How is that?"

"Oh, one of them d—d Abolitionists was lecturin' there; he had been invited to the town by a young fellow named Whittier; but they made it pretty hot for him, and I guess neither he nor Whittier will be in a hurry to repeat the thing."

"What kind of a fellow is this Whittier?"

"Oh, he's an ignorant sort of fellow; he don't know much."

"And who is this Thompson they're talking about?"

"Why, he's a man sent over here by the British to make trouble in our government."

As the two friends were stepping into the buggy, Mr. Whittier, with one foot on the step, turned and said to the host, who was standing by with several tavern loafers: —

"You've been talking about Thompson and Whittier. This is Mr. Thompson, and I am Whittier. Good morning."

"And jumping into the buggy," said the poet, with a twinkle in his eye, "we whipped up, and stood not on the order of our going." As for the host he stood with open mouth, being absolutely tongue-tied with astonishment. "And for all I know," said the narrator, "he's standing there still with his mouth open."

Mr. Thompson was secreted at the Whittier farm-house in Haverhill for two weeks after this affair.

Some two months after the disgraceful

scenes just described occurred the mobbing
of William Lloyd Garrison in Boston. He
had gone in the evening to deliver a lecture
before the Female Anti-Slavery Society.
A furious mob of "gentlemen of property
and standing" surrounded the building.
Mr. Garrison took refuge in a carpenter's
shop in the rear of the hall, but was vio-
lently seized, let down from a window by a
rope, and dragged by the mob to the City
Hall.   Mr. Whittier was staying at the
house of Rev. Samuel J. May. His sister
had gone to the lecture, and Mr. Whittier,
on hearing of the disturbance, had fears for
her safety, and went out to seek her. He
said to the writer that when he reached the
City Hall he saw before him the best
dressed mob imaginable. Presently he
heard a cry, "They've got him!" After a
short, sharp scuffle Garrison was got into a
carriage by the police, and taken to the
Leverett Street jail, as the only place where
he could be safe that night in Boston. Mr.
Whittier and Mr. May immediately went
down to the jail to see him. Garrison said
that he could not say, with Paul, that he was
dwelling in his own hired house, and so he

could not ask them to stay all night with him! His coat was not entirely gone, but was pretty badly torn. He was at first a good deal agitated by the affair, but when they left him he had become calm and assured. On the same evening, the mob threatened to make an attack upon Mr. May's house. Mr. Whittier got his sister Elizabeth safely bestowed for the night in the dwelling of another friend. He and Mr. May passed a sleepless night, and at one time half thought that, for safety's sake, they should have stayed in the jail with Garrison. However, they were not molested.

It is a remarkable testimony to the esteem in which Mr. Whittier must have been held by the citizens of Haverhill that, notwithstanding their bitter hatred of Abolitionism, they elected him their representative to the State Legislature in 1835, and again in 1836. In 1837 he declined re-election. In the legislative documents for 1835 he figures as a member of the standing committee on engrossed bills. His name does not appear in the State records for 1836: it was undoubtedly owing to his secretarial duties, mentioned below, that he was unable to take his seat as a member of the Legislature in the second year of his election.

In 1836 Whittier published " Mogg Megone," a poem on an episode in Indian life. It will be reviewed, with the rest of his poems, in the second part of this volume. In the same year he was appointed Secretary of the American Anti-Slavery Society, and removed to Philadelphia. In 1838–39, while in that city, he edited a paper which he named the *Pennsylvania Freeman.* It had formerly been edited by Benjamin Lundy, under the title of the *National Enquirer.* The office of the *Pennsylvania Freeman* was in 1838 sacked and burned by a mob. It was about the same time that Pennsylvania Hall in Philadelphia was burned to the ground by the citizens, on the very day after its dedication. Mr. Whittier had read an original poem on that occasion. The hall had been built at considerable sacrifice by the lovers of freedom, in order that one place at least might be open for free discussion. And it was just in order that it might not be used thus that it was burned by the guilty-thoughted mob. The keys had been given to the mayor, but neither he nor the police interfered to prevent the atrocious deed.

In 1837 Mr. Whittier edited, and wrote a preface for, the "Letters of John Quincy Adams to his Constituents." These stirring letters of Mr. Adams were called forth by the attacks that had been made on him by members of Congress for defending the right of negroes to petition the Government. Mr. Whittier, in his introductory remarks, speaks of the "Letters" as follows: —

"Their sarcasm is Junius-like, cold, keen, unsparing. In boldness, directness, and eloquent appeal, they will bear comparison with O'Connell's celebrated letters to the Reformers of Great Britain. . . . It will be seen that, in the great struggle for and against the Right of Petition, an account of which is given in the following pages, their author stood in a great measure alone, and unsupported by his northern colleagues. On 'his gray, discrowned head' the entire fury of slaveholding arrogance and wrath was expended. He stood alone,— beating back, with his aged and single arm, the tide which would have borne down and overwhelmed a less sturdy and determined spirit."

In the same year (1837) Mr. Whittier edited a pamphlet called "Views of Slavery and Emancipation," taken from Harriet Martineau's "Society in America." The whole subject of slavery is canvassed by Miss Martineau in the most searching and judicial manner.

In closing this account of our author's anti-slavery labors, we may bestow a word on the attitude assumed toward the Abolition movement by the Quakers as a sect. Through the labors of John Woolman, Benjamin Lundy, Anthony Benezet, and others, they had early been brought to see the wickedness of slaveholding, and in 1780 had succeeded in entirely ridding their denomination of the wrong. They not only emancipated their slaves, but remunerated them for their past services. Indeed, their record in this respect is unique for its fine ideal devotion to exact justice. They were the first religious body in the world to remove the pollution of slavery from their midst. But the cautious, acquisitive, peace-loving

Quakers seemed content to rest **here**, satisfied with having cleared their own skirts of wrong. They could not see the good side of the Abolition movement. They were scandalized by the violence and fanaticism of many Abolitionists. Mr. Whittier felt aggrieved by this attitude of the Friends, but did not on that account break with the denomination, or abandon the religion of his fathers. In 1868 he wrote as follows to the *New Bedford Standard*, which had spoken of him in an article on Thomas A. Greene: "My object in referring to the article in the paper was mainly to correct a statement regarding myself, viz.: That in consequence of the opposition of the Society of Friends to the anti-slavery movement, I did not for years attend their meetings. This is not true. From my youth up, whenever my health permitted, I have been a constant attendant of our meetings for religious worship. *This* is true, however, that after our meeting-houses were denied by the yearly meeting for anti-slavery purposes, I did not feel it in my way, for some years, to attend the annual meeting at Newport. From a feeling of duty I protested against that decision when

it was made, but was given to understand
pretty distinctly that there was no 'weight'
in my words.   It was a hard day for reformers; some stifled their convictions; others,
not adding patience to their faith, allowed
themselves to be worried out of the Society.
Abolitionists holding office were very generally 'dropped out,' and the ark of the church
staggered on with no profane anti-slavery
hands upon it."

CHAPTER VI.

AMESBURY.

AFTER the sacking and burning of the office of the *Pennsylvania Freeman*, Whittier returned to Haverhill, and soon after (in 1840) he sold the old farm and removed with his mother to Amesbury, a small town some nine miles nearer the sea than Haverhill. It is a rural town of over three thousand inhabitants, and contains nothing of note except the poet Whittier. The business of the place is the manufacture of woollen and cotton goods, and of carriages. The landscape is rugged and picturesque. The town covers a sloping hillside that stretches down to the Merrimack. Across this river rises a high hill, crowned with orchards and meadows. In summer time a sweet and quiet air reigns in the place. There are old vine-covered houses, grassy lawns, cool crofts, and sunken orchards; bees are humming, birds singing, and here and there through the trees slender columns of blue wood-smoke float upward in airy evanescence. Mr. Whittier's residence is on Friend Street, and not far beyond, on the same street, or rather in the delta formed by the meeting of two streets, stands the Friends' Meeting-House, where the poet has been an attendant nearly all his life:—

> "For thee, the priestly rite and prayer,
>   And holy day, and solemn psalm;
> For me, the silent reverence where
>   My brethren gather, slow and calm."

This old meeting-house is alluded to by the poet in "Abram Morrison," a fine humorous poem published in "The King's Missive" (1881). We there read how—

> "On calm and fair First Days
> Rattled down our one-horse chaise
> Through the blossomed apple-boughs
> To the old, brown meeting-house."

Whittier's house is a plain, white-painted structure, standing at the corner of two streets, and having in front of it numerous forest trees, chiefly maple. Since 1876 the

THE WHITTIER HOUSE, AMESBURY, MASS.

poet has passed only a part of each year at Amesbury, his other home being Oak Knoll in Danvers, where he resides with distant relatives.

The study at Amesbury of course possesses great interest for us as the place where most of the poet's finest lyrics have been written. It is a very cosey little study, and is entered by one door from within and another from without. The upper half of the outer door is of glass. This door is at the end of the left-hand porch shown in the view on page 125. The two windows in the study look out upon a long strip of yard in the rear of the house, — very pretty and quiet, and filled with pear-trees and other trees and vines. Upon one side of the room are shelves holding five or six hundred well-used volumes. Among them are to be noticed Charles Reade's novels and the poems of Robert Browning. A side-shelf is completely filled with a small blue and gold edition of the poets. On the walls hang oil paintings of views on the Merrimack River and other Essex County scenes, including Mr. Whittier's birthplace. In one corner is a handsome writing-desk, littered with papers and letters. Upon the hearth of the Franklin stove, high andirons smile a fireside welcome from their burnished brass knobs. Indeed, everything in the room is as neat and cosey as the wax cell of a honey-bee. And over all is shed the genial glow of the gentlest, tenderest nature in all the land.

In the autumn of 1844 was written "The Stranger in Lowell," a series of light sketches suggested by personal experiences. The style of these essays reminds one of that of "Twice Told Tales," but it is not so pure. The thought is developed too rhetorically, and the essays betray the limitations attending the life of a recluse. But these sketches are interesting as exhibitions of the growth of the author toward this peculiar form of essay-writing, and are valuable on that account.

In 1847 James G. Birney's anti-slavery paper, *The Philanthropist*, published in Cincinnati, was merged with the *National Era*, of Washington, D. C., with Dr. Gamaliel Bailey as managing editor, and John G. Whittier as associate or corresponding editor. Dr. Bailey had previously helped edit *The Philanthropist*. Both papers were treated to mobocratic attacks. The *Era* became an important organ of the Abolition party in Washington. To it Mr. Whittier contributed his "Old Portraits and Modern Sketches" as well as other reform papers.

In the same year (1847) our author published his "Supernaturalism of New England." [New York and London; Wiley and Putnam.] This pleasant little volume shows a marked advance upon Whittier's previous prose work. In its nine chapters he has preserved a number of oral legends and interesting superstitions of the farmer-folk of the Merrimack region. Parts of the work have been quoted elsewhere in this volume. One of the chapters closes with the following fine passage:—

"The witches of Father Baxter and 'the Black Man' of Cotton Mather have vanished; belief in them is no longer possible on the part of sane men. But this mysterious

universe, through which, half veiled in its
own shadow, our dim little planet is wheel-
ing, with its star-worlds and thought-weary-
ing spaces, remains. Nature's mighty mir-
acle is still over and around us; and hence
awe, wonder, and reverence remain to be
the inheritance of humanity: still are there
beautiful repentances and holy death-beds,
and still over the soul's darkness and confu-
sion rises star-like the great idea of duty.
By higher and better influences than the
poor spectres of superstition man must
henceforth be taught to reverence the Invis-
ible, and, in the consciousness of his own
weakness and sin and sorrow, to lean with
childlike trust on the wisdom and mercy of
an overruling Providence."

In 1849 Mr. Whittier collected and published his anti-slavery poems, under the title
"Voices of Freedom." The year 1850
marks a new era in his poetical career.
He published at that time his "Songs of
Labor," — a volume which showed that his
mind had become calmed by time, and was
now capable of interesting itself in other
than reform subjects.

There is not much of outward incident and circumstance to record of the quiet poetical years passed since 1840 at Amesbury and Danvers. Almost every year or two a new volume of poems has been issued, each one establishing on a firmer foundation the Quaker Poet's reputation as a creator of sweet and melodious lyrical poetry.

In 1868 an institution called "Whittier College" was opened at Salem, Henry County, Iowa. It was founded in honor of the poet, and is conducted in accordance with the principles of the Society of Friends.

In 1871 Whittier edited "Child-Life: A Collection of Poems," by various home and foreign authors. In the same year he edited, with a long introduction, the "Journal of John Woolman."

The name John Woolman is not widely known to persons of the present generation; and yet, as Whittier says, it was this humble Quaker reformer of New Jersey who did more than any one else to inspire all the great modern movements for the emancipation of slaves, first in the West Indies, then in the United States, and in Russia. Warner Mifflin, Jean Pierre Brissot, Thomas Clarkson, Stephen Grellet, William Allen, and Benjamin Lundy, — all these philanthropists owed much of their impulse to labor for the freedom of the slave to humble John Woolman. His journal or autobiography was highly praised by Charles Lamb, Edward Irving, Crabb Robinson, and others. "The style is that of a man unlettered, but with natural refinement and delicate sense of fitness, the purity of whose heart enters into his language."

Woolman was born in Northampton, West Jersey, in 1720. One day, in the year 1842, while clerk in a store in the village of Mount Holly, township of Northampton, N. J., he was asked by his employer to make out the bill of sale of a negro. He drew up the instrument, but his conscience was awakened, and some years after he began his life-work as a pedestrian anti-slavery preacher. He refused to ride in, or have letters sent him by, the stage-coaches, because of the cruelty exercised toward the horses by the drivers. Neither would he accept hospitality from those who kept slaves, always paying either the owners or the slaves for his entertainment. Woolman was most gentle and kind in his appeals to slave-owners, and rarely met with any violent remonstrance. Much of his work was within the limits of his own sect, and Mr. Whittier's introduction gives a valuable and succinct historical *résumé* of the steps taken by the Friends to rid their sect of the stigma of slaveholding.

Mount Holly, in Woolman's day, says Whittier, " was almost entirely a settlement of Friends. A very few of the old houses with their quaint stoops or porches are left. That occupied by John Woolman was a small, plain, two-story structure, with two windows in each story in front, a four-barred fence enclosing the grounds, with the trees he planted and loved to cultivate. The house was not painted, but whitewashed. The name of the place is derived from the highest hill in the county, rising two hundred feet above the sea, and commanding a view of a rich and level country of cleared farms and woodlands."

Very amusing is the picture given by Mr. Whittier of the eccentric Benjamin Lay, once a member of the Society of Friends in England, and afterward an inhabitant for some time of the West Indies, whence he was driven away on account of the violence and extravagance of his denunciations of slavery. He was a contemporary of Woolman. He lived in a cave near Philadelphia, as a sort of Jonah or Elijah, prophesying woe against the city on account of its participation in the crime of slavery. He wore clothes made of vegetable fibre, and ate only vegetable food. "Issuing from his cave, on his mission of preaching ' deliverance to the captive,' he was in the habit of visiting the various meetings for worship and bearing his testimony against slaveholders, greatly to their disgust and indignation. On one occasion he entered the Market Street Meeting, and a leading Friend requested some one to take him out. A burly blacksmith volunteered to do it, leading him to the gate and thrusting him out with such force that he fell into the gutter of the street. There he lay until the meeting closed, telling the bystanders that he did not feel free to rise himself. 'Let those who cast me here raise me up. It is their business, not mine.'

"His personal appearance was in remarkable keeping with his eccentric life. A figure only four and a half feet high, hunch-backed, with projecting chest, legs small and uneven, arms longer than his legs; a huge head, showing only beneath the enormous white hat large, solemn eyes and a prominent nose; the rest of his face covered with a snowy semicircle of beard falling low on his breast,—a figure to recall the old legends of troll, brownie, and kobold. Such was the irrepressible prophet who troubled the Israel of slaveholding Quakerism, clinging like a rough chestnut-burr to the skirts of its respectability, and settling like a pertinacious gad-fly on the sore places of its conscience.

"On one occasion, while the annual meeting was in session at Burlington, N. J., in the midst of the solemn silence of the great assembly, the unwelcome figure of Benjamin Lay, wrapped in his long white overcoat, was seen passing up the aisle. Stopping midway, he exclaimed, 'You slaveholders! Why don't you throw off your Quaker coats as I do mine, and show yourselves as you are?' Casting off as he spoke his outer garment, he disclosed to the astonished assembly a military coat underneath, and a sword dangling at his heels. Holding in one hand a large book, he drew his sword with the other. 'In the sight of **God**,' he cried, 'you are as guilty as if you stabbed your slaves to the heart, as I do this book!' suiting the action to the word, and piercing a small bladder filled with the juice of poke-weed (*phytolacca decandra*), which he had concealed between the covers, and sprinkling as with fresh blood those who sat near him."

There is something overwhelmingly ludicrous about this bladder of poke-weed juice! And what a subject for a painter!— the portentous, white-bearded dwarf standing there in the midst of the church, in act to plunge his gigantic sword tragically into the innermost bowels of the crimson poke-juice bladder, and from all parts of the house the converging looks of the broad-brimmed and shovel-bonneted Quakers!

Mr. Whittier further says that "Lay was

well acquainted with Dr. Franklin, who sometimes visited him. Among other schemes of reform he entertained the idea of converting all mankind to Christianity. This was to be done by three witnesses,—himself, Michael Lovell, and Abel Noble, assisted by Dr. Franklin. But, on their first meeting at the doctor's house, the three 'chosen vessels' got into a violent controversy on points of doctrine, and separated in ill-humor. The philosopher, who had been an amused listener, advised the three sages to give up the project of converting the world until they had learned to tolerate each other."

In 1873 Mr. Whittier edited "Child-Life in Prose." It is a collection of pretty stories, chiefly about the childhood of various eminent persons. One of the stories is by the editor, and is about "A Fish that I Didn't Catch."

In 1875 appeared "Songs of Three Centuries." The poet's design in this work was (to use his own words) "to gather up in a comparatively small volume, easily accessible to all classes of readers, the wisest thoughts, rarest fancies, and devoutest hymns of the metrical authors of the last three centuries." He says, "The selections I have made indicate, in a general way, my preferences." It is a choice collection, rich in lyrical masterpieces.

CHAPTER VII.

LATER DAYS.

About a mile westward from the village of Danvers, Mass., a grassy road, named Summer Street, branches off to the right and north. It is a pleasant, winding road, bordered by picturesque old stone fences and lined with barberry and raspberry bushes and gnarled old apple-trees. On either side are cultivated fields. Oak Knoll, the winter residence of Whittier, is the second house on the left, some half a mile up the road.

This fine old estate had been occupied for half a century by a man of wealth and taste. About the year 1875 it passed into the hands of Col. Edmund Johnson, of Boston, whose wife was Whittier's cousin.

It was planned that the poet should be a member of the household ; rooms were set apart and arranged for him, and he gave the estate its present name.

It is a spot full of traditions, and well suited to any poet's residence, most of all for one so versed in New England legends. It is the very spot once occupied by the Rev. George Burroughs, a clergyman who was hung for witchcraft in 1692, on the charge, among other things, of "having performed feats of extraordinary physical strength." He could hold out a gun seven feet long, tradition says, by putting his finger in the muzzle, and could lift a barrel of molasses in the same way by the bung-hole. For acts like these — deemed unclerical, at least, if not unnatural — he was convicted and hanged; and a well on the premises of Oak Knoll is still known as the "witch well."

Here, in the home of relatives, the poet has lived since 1876. A lovelier and more poetical place it would be difficult to imagine. The extensive, carefully kept grounds, and the antique elegance of the house, give to the estate the air of an old English manor, or gentleman's country hall. The house is approached by a long, upward-sweeping lawn, diversified with stately forest trees, clumps of evergreens and shrubs and flowers. Down across the road stands a large and hand-

VIEW FROM THE PORCH AT OAK KNOLL, DANVERS, MASS.

some barn, which is as neat as paint and care can make it. In front of the house the eye ranges downward over an extensive landscape, as far as to the town of Peabody, in the direction of Salem. Indeed, on every side of the estate there are broad and distant views of the blue hills of Essex and Middlesex.

In the summer, as you ascend the carriage-road that winds through the grounds, your eye is captured by the rare beauty of the scene. Yonder is a tall living wall of verdure, with an archway cut through it. To the left the grounds sweep gently down to a deep ravine, where a little rivulet, named Beaver Brook, creeps leisurely out and winds seaward through green and marish meadows. It is in this portion of the grounds that the fine oak-trees grow which give to the place its name. Here, too, is a large grove of pines, with numerous seats within it. There are trees and trees at Oak Knoll, — smooth and shapely hickories, glistering chestnuts with cool foliage, maples, birches, and the purple beech. Add to the picture the rural accessories of bee-haunted clover-fields, apple and pear orchards, and beds of tempting strawberries. The house is of wood, salmon-colored, with tall porches on each side, up-propped by stately Doric columns. In front, with wide sweep of closely cropped grass intervening, is the magnificent Norway spruce that Oliver Wendell Holmes, a year or two before Mr. Whittier's death, on one of those periodical visits to his brother poet that so delighted their two souls, named " The Poets' Pagoda." A luxuriant vine clusters about the eaves of the house. On the long porch a mocking-bird and a canary-bird fill the green silence with gushes of melody, and near at hand, in his study in the wing of the building, sits one with a singing pen and listens to their song. To their song and to the murmur of the tall pines by his window he listens, then looks into his heart and writes, — this sweet-souled magician, — and craftily imprisons between the covers of his books, echoes of bird and tree music, bits of blue sky, glimpses of green landscape, winding rivers, and idyls of the snow, — all suffused and interfused with a glowing atmosphere of human and divine love, such as the poet found in this home of his choosing at Oak Knoll. It will not perhaps be

intruding upon the privacies of home to say
that the members of the cultured household
at Oak Knoll ever, found in their happy
circle, their highest pleasure in ministering
to all needs, social or otherwise, of their
loved cousin the poet. Three sisters dis-
pense the hospitalities of the house, and a
young daughter of Mrs. Woodman's adds
the charm of girlhood to the family life.

Readers of Whittier, who know how
deeply his writings are tinged with the
scenery, legendary lore and folk-life of his
native Merrimack Valley, will not wonder
that a certain *Heimweh*, or home-sickness,
draws him northward, when

> " Flows amain
> The surge of summer's beauty."

and

> " Pours the deluge of the heat
> Broad northward o'er the land.'

It is but one hour's ride by cars from
Danvers to Amesbury; and part of the time
in the latter place, and part of the time at

the Isles of Shoals, and in the beautiful lake and mountain region of New Hampshire, Mr. Whittier passes the warm season. For many years it was his custom to spend a portion of each summer at the Bearcamp River House, in West Ossipee, N. H., some thirty miles north of Lake Winnipiseogee. The hotel was situated on a slight eminence, commanding a view of towering "Mount Israel" and of "Whittier Mountain," named after the poet. It is a region full of noble prospects, being just in the outskirts of the White Mountain group. Several of the poems of Whittier were inspired by this scenery, notably "Among the Hills," "Sunset on the Bearcamp," and "The Seeking of the Waterfall." In the first of these we read how —

"Through Sandwich notch the west-wind sang,"

and —

> "Above his broad lake Ossipee,
>   Once more the sunshine wearing,
> Stooped, tracing on that silver shield
>   His grim armorial bearing."

"Sunset on the Bearcamp" contains a

stanza considered by some to be one of the
poet's finest: —

> "Touched by a light that hath no name,
>   A glory never sung,
> Aloft on sky and mountain wall
>   Are God's great pictures hung.
> How changed the summits vast and old!
>   No longer granite-browed,
> They melt in rosy mist; the rock
>   Is softer than the cloud;
> The valley holds its breath; no leaf
>   Of all its elms is twirled:
> The silence of eternity
>   Seems falling on the world."

The Bearcamp River House (now no
more) was a hostelry whose site, antique
hospitality, and eminent guests were every
whit as worthy to be embalmed in lasting
verse as were those of the Wayside Inn of
Sudbury. Before the red, crackling flames
of its huge fireplace such literary characters
as Whittier, Gail Hamilton, Lucy Larcom,
and Hiram Rich used to gather on chill summer evenings for the kind of talks that only
a wood fire can inspire. The Quaker poet
is a charming conversationalist, and can
tell a story as capitally as he can write one.

He has a goodly *répertoire* of ghost tales and legends of the marvellous. One of his best stories is about a scene that took place in Independence Hall in Philadelphia, when the court remanded a negro to slavery. The poet says that an old sailor who was present became so infuriated by the spectacle that he made the air blue with oaths uttered in seven different languages.*

December 17, 1877, was the poet's seventieth birthday, and the occasion was celebrated in a twofold manner, namely, by a Whittier Tribute in the *Literary World*, and by a Whittier Banquet given at the Hotel Brunswick, in Boston, by Messrs. H. O. Houghton and Co., the publishers of Whittier's works. The *Literary World* tribute contained poems by Henry Wadsworth Longfellow, Bayard Taylor, E. C. Stedman, O. W. Holmes, William Lloyd Garrison, and others. Mr. Longfellow's poem, "The Three Silences," is one of unusual beauty.

* For these details about days on the Bearcamp, the writer is indebted to Dr. Robert R. Andrews, an acquaintance of the poet.

THE THREE SILENCES OF MOLINOS.

"Three Silences there are : the first of speech,
  The second of desire, the third of thought;
  This is the lore a Spanish monk, distraught
  With dreams and visions, was the first to teach.
These Silences, commingling each with each
  Made up the perfect Silence, that he sought
  And prayed for, and wherein at times he caught
  Mysterious sounds from realms beyond our reach.
O thou, whose daily life anticipates
  The life to come, and in whose thought and word
  The spiritual world preponderates,
Hermit of Amesbury! thou too hast heard
  Voices and melodies from beyond the gates,
  And speakest only when thy soul is stirred!"

There were letters from the poet Bryant, the historian George Bancroft, Colonel T. W. Higginson, and Mrs. H. B. Stowe; and there was a pleasant description of the Danvers home by Charles B. Rice. Mr. Whittier's "Response" was published in the January number of the paper:—

"Beside that milestone where the level sun,
  Nigh unto setting, sheds his last, low rays
On word and work irrevocably done,
Life's blending threads of good and ill outspun,
  I hear, O friends! your words of cheer and praise,
Half doubtful if myself or otherwise.
  Like him who, in the old Arabian joke,
  A beggar slept and crownèd Caliph woke."

The anniversary of the founding of the *Atlantic Monthly* happening to be synchronous with Whittier's birthday, the publishers determined to make a double festival of the occasion. The gathering at the Hotel Brunswick was a brilliant one, and the invitations were not limited by any clique or any sectional lines.

In this same month the admirers of Mr. Whittier in Haverhill, Newburyport, and neighboring towns, formed a Whittier Club, its annual meetings to be held on December 17.

The ladies of Amesbury presented to the poet on his birthday a richly finished Russia-leather portfolio, containing fourteen beautiful sketches in water-colors of scenes in and about Amesbury, by a talented Amesbury artist. The subjects of the sketches are those scenes which he has immortalized in his poems, and include his home, birthplace, the old school-house, old Quaker Meeting-House, Rivermouth Rocks, etc. The portfolio was presented to him at Oak Knoll, accompanied by a basket of exquisite flowers.

Since taking up his residence in Danvers,

the poet has published "The Vision of
Echard, and Other Poems," — including
the beautiful ballad, "The Witch of Wenham," — and "The King's Missive, and
Other Poems."

11

CHAPTER VIII.

PERSONAL.

As a boy, Whittier grew up slender, delicate, and shy, with dark hair and dark eyes; his nature silent and brooding, gentle, compassionate, religious, and sensitive to the beauty of the external world. He is of the nervous temperament, and his health has never been robust. Indeed, in later life the state of his health has often been precarious, and his plans for work have been at the mercy of his nerves. As a young man, and crowned Laureate of Freedom, Whittier must have presented a striking appearance, with his raven hair, and glittering black eyes flashing with the inspiration of a great cause. Mr. J. Miller McKim, a member with Whittier of the famous Anti-Slavery Convention held in Philadelphia in 1833, thus describes the poet: --

"He wore a dark frock-coat with standing collar, which, with his thin hair, dark and sometimes flashing eyes, and black whiskers, — not large, but noticeable in those unhirsute days, — gave him, to my then unpractised eye, quite as much of a military as a Quaker aspect. His broad, square forehead and well-cut features, aided by his incipient reputation as a poet, made him quite a noticeable feature in the convention."

Frederika Bremer, in her "Sketches of American Homes," gives an outline portrait of Whittier as he appeared when forty years of age: —

"He has a good exterior, a figure slender and tall, a beautiful head with refined features, black eyes full of fire, dark complexion, a fine smile, and lively but very nervous manner. Both soul and spirit have overstrained the nervous cords and wasted the body. He belongs to those natures who would advance with firmness and joy to martyrdom in a good cause, and yet who are never comfortable in society, and who look as if they would run out of the door every moment. He lives with his mother and sister in a country-house to which I have promised to go. I feel that I should enjoy myself with Whittier, and could make him feel at ease with me. I know from my own experience what this nervous bashfulness, caused by the over-exertion of the brain, requires, and how persons who suffer therefrom ought to be met and treated."

George W. Bungay, in his "Crayon Sketches" of distinguished Americans, published in 1852, gives the following picture of Whittier: "His temperament is nervous-bilious; [he] is tall, slender and straight as an Indian; has a superb head; his brow looks like a white cloud under his raven hair; eyes large, black as sloes, and glowing with expression, — . . . those starlike eyes flashing under such a magnificent forehead."

A writer in the *Democratic Review* for August, 1845, speaks of "the fine intellectual beauty of his expression, the blending brightness and softness of the clear dark eye, the union of manly firmness and courage with womanly sweetness and tenderness alike in countenance and character."

Mr. David A. Wasson says that Whittier is of the Saracenic or Hebrew prophet type: "The high cranium, so lofty, especially in the dome,—the slight and. symmetrical backward slope of the *whole* head,—the powerful level brows, and beneath these the dark, deep eyes, so full of shadowed fire,—the Arabian complexion,—the sharp-cut, intense lines of the face,—the light, tall, erect stature,—the quick, axial poise of the movement,"—all these traits reveal the fiery Semitic prophet.

The long backward and upward slope of the head, alluded to by Mr. Wasson, is very striking. It is the head of Walter Scott or of Emerson. Whittier is now an old man, somewhat hard of hearing, and with the fixed sadness of time upon his pleasant face. But ever and anon, as you converse with him, his countenance is irradiated by a sudden smile, sweet and strange and full of benignity,—like a waft of per-

fume from a bed of white violets, or a glint
of rich sunlight on an April day.   His is one
of those Emersonian natures that everybody
loves at first sight.   The very mole under
the right eye seems somehow the birth-mark
or sign-manual of kindliness.   The quaint
grammatical solecisms of the Quaker and the
New England farmer—the "thee's" and the
omission of the *g*'s from present participles
and other words ending in "ing"—give
to the poet's conversation a certain slight
piquancy and picturesqueness.*   About half-
past nine every morning, when at Amesbury,
Mr. Whittier walks down for the mail and
the news, and perhaps has a chat with some
neighbor on the street, or with the country
editor who is setting up in type his own
editorials while he grimly rolls his quid of
tobacco in his cheek.   In the spring and

---

* The writer remembers once speaking with a laborer whom
Mr. Whittier had employed. The good fellow could not
conceal his admiration for the poet. "Why," he said, "you
wouldn't think it, would you, but he talks just like common folks. We was talkin' about the apples one day, and
he said, 'Some years they ain't wuth pickin','—just like anybody, you know; ain't stuck up at all, and yet he's a great
man, you know. He likes to talk with farmers and common
folks; he don't go much with the bigbugs;—one of the
nicest men, and liberal with his money, too."

early summer the poet's dress will be after this fashion: black coat and vest, gray pantaloons, cinnamon-colored overcoat, drab tile hat, and perhaps a small gray tippet around his neck. As he walks, he salutes those whom he meets with a little jerky bow. A forty years' residence in Amesbury has made him acquainted with almost everybody, and he might, therefore, very properly be somewhat economical of exertion in his salutations. But his abrupt bow is really the expression of that unbending rectitude and noble pride in individual freedom that made him the reformer and the poet of liberty. As a single instance of Whittier's kind-heartedness, take the following incident, narrated by an anonymous writer in the *Literary World* for December, 1877: "When I was a young man trying to get an education, I went about the country peddling sewing-silk to help myself through college; and one Saturday night found me at Amesbury, a stranger and without a lodging-place. It happened that the first house at which I called was Whittier's, and he himself came to the door. On hearing my request he said he was very sorry that he could not keep me, but it was quarterly meeting and his house was full. He, however, took the trouble to show me to a neighbor's, where he left me; but that did not seem to wholly suit his idea of hospitality, for in the course of the evening he made his appearance, saying that it had occurred to him that he could sleep on a lounge, and give up his own bed to me,— which it is, perhaps, needless to say, was not allowed. But this was not all. The next morning he came again, with the suggestion that I might perhaps like to attend meeting, inviting me to go with him; and he gave me a seat next to himself. The meeting lasted an hour, during which there was not a word spoken by any one. We all sat in silence that length of time, then all arose, shook hands and dispersed; and I remember it as one of the best meetings I ever attended."

Dom Pedro II., Emperor of Brazil, is a reader of Mr. Whittier's poems, and an ardent admirer of his genius. He has exchanged letters with him, both in regard to poetry and to the emancipation of slaves.* When his Majesty was in this country, in 1876, he expressed a wish to meet Mr. Whittier, and on Wednesday evening, June 14, a little reception was arranged by Mrs. John T. Sargent at her Chestnut Street home, a few prominent persons having been invited to be present. "When the Emperor arrived, the other guests had already assembled. Sending up .his card, his Majesty followed it with the quickness of an enthusiastic school-boy; and his ,first question, after somewhat hastily paying his greetings, was for Mr. Whittier. The poet stepped forward to meet his imperial admirer, who would fain have caught him in his arms and embraced him warmly, with all the enthusiasm of the Latin race. The diffident Friend seemed somewhat abashed at so demonstrative a greeting, but with a cordial grasp of the hand drew Dom Pedro to the sofa, where the two chatted easily and with the familiarity of old friends.

"The rest of the company allowed them

* The Emperor has translated Whittier's "Cry of a Lost Soul" into Portuguese, and has sent to the poet several specimens of the Amazonian bird whose peculiar note suggested the poem.

to enjoy their *tête-à-tête* for some half hour, when they ventured to interrupt it, and the Emperor joined very heartily in a general conversation."

As the Emperor was driving away, he was seen standing erect in his open barouche, and " waving his hat, with a seeming hurrah, at the house which held his venerable friend." *

As a specimen of Mr. Whittier's genial and winning epistolary style, it is permissible to quote here a letter of his, addressed to Mrs. John T. Sargent, and included by her in her sketches of the Radical Club: —

" AMESBURY, Wednesday Eve.

" MY DEAR MRS. SARGENT, — Few stronger inducements could be held out to me than that in thy invitation to meet Lucretia Mott and Mary Carpenter. But I do not see that I can possibly go to Boston this week. None the less do I thank thee, my dear friend, in thinking of me in connection with their visit.

---

* Mrs. Sargent's " Sketches and Reminiscences of the Radical Club," pp. 301, 302.

"My love to Lucretia Mott, and tell her I have never forgotten the kind welcome and generous sympathy she gave the young abolitionist at a time when he found small favor with his 'orthodox' brethren. What a change she and I have lived to see! I hope to meet Miss Carpenter before she leaves us. For this, and for all thy kindness in times past, believe me gratefully thy friend,

"JOHN G. WHITTIER."

The modesty and shyness of the poet have already been more than once alluded to. They form his most distinctive personal or constitutional peculiarity. It is unnecessary to quote from his writings to illustrate what is patent to everybody who reads his books, or knows anything about him.

The poet's personal friends know well that he has a good deal of genial, mellow humorousness in his nature. To get an idea of it, read his charming prose sketches of home and rural life, and such poems as the whimsical, enigmatical "Demon of the Study," as well as "The Pumpkin," "To My

Old Schoolmaster," and the "Double-Headed Snake of Newbury." These poems almost equal Holmes's for rich and *riant* humor.

It is not so well known as it ought to be that the author of "Snow-Bound" has as deep a love of children as had Longfellow. Before the Bearcamp House was burned to the ground in 1880, Mr. Whittier used sometimes to come up from Amesbury with a whole bevy of little misses about him, and at the hotel the wee folk hailed him as one of those dear old fellows whom they always love at sight. It is said that Edward Lear — the friend of Tennyson, and author of "Nonsense Verses" for children — used to make a hobby-horse of himself in the castles of Europe, and treat his little friends to a gallop over the carpet on his back. If Mr. Whittier never got quite so far as this in juvenile equestrianism, he has at least equally endeared himself to the children who have had the good fortune to look into his loving eyes and enjoy the sunshine of his smile. When sitting by the fireside, or stretched at ease on the fragrant hay in the barn or field, or walking among the hills, nothing pleases him better than to have an audience of young folks eagerly listening to one of his stories. If they are engaged in a game of archery, he will take a hand in the sport, and no one is better pleased than he to hit the white. His unfailing kindness in answering the many letters addressed to him by young literary aspirants, or by others who desire his advice and help, is something admirable: no one knows how to win hearts better than he.

To these notes of personal traits it only remains to add a list of the offices of dignity and honor which have been held by Mr. Whittier. Besides his various editorial, secretarial, and legislative positions, he served as Overseer of Harvard College from 1858 to 1863. He was a member of the Electoral College in 1860 and in 1864. The degree of Master of Arts was bestowed upon him by Harvard College in 1860, and the same degree by Haverford College in the same year. He was elected a resident member of the American Philosophical Society in 1864, but never accepted the honor, notwithstanding the fact that his name appeared for two or three years on the Society's roll. In 1871 he was made a Fellow of the American Academy of Arts and Sciences.

Part II.

ANALYSIS OF HIS GENIUS AND WRITINGS.

CHAPTER I.

THE MAN.

"Not by the page word-painted
Let life be banned or sainted :
Deeper than written scroll
The colors of the soul."

MY TRIUMPH.

To analyze and describe the *poetry* of Whittier is a comparatively easy task, for it is all essentially lyrical or descriptive, and is resolvable into a few simple elements. His poetry is not profound; but it is sweet and melodious, — now flashing with the fire of freedom and choked with passionate indignation, and now purling and rippling through the tranquil meadows of legend and song. Such a poem as Emerson's "Sphinx," groaning with its weight of mystical meaning, Whittier never wrote, nor could write. Neither is he dramatic, nor skilled in the subtile harmonies of rhythm and metre. As an artist he is easily comprehensible.

But to fathom the *man*, — to drop one's plummet into the infinite depths of the human mind, to peer about with one's little candle among the dusty phantoms and spent forces of the past, and through the endlessly crossing and interblending meshes trace confidently up all the greater and the finer hereditary influences that have moulded a human character, — and then discover and weigh the post-natal forces that have acted upon that character through a long and varied life, — this is a very difficult task, and demands in him who would undertake it a union of historic imagination with caution and modesty.

The moral in Whittier predominates over the æsthetic, the reformer over the artist. "I am a man, and I feel that I am above all else a man." What is the great central element in our poet's character, if it is not that deep, never-smouldering moral fervor, that unquenchable love of freedom, that —

> "Hate of tyranny intense,
> And hearty in its vehemence,"

which, mixed with the beauty and melody

John G. Whittier

of his soul, gives to his pages a delicate glow as of gold-hot iron; which crowns him the Laureate of Freedom in his day, and imparts to his utterances the manly ring of the prose of Milton and Hugo and the poetry of Byron, Swinburne, and Whitman,— all poets of freedom like himself?

And what is love of freedom but the mainspring of Democracy? And what is Democracy but the rallying-cry of the age, the one word of the present, the one word of the future, the word of all words, and the white, electric beacon-light of modern life?

At the apex of modern Democracy stands Jesus of Nazareth; at its base stand the poets and heroes of freedom of the past hundred years. Christian Democracy has had its revolutions, its religious ferments and revolts, and its emancipations of slaves. Quakerism is one of its outcomes. Democracy produced George Fox; George Fox produced Quakerism; Quakerism produced Whittier; Whittier helped destroy slavery. He could not help doing so, for with slavery both Democracy and Quakerism are incompatible.   Whittier fought slavery as a Quaker, he has lived as a Quaker, and written as a Quaker; he has never fully emancipated himself from the shackles of the sect. To understand him, therefore, we must understand his religion.

The principles of the sect are all summed up in the phrases *Freedom* and the *Inner Light.*   Historically considered, Quakerism is a product of the ferment that followed the civil war in England two centuries ago.   Considered abstractly, or as a congeries of principles, it has a sociological and a philosophical root, both of these running back into the great tap-root, love of freedom, whose iron-tough, writhen fibres enwrap the dark foundation rocks of human nature itself.

Sociologically speaking, Quakerism is pure democracy, an exaltation of the majesty of the individual and of the mass of the people.   It is the pure precipitate of Christianity.   It is a protest against the hypocrisy, formalism, tyranny, of priestcraft, kingcraft, and aristocracy.

Philosophically, its theory of the Inner

Light is identical with the doctrine of idealism or innate ideas, held by Descartes, Fichte, Schelling, Cousin. It means individualism, a return to the primal sanities of the soul. "I think, therefore I am." My thinking soul is the ultimate source of ideas and truth. In that serene holy of holies full-grown ideas leap into being, — subjective, *a priori*, needing no sense-perception for their genesis.

But Transcendentalism differed from Quakerism in this: the former held that the illumination of the mind was a natural process; but Quakerism maintains that it is a supernatural process, the work of the "Holy Ghost." And herein Quakerism is inferior to Transcendentalism. But it is superior to it in that it does not believe in the infallibility of individual intuitions, but considers the true criterion of truth to be the universal reason, the "consensus of the competent." Yet the great danger that pertains to all moonshiny, or subjective, systems of philosophy is that their individualism will spindle out into wild extravagances of theory, and foolish eccentricities of manner and dress; and we shall find that, practically, Quakerism has as Quixotic a record as Transcendentalism. To say that both systems have performed noble and indispensable service in the development of mind is but to utter a truism.

We may now consider a little more closely the peculiarities of doctrine and life which characterize the Friends. The doctrine of the Inner Light, or pure spirituality, resulted in such tenets as these: the freedom of conscience; the soul the fountain of all truth, worthlessness of tradition and unsanctified learning ; the conscience or voice within the judge of the Bible or Written Word ; disbelief in witchcraft, ghosts, and other superstitions; love of friends and enemies, the potency of moral suasion, moral ideas, and as a consequence the wickedness of war, and a belief in human progress as the result of peaceable industry; universal enfranchisement, every man and woman may be enlightened by the Inner Light, — hence equality of privilege, no distinction between clergy or laity or between sex and sex,— the right of woman to develop her entire nature as she sees fit. In the principles which define the attitude of the Quaker toward social conventions, we find a queer jumble of the doctrines of primitive Christianity with the ideas of individual independence innate in the Germanic mind, and especially in the popular mind.* The Christian gospel of love forbids the Quakers to countenance war, capital punishment, imprisonment for debt, slavery, suppressment of the right of free speech and the right of petition. Their doctrine of equality in virtue of spiritual illumination forbids them to remove their hats in presence of any human being, even a king; leads them to avoid the use of the plural "you," as savoring of man-worship, and to refuse to employ a hired priesthood. Their doctrine of pure spirituality is inconsistent with sacerdotal

---

* The same sterling material that went to the making of the Quaker went also to the making of the Puritan farmer-and-artisan victors of Naseby, and Worcester, and Marston Moor. The same faults characterized each class. In stiff-backed independence and scorn of the gilt-edged poetry of conventional manners, and in the absurd extreme to which they carried that independence and scorn, the Quaker and the Puritan were alike. Only the Quaker out-puritaned the Puritan, — was much more consistent in his fanatical purism, scrawny asceticism, and contempt for distinguished manners and the noble imaginative arts.

rites and mummeries, such as baptism, the eucharist, forms of common prayer, etc. Music, poetry, painting, and dancing also have a worldly savor and tend to distract the mind from its spiritual life. So do rich and gaudy robes: we must therefore have simplicity of dress. Hear William Penn on this subject: *—

"I say, if sin brought the first coat, poor Adam's offspring have little reason to be proud or curious in their clothes. . . . It is all one as if a man who had lost his nose by a scandalous distemper, should take pains to set out a false one, in such shape and splendor as should give the greater occasion for all to gaze upon him; as if he would tell them he had lost his nose, for fear they would think he had not. But would a wise man be in love with a false nose, though ever so rich, and however finely made?"

A natural corollary of the Friends' doctrine of inward supernatural illumination is their habit of silent worship, or silent wait-

* In his work " No Cross, No Crown."

ing.* It is probable that this feature of their religious gatherings has done much to cultivate that peculiar tranquillity of demeanor which distinguishes them.† They meet the burdens, bereavements, and disappointments of life with a placid equanimity in strong antithesis to the often passionate grief and rebellion of other classes of religious people. Finally, we may add to the list of their characteristics their great moral sincerity. "With calm resoluteness they tell you your faults face to face, and without exciting your ill-will."

The objections to the Quakerism of our day are that it is retractile, stationary, negative; it is selfish, narrow, ascetic, tame; it has no iron in its blood; it rarely adds anything to the world's thought. The Quakers are a hopelessly antiquated sect,

---

* Their ideas on this subject are very well stated in the following words taken from a Quaker pamphlet by Mary Brook: "Solomon saith, 'The preparations of the heart in man, and the answer of the tongue, are from the Lord.' If the Lord alone can prepare the heart, stir it up, or incline it towards unfeigned holiness, how can any man approach him acceptably, till his heart be prepared by him?—and how can he know this preparation except he wait in silence to feel it?"

† See Appendix I.

a dying branch almost wholly severed from connection with the living forces of the tree of modern society. There are, it is true, a goodly number of liberal Quakers, who, in discarding the peculiar costume of the time of Charles II., which many of them even yet wear, have also thrown off the intellectual mummy-robes of the sect. Many adopt the tenets of Unitarianism, or make that religious body the stepping-stone to complete emancipation from an obsolete system of thought. But the mass of them are immovable. They have been characterized substantially in the following words by Mr. A. M. Powell, himself a Quaker by birth, and an unwilling witness to the faults of a system of doctrines in which he sees much to admire:—

"In its merely sectarian aspect, Quaker-ism is as uninteresting, narrow, timid, self-ish, and conservative as is mere sectari-anism under any other name. The Quakers have little comprehension of the meaning of Quakerism beyond a blind observance of the peculiarities of dress and speech and the formality of the Meeting. They cling to the now meaningless protests of the past.

They are inaccessible to new conceptions of truth. They have dishonored the important fundamental principle [of the Inner Light] and tarnished the Society's good name by subordinating it to narrow views of religion, to commercial selfishness, and to the prevalent palsying conservatism of the outside world."*

In all that is said in these pages by way of criticism of the Quakers, reference is had solely to their doctrines as a system of thought. Of their sweet and beautiful *lives* it is hardly necessary to speak at length. Volumes might be filled with instances of their large-hearted benevolence and personal self-sacrifice in care for others. The loveliness of their lives is like a beautiful perfume in the society in which they move. As you see the Quaker women of Philadelphia, with their pure, tranquil faces, and plain, immaculate dress, moving about among the greedy and vile-mannered non-Quaker *canaille* of that democratic city, they seem like Christian and Faithful

* Mrs. John T. Sargent's "Sketches and Reminiscences of the Radical Club."

amid the crowds of Vanity Fair. Their faces are like a benediction, and you thank heaven for them. The liberal Friends in America have many great and noble names on their roll of honor. And surely a sect that has produced such characters as Lucretia Mott, John Bright, and John G. Whittier, must win our intellectual respect. But it is only because these persons, like Milton, were in most respects above their sect that we admire them. There are proofs manifold, however, throughout the prose and poetry of Whittier that he has nominally remained within the pale of Quakerism all his days. Doubtless such a course was essential to the very existence in him of poetic inspiration. His genius is wholly lyrical. A song or lyric is the outgushing of pure emotion. Especially in the case of the religious and ethical lyrist is faith life, and doubt death. Doubt, in Whittier's case, would have meant the cessation of his songs. To break away entirely from the faith of his fathers would have chilled his inspiration. He has not, it is true, escaped the conflict with doubt. As we shall see, no man has had a severer struggle to reconcile his faith with the terror and mystery of life. But, although his religious views have been liberalized by science, yet he has never ceased to retain a hearty sympathy with, and belief in, the Quaker principles of the Inner Light, silent waiting, etc.

That he has remained within the pale of Quakerism has been an injury to him as well as a help. It makes him obtrude his sectarianism too frequently, especially in his prose writings. By the very nature of the creed, he must either be blind to its faults, or constantly put on the defensive against the least assault, from whatever quarter it may come. When he dons the garb of the sectary, he naturally becomes weakened, and loses his chief charm. We see then that he is a man hampered by a creed which forbids a catholic sympathy with human nature. He is shut up in the narrow field of sectarian morals and religion. He cannot, for example, enter, by historical imagination, into poetical sympathy with the gorgeous ritual and dreamy beauty of a European cathedral service. And yet so pure, gentle, and sweet is his nature that it is hard to censure him for this peculiarity. It is regret rather than censure that we feel, regret that he has

been so bound by circumstances that prevented his breaking wholly away from ham-
pering limitations, and to be always, what
he so often is, the strong and sweet-voiced
spokesman of the heart of humanity.

Let us hear his gentle confessions of faith.
In the autobiographical poem, "My Namesake," we read: —

> "He worshipped as his fathers did,
>   And kept the faith of childish days,
> And, howsoe'er he strayed or slid,
>   He loved the good old ways.
>
> The simple tastes, the kindly traits,
>   The tranquil air, and gentle speech,
> The silence of the soul that waits
>   For more than man to teach."

In "The Meeting" he has given us an
"Apologia pro Vita Sua,"— a defence of his
religious habits. He says he is accustomed
to meet with the Friends twice a week in
the little Meeting" at Amesbury, chiefly for
two reasons: first, because in the silent, un-
adorned house, with "pine-laid floor," his
religious communings are not distracted by
outward things as they would be if he worshipped always amid the solitudes of nature;
and, secondly, he finds in "The Meeting" a

heart-solace in the memories of dear ones passed away, who once sat by his side there. He says, in reference to the Quaker service: —

> "I ask no organ's soulless breath
>   To drone the themes of life and death,
>   No altar candle-lit by day,
>   No ornate wordsman's rhetoric-play,
>   No cool philosophy to teach
>   Its bland audacities of speech,
>
>   .   .   .   .
>
>   No pulpit hammered by the fist
>   Of loud-asserting dogmatist."

In " Memories " he says: —

> "Thine the Genevan's sternest creed,
>   While answers to my spirit's need
>   The Derby dalesman's simple truth.
>   For thee, the priestly rite and prayer,
>   And holy day and solemn psalm;
>   For me, the silent reverence where
>   My brethren gather slow and calm."

There are two epochs in the religious or philosophical development of Whittier. The first — that of simple piety unclouded by doubt, the epoch of unhesitating acceptance of the popular mythology — seems to have lasted until about 1850, or the period of early Darwinism and Spencerianism, —

the most momentous epoch in the religious history of the world. This pivotal point is very well marked by the publication, in 1853, of "The Chapel of the Hermits" and "Questions of Life." It is now that harrowing doubt begins, and restless striving to retain the faith amid new conditions and a vastly widened mental horizon. Transcendentalism, too, had just passed the noon meridian of its splendor. Emerson had written many of his exquisite philosophical poems, and Parker had blown his clear bugle-call to a higher religious life. It is evident that Whittier was — as, indeed, he could not help being — profoundly moved by the new spirit of the times.

With Transcendentalism he must have had large sympathy, owing to the similarity of its principles to those of Quakerism. And that he was profoundly agitated by the revelations of science his poetry shows. In "My Soul and I" (a poem remarkable for its searching subjective analysis), and in the poem "Follen," he had given expression to religious doubt, over which, as always in his case, faith was triumphant. But it is in "The Chapel of the Hermits" and succeeding poems that he first gave free and full utterance to the doubt and struggle of soul that was not his alone, but which was felt by all around him. In respect of doubt "My Soul and I" and "Questions of Life" resemble "Faust," as well as Tennyson's "Two Voices" and the "In Memoriam."

> " Life's mystery wrapped him like a cloud ;
>   He heard far voices mock his own,
> The sweep of wings unseen, the loud,
>   Long roll of waves unknown.
>
> The arrows of his straining sight
>   Fell quenched in darkness ; priest and sage
> Like lost guides calling left and right,
>   Perplexed his doubtful age.
>
> Like childhood, listening for the sound
>   Of its dropped pebbles in the well,
> All vainly down the dark profound
>   His brief-lined plummet fell."

My Namesake.

The "Questions of Life" are such as these : —

> "I am : but little more I know !
> Whence came I ? Whither do I go ?
> A centred self, which feels and is ;
> A cry between the silences."

> "This conscious life, — is it the same
> Which thrills the universal frame?"

> "Do bird and blossom feel, like me,
> Life's many-folded mystery, —
> The wonder which it is *To Be?*
> Or stand I severed and distinct,
> From Nature's chain of life unlinked?"

Such questions as these he confesses himself unable to answer. He shrinks back terrified from the task. He will not dare to trifle with their bitter logic. He will take refuge in faith; he will trust the Unseen; let us cease foolish questioning, and live wisely and well our present lives. He comes out of the struggle purified and chastened, still holding by his faith in God and virtue. A good deal of the old Quakerism is gone, — the belief in hell, in the Messianic and atonement machinery, in local and special avatars, etc. Again and again, in his later poems, he asserts the humanity of Christ and the co-equal divinity of all men: see "Miriam," for example. His opinion about hell he embodies in the sweet little poem, "The Minister's Daughter," published in "The King's Missive." In short, his religion is a simple and trustful theism. But there is no evidence that he has ever incorporated into his mind the principles of the development-science, — the evolution of man, the correlation of forces, the development of the universe through its own inner divine potency; or, in fine, any of the unteleological, unanthropomorphic explanations of things which are necessitated by science, and admitted by advanced thinkers, both in and out of the Churches.

As witnesses to his trustful attitude, we may select such a cluster of stanzas as this: —

> "Yet, sometimes glimpses on my sight,
> Through present wrong, the eternal right;
> And, step by step, since time began,
> I see the steady gain of man;
>
> That all of good the past hath had
> Remains to make our own time glad,—
> Our common daily life divine,
> And every land a Palestine.
>
> .   .   .   .   .
>
> Through the harsh noises of our day
> A low, sweet prelude finds its way;
> Through clouds of doubt, and creeds of fear,
> A light is breaking calm and clear."
>
> *Chapel of the Hermits.*

"Yet, in the maddening maze of things,
    And tossed by storm and flood,
To one fixed stake my spirit clings;
    I know that God is good !

       .   .   .   .

I know not where His islands lift
    Their fronded palms in air;
I only know I cannot drift
    Beyond His love and care."

The Eternal Goodness.

"When on my day of life the night is falling,
    And in the winds from unsunned spaces blown,
I hear far voices out of darkness calling
    My feet to paths unknown,

Thou who hast made my home of life so pleasant,
    Leave not its tenant when its walls decay;
O love divine, O Helper ever present,
    Be Thou my strength and stay !"

At Last.

"Dear Lord and Father of mankind,
    Forgive our foolish ways !
Reclothe us in our rightful mind,
In purer lives thy service find,
    In deeper reverence, praise."

The Brewing of Soma.

But Whittier is as remarkable for his faith in man as for his faith in God.   He is in the highest degree patriotic, American.   He loves America because it is the land of freedom. It has been charged against him that he is no true American poet, but a Quaker poet. The American, it is said, is eager, aggressive, high-spirited, combative; the Quaker, subdued and phlegmatic. The American is loud and boastful and daring and reckless; the Quaker, cautious, timid, secretive, and frugal. This is undoubtedly true of the classes as types, but it is far from being true of Whittier personally. He has blood militant in him. He comes of Puritan as well as Quaker stock. The Greenleafs and the Batchelders were not Quakers. The reader will perhaps remember the Lieutenant Greenleaf, already mentioned, who fought through the entire Civil War in England.* But his writings alone

* Hear Whittier himself on the subject : —

"Without intending any disparagement of my peaceable ancestry for many generations, I have still strong suspicions that somewhat of the old Norman blood, something of the grim Berserker spirit, has been bequeathed to me. How else can I account for the intense childish eagerness with which I listened to the stories of old campaigners who sometimes fought their battles over again in my hearing? Why did I, in my young fancy, go up with Jonathan, the son of Saul, to smite the garrisoned Philistines of Michmash, or with the fierce son of Nun against the cities of Canaan? Why was Mr. Greatheart, in Pilgrim's Progress, my favorite character? What gave such fascination to the grand Homeric encounter furnish ample proof of his martial spirit. The man and the Quaker struggle within him for the mastery; and the man is, on the whole, triumphant. Whenever his Quakerism permits, he stands out a normal man and a genuine American.   As Lowell says: —

> " There is Whittier, whose swelling and vehement heart
> Strains the strait-breasted drab of the Quaker apart,
> And reveals the live Man still supreme and erect
> Underneath the bemummying wrappers of sect."

If anybody will take the trouble to glance over the complete works of Whittier, he or she will find that one of the predominant characteristics of his writings is their indigenous quality, their national spirit.   Indeed, this is almost too notorious to need mention.   He, if any one, merits the proud title of "A Representative American Poet."   His whole soul is on fire with love of country.

between Christian and Apollyon in the valley? Why did I follow Ossian over Morven's battle-fields, exulting in the vulture-screams of the blind scald over his fallen enemies? Still, later, why did the newspapers furnish me with subjects for hero-worship in the half-demented Sir Gregor McGregor, and Ypsilanti at the head of his knavish Greeks? I can account for it only on the supposition that the mischief was inherited, — an heirloom from the old sea-kings of the ninth century." — *Prose Works, II.*, 390, 391.

As in the case of Whitman, his country is his bride, and upon it he has showered all the affectional wealth of his nature. The Quaker may be too obtrusive in his prose writings, but it is not so in the greater and better portion of his poetry. When the rush and glow of genuine poetical inspiration seize him, he invariably rises in spirit far above the weltering and eddying dust-clouds of faction and sect into the serene atmosphere of genuine patriotism. Read his "Last Walk in Autumn," where he says: —

> "Home of my heart! to me more fair
>   Than gay Versailles or Windsor's halls,
> The painted, shingly town-house where
>   The freeman's vote for Freedom falls!"

Read his "Eve of Election": —

> "Not lightly fall
>   Beyond recall
> The written scrolls a breath can float;
>   The crowning fact,
>   The kingliest act
> Of Freedom is the freeman's vote!"

Or take "After Election," a poem that cannot be read without a thrill of the nerves and a leaping of the heart. You have concentrated

in that wild lyric burst the purest essence
of democratic patriotism,—the trembling
anxiety and yearning of a mother-heart.   It
is a poem celebrating a victory of peace with
all the fiery energy of a war-ode (a significant fact that the advocates of gory war, as
a source of poetic inspiration, would do well
to ponder) : —

> "The day's sharp strife is ended now,
>   Our work is done, God knoweth how!
>   As on the thronged, unrestful town
>   The patience of the moon looks down,
>   I wait 'to hear, beside the wire,
>   The voices of its tongues of fire.
>
>   Slow, doubtful, faint, they seem at first:
>   Be strong, my heart, to know the worst!
>   Hark!—there the Alleghanies spoke;
>   That sound from lake and prairie broke,
>   That sunset gun of triumph rent
>   The silence of a continent!
>
>   That signal from Nebraska sprung,
>   This, from Nevada's mountain tongue!
>   Is that thy answer, strong and free,
>   O loyal heart of Tennessee?
>   What strange, glad voice is that which calls
>   From Wagner's grave and Sumter's walls?
>
>   From Mississippi's fountain-head
>   A sound as of the bison's tread!

> There rustled freedom's Charter Oak!
> In that wild burst the Ozarks spoke!
> Cheer answers cheer from rise to set
> Of sun. We have a country yet!"

To sum up now our analysis of the poet's character. We have seen that the central trait of his mind is love of freedom. (Even his religion, which is so profound an element in his nature, and so all-pervasive in his writings, will be found, on a deep analysis, to be a yearning for freedom from the trappings of sense and time, in order to attain to a spiritual union with the Infinite.) This love of freedom, this hatred of oppression, intensified by persecution, both ancestral and personal, stimulated by contact with Puritan democracy, as well as by the New England Transcendental movement, and flowering out luxuriantly in the long struggle against slavery, — this noble sentiment, and that long self-sacrificing personal warfare in behalf of the oppressed, form the true glory of Whittier's character. Shy, timid, almost an invalid, having a nervous horror of mobs and personal indignities, he yet forgot himself in his love of Man, overcame and underwent, — suffered social martyrdom for a quarter of a century, never flinching, never holding his peace for bread's sake or fame's sake, not stopping to count the cost, taking his life in his hand, and never ceasing to express his high-born soul in burning invective and scathing satire against the oppressor, or in words of lofty hope and cheer for the suffering idealist and lover of humanity, whoever and wherever he was. Whittier is a hero as well as a poet. He will be known to posterity by a few exquisite poems, but chiefly by his moral heroism and patriotism. As a thinker and a poet he belongs, with Bryant and Longfellow, to the pre-scientific age. The poetry of the future (of the new era of self-consciousness) will necessarily differ widely from that of the first half of this century. It will not be distinctively the poetry of Wordsworth, or Cowper, or Byron, or Longfellow, or Whittier. When the present materialistic and realistic temper of mind disappears from literature, and really noble ideal poetry returns, it will be vast in its scope and range, robust in its philosophy, unfettered by petty rhymes and classicisms, but powerfully rhythmic and harmonious. The writings of Shakspere, Goethe,

Jean Paul, Hugo, Tennyson, Whitman, and Emerson are the magnificent proem to it. It will be built upon a scientific and religious cosmism. It will not discuss Apollo and Luna and Neptune, and the nymphs and muses, but will draw its imagery from the heaven-staining red-flames of the sun, the gulfs of space, the miracles of organic and inorganic life, and human society. It will draw its inspiration not more from the storied past than from the storied future foreseen by its prophetic eye. It will idealize human life and deify nature. It will fall in the era of imagination. (After it will come another age of criticism.) It will fall in the age of splendid democracies. And in that age men will look back with veneration, not so much, perhaps, to the scholar-poets as to the hero-poets, like Whittier, who put faith in the rights of man and woman, who did believe in divine democracy, and were not ashamed of it, but nursed it patiently through its puling infancy, well assured of its undying grandeur when it should come to man's estate.

We subjoin fittingly to this chapter a characteristic letter of Mr. Whittier's, in which he speaks lovingly of Robert Burns, that other poet of freedom and independence of thought for all men.

At the Burns festival in Washington, 1869, the following letter from John G. Whittier was read:

"AMESBURY, 1st month, 18th day, 1869.

"DEAR FRIEND,— I thank the club represented by thee for remembering me on the occasion of its annual festival. Though I have never been able to trace my ancestry to the Land o' Cakes, I have— and I know it is saying a great deal— a Scotchman's love for the poet whose fame deepens and broadens with years. The world has never known a truer singer. We may criticise his rustic verse and compare his brief and simple lyrics with the works of men of longer scrolls and loftier lyres; but after rendering to Wordsworth, Tennyson and Browning the homage which the intellect owes to genius, we turn to Burns, if not with awe and reverence, [yet] with a feeling of personal interest and affection. We admire others; we love him. As the day of his birth comes round, I take down his well-worn volume in grateful commemoration, and feel that I am communing with one whom living I could have loved as much for his true manhood and native nobility of soul as for those wonderful songs of his which shall sing themselves forever.

"They know little of Burns who regard him as an aimless versifier — 'the idle singer of an idle lay.' Pharisees in the Church, and oppressors in the State, knew better than this. They felt those immortal sarcasms which did not die with the utterer, but lived on to work out the divine commission of Providence. In the shout of enfranchised millions, as they lift the untitled Quaker of Rochdale into the British Cabinet, I seem to hear the voice of the Ayrshire poet : —

> "'For a' that and a' that,
> It's comin' yet for a' that ;
> That man to man the world o'er
> Shall brothers be for a' that.'

"With hearty sympathy and kind greetings for the Burns Club of Washington,
"I am, very truly, thy friend,
"JOHN G. WHITTIER."

CHAPTER II.

THE ARTIST.

THE title of this chapter is almost a misnomer; for the style, or technique, of the poet whose works we are considering is so very simple and unoriginal that he can hardly be said to have a distinctive style of his own, — unless a few persistent mannerisms establish a claim to it. His diction, however, is always pictorial, and glows with an intense Oriental fervor. Fused in this interior vital heat, his thoughts do not sink, like powerful Jinn, into the deep silence-sphere of the mind, to fetch thence sparkling treasures, rich and strange: rather, they run to and fro with lightning swiftness amid the million surface-pictures of the intellect; rearranging, recombining, and creatively blending its images, and finally pouring them out along the page to charm our fancy and feeling with old thoughts and scenes painted in fresh colors and from new points of view. There is more of fancy than of creative imagination in Whittier.

The artistic quality, or tone, of his mind is a fusion of that of Wordsworth and that of Byron. In his best ballads and other lyrics you have the moral sincerity of Wordsworth and the sweet Wordsworthian simplicity (with a difference); and in his reform poems you have the Byronic indignation, and scorn of Philistinism and its tyrannies. As a religious poet, he reveals the quiet piety and devoutness of Cowper; and his rural and folk poems show that he is a debtor to Burns.

He has been a diligent reader, — "a close-browed miser of the scholar's gains," — and his writings are full of bookish allusions. But, if the truth must be told, his doctor's gown does not often sit gracefully upon his shoulders. His readers soon learn to know that his strength lies in his moral nature, and in his power to tell a story melodiously, simply, and sweetly. Hence it is, doubtless, that they care little for his literary

14

allusions, — think, perhaps, that they are
rather awkwardly dragged in by the ears,
and at any rate hasten by them impatiently
that they may inhale anew the violet-fresh-
ness of the poet's own soul. What has just
been said about bookish allusions does not
apply to the beautiful historical ballads produced by Whittier in the mellow maturity
of his powers. These fresh improvisations
are as perfect works of art as the finest
Greek marbles.   In them Whittier at length
succeeds in freeing himself completely from
the shackles of didacticism. Such ballads as
"The Witch's Daughter" and "Telling the
Bees" are as absolutely faultless productions
as Wordsworth's "We are Seven" and his
"Lucy Gray," or as Uhland's "Des Sänger's
Fluch," or William Blake's "Mary." There
is in them the confident and unconscious
ease that marks the work of the highest
genius. A shower of lucid water-drops falls
in no truer obedience to the law of perfect
sphericity than flowed from the pen of the
poet these delicate creations in obedience to
the law of perfect spontaneity. Almost all
of Whittier's lyrics have evidently been rapidly written, poured forth in the first glow

of feeling, and not carefully amended and polished as were Longfellow's works. And herein he is at fault, as was Byron. But the delicate health of Whittier, and his toilsome early days, form an excuse for his deficiency in this respect. His later creations, the product of his leisure years, are full of pure and flawless music. They have no harmony or rhythmic volume of sound, as in Tennyson, Swinburne, Milton, and Shakspere; but they set themselves to simple melodious airs spontaneously. As you read them, your feet begin to tap time,— only the music is that of a good rural choir rather than that of an orchestra.

The thought of each poem is generally conveyed to the reader's understanding with the utmost lucidity. There is no mysticism, no obscurity. The story or thought unfolds itself naturally, and without fatigue to our minds. A great many poems are indeed spun out at too great length; but the central idea to be conveyed is rarely lost sight of.

To the list of his virtues as an artist, it remains to add his frequent surprising strength. This is naturally most marked in the anti-slavery poems. When he wrote these, he was in the flush of manhood, his soul at a white heat of moral indignation. He is occasionally nerved to almost superhuman effort: it is the battle-axe of Richard thundering at the gates of Front de Bœuf. For nervous energy, there is nothing in the Hebrew prophets finer than such passages as these:—

> "Strike home, strong-hearted man!
> Down to the root
> Of old oppression sink the Saxon steel."
>
> To Ronge.

> "Maddened by Earth's wrong and evil,
> 'Lord!' I cried in sudden ire,
> 'From thy right hand, clothed with thunder,
> Shake the bolted fire!'"
>
> What the Voice Said.

> "Hands off! thou tithe-fat plunderer! play
> No trick of priestcraft here!
> Back, puny lordling! darest thou lay
> A hand on Elliott's bier?
> Alive, your rank and pomp, as dust,
> Beneath his feet he trod:
> He knew the locust-swarm that cursed
> The harvest-fields of God.

> "On these pale lips, the smothered thought
> Which England's millions feel,

A fierce and fearful splendor caught,
    As from his forge the steel.
Strong-armed as Thor, — a shower of fire
    His smitten anvil flung;
God's curse, Earth's wrong, dumb Hunger's ire, —
    He gave them all a tongue!"

Elliott.

" And Law, an unloosed maniac, strong,
    Blood-drunken, through the blackness trod,
    Hoarse-shouting in the ear of God
The blasphemy of wrong."

The Rendition.

" All grim and soiled, and brown with tan,
    I saw a Strong One, in his wrath,
Smiting the godless shrines of man
    Along his path."

The Reformer.

As Whittier has grown older, and the battles of his life have become (as he expressed it to the writer) like " a remembered dream," his genius has grown mellow and full of graciousness. His art culminated in " Home Ballads," " Snow-Bound," and " The Tent on the Beach." He has kept longer than most poets the lyric glow; only in his later poems it is " emotion remembered in tranquillity."

If asked to name the finest poems of Whittier, would not the following instinctively recur to the mind: "Snow-Bound," "Maud Muller," "Barbara Frietchie," "The Witch's Daughter," "Telling the Bees," "Skipper Ireson's Ride," "King Volmer and Elsie," and "The Tent on the Beach"?

To these one would like to add several exquisite hymns and short secular lyrics. But the poems mentioned would probably be regarded by most critics as Whittier's finest works of art. They merit this distinction certainly; and they furnish remarkable instances for those who desire to study the poet's greater versatility in the ballad line, as they are all good representatives of his wonderfully long range.

The foregoing remark must be our cue for beginning to pass in review the artistic deficiencies of Whittier. He has three crazes that have nearly ruined the mass of his poetry. They are the reform craze, the religious craze, and the rhyme craze. Of course, as a man, he could not have a superfluity of the first of these; but, as a poet, they have been a great injury to him. We need not deny that he has taken the manlier course in subordinating the artist to the reformer and preacher; but in estimating his poetic merits we ought to regard his work from an absolute point of view. Let us not be misunderstood. It is gladly and freely conceded that the theory that great poetry is not necessarily moral, and that the aim of poetry is only to please the senses, is a petty and shallow one, and that the true function of the great poet is also to bear witness to the ideal and noble, to the moral and religious. Let us heartily agree with Principal Shairp when he says that the true end of the poet " is to awaken men to the divine side of things; to bear witness to the beauty that clothes the outer world, the nobility that lies hid, often obscured, in human souls; to call forth sympathy for neglected truths, for noble but oppressed persons, for downtrodden causes, and to make men feel that through all outward beauty and all pure inward affection God himself is addressing them." We may admit all this, and yet find fault with the moralizations and homilies of Whittier. The poetry of Dante and Milton is full of ethical passion, and occasionally a little sermon is wedged in; yet they do not treat us to endless broadsides

of preaching, as Whittier does in his earlier
poems, and in some of his later ones. But
there is this distinction: the moral in Dante
and Milton and Shakspere and Emerson
is so garnitured with beauty that while our
souls are ennobled our imaginations are
gratified.   But in many of Whittier's poems
we have the bare skeleton of the moral,
without the rounded contour and delicate
tints of the living body of beauty. His
reform poems have been called stump-
speeches in verse.   His anti-slavery poems
are, with a few exceptions, devoid of beauty.
They should have been written in the manner he himself commends in a review of
Longfellow's "Evangeline": he should have
depicted the truth strongly and attractively,
and left to the reader the censure and the
indignation.   Mr. Whittier seems to know
his peculiar limitations as well as his critics.
He speaks of himself as one —

> "Whose rhyme
> Beat often Labor's hurried time,
> Or Duty's rugged march through storm and strife,"

and he has once or twice expressed himself
in prose in a way that seems to show that he

recognizes the artistic mistake in the construction of his earlier poems. The omission of the moral *envoi* from so many of his maturer creations strengthens one in this surmise. In 1867 Whittier published the following letter in the New York *Nation:*

"To the Editor of the Nation:

"I am very well aware that merely personal explanations are not likely to be as interesting to the public as to the parties concerned; but I am induced to notice what is either a misconception on thy part, or, as is most probable, a failure on my own to make myself clearly understood. In the review of 'The Tent on the Beach' in thy paper of last week, I confess I was not a little surprised to find myself represented as regretting my life-long and active participation in the great conflict which has ended in the emancipation of the slave, and that I had not devoted myself to merely literary pursuits. In the half-playful lines upon which this statement is founded, if I did not feel at liberty to boast of my anti-slavery labors and magnify my editorial profession, I certainly did not mean to underrate them, or express the shadow of a regret that they had occupied so large a share of my time and thought. The simple fact is that I cannot be sufficiently thankful to the Divine Providence that so early called my attention to the great interests of humanity, saving me from the poor ambitions and miserable jealousies of a selfish pursuit of literary reputation. Up to a comparatively recent period my writings have been simply episodical, something apart from the real object and aim of my life; and whatever of favor they have found with the public has come to me as a grateful surprise rather than as an expected reward. As I have never staked all upon the chances of authorship, I have been spared the pain of disappointment and the temptation to envy those who, as men of letters, deservedly occupy a higher place in the popular estimation than I have ever aspired to.

"Truly thy friend,

"JOHN G. WHITTIER.

"AMESBURY, 9th, 3d mo., 1867."

One is reminded by this letter that Wordsworth once said to Dr. Orville Dewey, of Boston, that, "although he was known to the world only as a poet, he had given twelve hours' thought to the condition and prospects of society for one to poetry." In a letter read at the third decade meeting of the American Anti-Slavery Society in Philadelphia, Mr. Whittier said: "I am not insensible to literary reputation; I love, perhaps too well, the praise and good-will of my fellow-men; but I set a higher value on my name as appended to the Anti-Slavery Declaration of 1833 than on the title-page of any book."

In his earlier years our poet was wholly ignorant of the fact that an artist should love beauty for its own sake. The simple-hearted Quaker and Puritan farmer-youth thought it almost a sin to spend his time in the cultivation of the beautiful. In his dedication of the "Supernaturalism of New England" to his sister, he says: —

> "And knowing how my life hath been
>   A weary work of tongue and pen,
>   A long, harsh strife with strong-willed men,
>   Thou wilt not chide my turning,
>   To con, at times, an idle rhyme,
>   To pluck a flower from childhood's clime,
>   Or listen, at Life's noon-day chime,
>   For the sweet bells of Morning!"

" Poor fellow!" we say at first.   And yet there is something refreshing and noble in such a spirit.   It is with difficulty that the Germanic mind can bring itself to the study of the beautiful as something of co-equal worth with the moral.   Let us leave that, says the Teuton, to the nation whose word for love of art is " virtue."   How Whittier would have abhorred in his youth and early manhood the following sentiment by one of the Latin race : —

" The arts require idle, delicate minds, not stoics, especially not Puritans, easily shocked by dissonance, inclined to sensuous pleasure, employing their long periods of leisure, their free reveries, in harmoniously arranging, and with no other object but enjoyment, forms, colors, and sounds." (Taine's *English Literature*, II. 332.)   Or the following from the same work :—

" The Puritan destroys the artist, stiffens the man, fetters the writer, and leaves of artist, man, writer, only a sort of abstract being, the slave of a watchword.   If a Milton springs up among them, it is because, by his wide curiosity, his travels, his comprehensive education, and by his independence of spirit, loftily adhered to even against the sectarians, Milton passes beyond sectarianism." (I. 397, 398.)

Here is another passage from Whittier on this same subject. It is almost a pity to give it, since the author has apparently repudiated the sentiment by omitting the lines from his complete works. In the introduction to "Supernaturalism of New England" he says: —

"If in some few instances, like Burns in view of his national thistle, I have—

> 'Turned my weeding-hook aside,
> And spared the symbol dear,'

I have been influenced by the comparatively innocent nature and simple poetic beauty of the traditions in question; yet not even for the sake of poetry and romance would I confirm in any mind a pernicious credulity, or seek to absolve myself from that stern duty which the true man owes to his generation, to expose error whenever and wherever he finds it."

One more instance. In one of his sketches he is describing an old custom called "Pope Night," which has been kept up in the Mer-

rimack Valley in unbroken sequence from
the time of the Guy Fawkes plot. The plot
is commemorated by bonfires and effigies of
the Pope and others, and Whittier quotes
these lines of a song which is sung on the
occasion : —

> "Look here ! from Rome
>   The Pope has come,
>   That fiery serpent dire;
>   Here's the Pope that we have got,
>   The old promoter of the plot;
>   We'll stick a pitchfork in his back,
>   And throw him in the fire."

Mr. Whittier was so broad-minded in regard to all matters pertaining to true growth,
and withal so conscientious a student of the
best versification, that is, the most natural,
that we soon find him striving, at least, to
free himself from all these minor faults.

Consequently his mannerisms more and
more drop away. He is a born preacher.
And presently we see in him a decided
advance toward the delineation of what is
simply true and beautiful, without the ap-
preciable pause by the way, "to point a
moral and adorn a tale." For a preacher is
not a poet; and true poetic fire. must be

dimmed at once, and the divine afflatus be
a lack-lustre thing, when appeals by pious
exhortation are brought in to fill out rhyme
and metre. Many of Whittier's purely religious poems are the most exquisite and
beautiful ever written. The tender feeling,
the warm-hearted trustfulness, and the reverent touch of his hymns speak directly to
our hearts. The prayer-hymn at the close
of "The Brewing of Soma" ("Dear Lord
and Father of mankind," etc.), and such
poems as "At Last" and "The Wish of
To-day," are unsurpassed in sacred song.
Some one has said that in Whittier's books
we rarely meet with ideas expressed in such
perfection and idiosyncrasy of manner that
ever afterward the same ideas must recur to
our minds in the words of this author and
no other; that is to say, there are few dicta,
few portable and universally-quoted passages
in his writings. But exception must be
made in favor of his best hymns. Their
stanzas haunt the mind with their beauty,
and you are obliged to learn them by heart
before you can have peace. These purely
religious productions show Whittier's work
at high-water mark, and as long as the

English language is spoken, they will be
employed by those who require a vehicle for
thought, by which the true worship may be
served. There is only one poet in the world
whose works will not suffer by reading his
entire poetical productions in consecutive
perusal, and that is Shakspere. Poetry
should be read solely for the refreshment
and elevation of the mind, and only when
one's mood requires it. Unquestionably, if
so read, all mannerisms that Mr. Whittier
might have been accused of at an early
stage in his authorship would not appear so
conspicuous.

One of the mannerisms of our poet is his
inclination toward the four-foot line with
consecutive or alternate rhymes. Almost
all of Burns's poetry is written as just described; and it is evident Mr. Whittier's ear
was naturally inclined to it, from his early
love for Burns, his patron saint, as it were,
in those then untrodden fields. An ear educated by Tennyson, and the other Victo-
rian poets, might be unable to grasp even
the beauty of thought unless conveyed by
their especial methods. One is pleased
when rhymes are so masked, so subtly inter-

twined, and parted by intervening lines, that each shall seem like a delicate echo of that which preceded it, — the assonance just remembered, and no more.

A minor mannerism of Whittier is his frequent use of the present participle in *ing*, with the verb *to be;* "is flowing," "is shining," etc. The jingle of the *ing* evidently caught the poet's rhyme-loving ear, and sometimes it really has a very pretty effect. Certain it is he has used it with great skill, and given his readers insight into another of his versatile gifts.

As to the originality of our poet there is this to be said: He has a distinctively national spirit or vision; he is democratic in his feelings, and treats of indigenous subjects. His vehicle, his poetic forms and handling, he has treated as minor subjects for thought. He is democratic, not so powerfully and broadly as Whitman, but more unaffectedly and sincerely. He has not the magnificent prophetic vision, or *Vorstellungskraft*, of Whitman, any more than he has the crushing mastodon-steps of Whitman's ponderous rhythm. But he has thrown himself

with trembling ardor and patriotism, into
the life of his country. It is this fresh,
New-World spirit that entitles him to be
called original: he is non-European. He
has not travelled much, nor mingled in the
seething currents of Western and Southern
life; but his strong sympathy has gone forth
over the entire land. He also reflects faithfully the quiet scenes of his own Merrimack
Valley. From his descriptions of these
scenes we receive the impression of freshness and originality; and we recognize a
master hand that can so portray them as to
make us see the same places, though only
on the printed page.

One regrets using a critical pen at all in
discussing such a writer. It would be ungracious to call to a severe account one who
places the most modest estimate upon his
own work, and who has distinctly stated
that, up to "about the year 1865, his writings were simply episodical, something apart
from the real object and aim of [his] life."
It is hard to criticise severely one who is
unjust to himself through excess of diffident
humility. In the exquisite Proem to his

complete poems he would fain persuade us that he cannot breathe such notes as those of —

> "The old melodious lays
> Which softly melt the ages through,
>   The songs of Spenser's golden days,
>   Arcadian Sidney's silvery phrase,
> Sprinkling our noon of time with freshest morning dew."

But not so, O gentle minstrel of Essex! There are poems of thine which thousands prefer to the best of Spenser's or Sidney's, and which will continue to exist as long as beauty is its own excuse for being. Thou too hast been in Paradise, to fetch thence armfuls of dewy roses for our delight; not mounting thither by the "stairway of surprise," but along the common highway of daily duty and noble endeavor, unmindful of the dust and heat and chafing burdens, but singing aloud thy songs of lofty cheer, all magically intertwined with pictures of wayside flowers, and the homely beauty of lowliest things. And thou hast imparted to us the "groping of the keys of the heavenly harmonies," that no one who loves thy songs, ever loses from his life.

CHAPTER III.

POEMS SERIATIM.

AMONG the three or four critical papers on Whittier that have up to this time been published, there is one that is marked by exceptional vigor; namely, the admirable philosophical analysis by Mr. David A. Wasson, published in the *Atlantic Monthly* for March, 1864. The author gladly acknowledges his indebtedness to this paper for several things, — chiefly for its keen *aperçu* into the nature of Whittier's genius, and the proper psychological grouping of his poems. Mr. Wasson's classification can hardly be improved upon in its general features. He divides the literary life of the poet into three epochs, — The Struggle for Life, The Culture Epoch, and The Epoch of Poetic Realism; and between each of these he places transitional periods. The lines of his classification, however, are too sharply drawn, and the epochs seem too minutely subdivided. Moreover, the present writer would add an introductory or preparatory period; in other respects it seems to him that the grouping is as correct as such mathematical measurements of a poet's development can be. Suppose we group and name the poet's mental epochs as follows:—

FIRST PERIOD. — INTRODUCTORY. 1830–1833.

During this quiet, purely literary epoch, Whittier published " Legends of New England" and "Moll Pitcher," and edited the " Literary Remains of Brainard."

SECOND PERIOD. — STORM AND STRESS. 1833–1853.

The beginning of this period was marked by the publication of "Justice and Expediency," and during its continuance were written most of the anti-slavery productions, the Indian poems, many legendary lays and prose pieces, religious lyrics, and "Songs of Labor." The latter, being partially free from didacticism, leads naturally up to the third period.

THIRD PERIOD. — TRANSITION.   1853–1860

This Mr. Wasson calls the epoch of culture and religious doubt, the central poems of which are " Chapel of the Hermits " and " Questions of Life."   We now begin to see a love of art for art's sake, and there are fewer moral stump-speeches.   The indignation of the reformer is giving place to the calm repose of the artist.   And such ballads as " Mary Garvin " and " Maud Muller " form the introduction to the culminating (or fourth) epoch in the poet's creative life.

FOURTH PERIOD. — RELIGIOUS AND ARTISTIC REPOSE.
1860–

During this time have been written nearly all the author's great works, namely, his beautiful ballads, as well as "Snow-Bound" and "The Tent on the Beach."   The literary style is now mature.   The beautiful is sought for its own sake, both in nature and in lowly life.   It is a season of trust and *naïve* simplicity.

The works produced during the Introductory period have already been discussed in the biographical portion of this volume.

Before passing rapidly in review some of the more important detached poems of the three latter periods (reserving a number of poems for consideration by groups), we must be allowed to offer a few criticisms on the earlier poems in general, meaning by this the ones published previous to the "Songs of Labor" in 1850. These earlier productions are to be commended chiefly for two things: (1) the subjects are drawn from original and native sources, and (2) the slavery poems are full of moral stamina and fiery indignation at oppression. There are single poems of great merit and beauty. But the style of most of them is unoriginal, being merely an echo of that of the English Lake School. Whittier's poetical development has been a steady growth. His genius matured late, and in his early poems there is little promise of the exquisite work of his riper years, unless it is a distinct indication of his rare power of telling a story in verse. It must be remembered that when Whittier began to write, American literature had yet to be created. There was not a single great American poem, with the exception of Bryant's "Thanatopsis."

The prominent poets of that time — Percival, Brainard, Trumbull, Joel Barlow, Hillhouse, Pierpont, Dana, Sprague — are all forgotten now. The breath of immortality was not upon anything they wrote. A national literature is a thing of slow growth. Every writer is insensibly influenced by the intellectual tone of his neighbors and contemporaries. Judged in the light of his early disadvantages, and estimated by the standard of that time, Whittier's first essays are deserving of much credit, and they have had a distinct æsthetic and moral value in the development of American literature and the American character. But their deficiencies are very grave. There is a good deal of commonplace, and much extravagance of rhetoric. There are a great many "Lines" called forth by circumstances not at all poetical in their suggestions. Emotion and rhyme and commonplace incident are not enough to make a poem. One cannot embalm the memory of all one's friends in verse. In casting about for an explanation of the circumstance that our poet has so often chosen tame and uninspiring themes for his poems, we reach the conclusion that it is due to his solitary and uneventful life, and to the subdued and art-chilling atmosphere of his Quaker religion. You get, at any rate, no true impression of the intellectual breadth of the poet's mind from many of the productions of the period we are considering: the theme is too weak to support the poetical structure reared upon it. The poems and essays are written by one untoughened and unvitalized by varied and cheerful intercourse with men and affairs, a state of mind that was changed considerably as Mr. Whittier emerged from his semi-obscurity into a larger comprehension of his own powers.

A minor fault of this period is the too frequent interruption of explanatory notes, that break and mar the free-flowing melody of versified thought. We find the same blemish in Longfellow's early work.

At the opening of the complete poetical works of Whittier stand two long Indian poems, with their war-paint and blood — like scarlet maples at the entrance of an aboriginal forest. The first of these poems, "Mogg Megone," is every way inferior to

the second, or " The Bridal of Pennacook."
" Mogg Megone " was published in 1836,
and " The Bridal of Pennacook " in 1848.
Mr. Whittier half apologizes for retaining
the former of these in his complete works.
There is, amongst much that, eliminated,
might not be missed, a certain fresh and
realistic diction, or nomenclature. It is picturesque, in portions somewhat dramatic and
thrilling, and now is valuable as a link between the early stage of his authorship and
the advanced culture of later years. In style
it is an echo of Scott's " Lady of the Lake "
or " Marmion."

In " The Bridal of Pennacook " we have
an Indian idyl of unquestionable power and
beauty, a descriptive poem full of the cool,
mossy sweetness of mountain landscapes,
and although too artificial and subjective
for a poem of primitive life, yet saturated
with the imagery of the wigwam and the
forest. A favorite article of food with the
Indians of Northern Ohio was dried bear's-
meat dipped in maple syrup. There is a
savor of the like ferity and sweetness in this
poem. It is almost wholly free from the
strongly-marked faults of " Mogg Megone,"

and (that test of all tests) it is pleasant reading. Its two cardinal defects are lack of simplicity of treatment, and tenuity or triviality of the subject, or plot. The story is sometimes lost sight of in a jungle of verbiage and description. In contrasting such a poem with " Hiawatha," we see the wisdom of Longfellow in choosing an antique vehicle, or rhythmic style. Aborigines have a dialect of their own; the sentences of an Indian brave being as abrupt and sharp as the wild screams of an eagle. The set speeches of the North American Indians are always full of divers stock metaphors about natural scenery, wild animals, totems, and spirits, and are so different from those of civilized life that an expert can instantly detect a forgery or an imitation, so that all incongruities that attribute the complex and refined emotions of civilized life to the savage, seriously mar the pleasure of the reader. The descriptions of natural scenery in these Indian legends of Mr. Whittier's are fine, as all such writing by his facile pen was ever felicitous. And by virtue of this descriptive power, these idyls will be held long in grateful remembrance.

In plan the poem is like the "Decameron," the "Princess," the "Canterbury Tales," and "Tales of a Wayside Inn." The different portions are supposed to be related by five persons, — a lawyer, a clergyman, a merchant and his daughter, and the poet, — who are all sight-seeing in the White Mountains. The opening description, in blank verse, conveys a vague but not very powerful impression of sublimity. The musical nomenclature of the red aborigines is finely handled, and such words as Pennacook, Babboosuck, Contoocook, Bashaba, and Weetamoo chime out here and there along the pages with as silvery a sweetness as the Tuscan words in Macaulay's "Lays." At the wedding of Weetamoo we have —

> "Pike and perch from the Suncook taken,
> Nuts from the trees of the Black Hills shaken,
> Cranberries picked from the Squamscot bog,
> And grapes from the vines of Piscataquog:
>
> And, drawn from that great stone vase which stands
> In the river scooped by a spirit's hands,
> Garnished with spoons of shell and horn,
> Stood the birchen dishes of smoking corn."

The following stanza on the heroine, Weetamoo, is a fine one: —

"Child of the forest!—strong and free,
  Slight-robed, with loosely flowing hair,
She swam the lake, or climbed the tree,
  Or struck the flying bird in air.
O'er the heaped drifts of winter's moon
  Her snow-shoes tracked the hunter's way;
And, dazzling in the summer noon,
The blade of her light oar threw off its shower of
    spray!"

The "Song of Indian Women," at the close of "The Bridal of Pennacook," is admirable for melody, weird and wild beauty, and naturalness. It is a lament for the lost Weetamoo, who, unfortunate in her married life, has committed suicide by sailing over the rapids in her canoe:—

"The Dark Eye has left us,
  The Spring-bird has flown;
On the pathway of spirits
  She wanders alone.
The song of the wood-dove has died on our shore,—
Mat wonck kunna-monee!—We hear it no more!

.   .   .   .   .

O mighty Sowanna!
  Thy gateways unfold,
From thy wigwams of sunset
  Lift curtains of gold!
Take home the poor Spirit whose journey is o'er,—
Mat wonck kunna-monee!—We see her no more!"

There are two minor Indian poems by
Whittier that have the true ring; namely,
the "Truce of Piscataqua" and "Funeral
Tree of the Sokokis." The latter well-
known poem is pitched in as high and solemn a key as Platen's "Grab im Busento,"
a poem similar in theme to Whittier's: —

> "They heave the stubborn trunk aside,
> The firm roots from the earth divide, —
> The rent beneath yawns dark and wide.
>
> And there the fallen chief is laid,
> In tasselled garbs of skins arrayed,
> And girded with his wampum-braid."
>
> *Whittier.*

> "In der wogenleeren Höhlung wühlten sie empor die
>   Erde,
> Senkten tief hinein den Leichnam, mit der Rüstung
>   auf dem Pferde.
> Deckten dann mit Erde wieder ihn und seine stolze
>   Habe."
>
> *Platen.*

In the empty river-bottom hurriedly they dug the death-
    pit,
Deep therein they sank the hero with his armor and his
    war-steed,
Covered then with earth and darkness him and all his
    splendid trappings.

When the reader, who has worked gloomily along through Whittier's anti-slavery and miscellaneous poems, reaches the "Songs of Labor," he feels at once the breath of a fresher spirit, — as a traveller who has been toiling for weary leagues through sandy deserts bares his brow with delight to the coolness and shade of a green forest through whose thick roof of leaves the garish sunlight scarcely sifts. We feel that in these poems a new departure has been made. The wrath of the reformer has expended itself, and the poet now returns, with mind elevated and more tensely keyed by his moral warfare, to the study of the beautiful in native themes and in homely life. "The Shipbuilders," "The Shoemakers," "The Fishermen," and "The Huskers" are genuine songs; and more shame to the craftsmen celebrated if they do not get them set to music, and sing them while at their work. One cannot help feeling that Walt Whitman's call for some one to make songs for American laborers had already been met in a goodly degree by these spirited "Songs of Labor." What workman would not be glad to carol such

stanzas as the following, if they were set to
popular airs?

> "Hurrah! the seaward breezes
>   Sweep down the bay amain;
>   Heave up, my lads, the anchor!
>   Run up the sail again!
>   Leave to the lubber landsmen
>   The rail-car and the steed:
>   The stars of heaven shall guide us,
>   The breath of heaven shall speed."
>
> *The Fishermen*

> "Ho! workers of the old time styled
>   The Gentle Craft of Leather!
>   Young brothers of the ancient guild,
>   Stand forth once more together!
>   Call out again your long array,
>   In the olden merry manner!
>   Once more, on gay St. Crispin's day,
>   Fling out your blazoned banner!

> Rap, rap! upon the well-worn stone
>   How falls the polished hammer!
>   Rap, rap! the measured sound has grown
>   A quick and merry clamor.
>   Now shape the sole! now deftly curl
>   The glossy vamp around it,
>   And bless the while the bright-eyed girl
>   Whose gentle fingers bound it!"
>
> *The Shoemakers.*

The publication of "The Chapel of the
Hermits" and "Questions of Life," in 1853,

marks (as has been said) the period of culture and of religious doubt, — doubt which ended in trust. In this period we have such genuine undidactic poems as " The Barefoot Boy."

> " Blessings on thee, little man,
> Barefoot boy, with cheek of tan!
> With thy turned-up pantaloons,
> And thy merry whistled tunes;
> With thy red lip, redder still
> Kissed by strawberries on the hill;
> With the sunshine on thy face,
> Through thy torn brim's jaunty grace."

Also, such fine poems as " Flowers in Winter" and " To My Old Schoolmaster;" as well as the excellent ballads, "Maud Muller," " Kathleen," and " Mary Garvin."

The period in Whittier's life from about 1858 to 1868 we may call the Ballad Decade,* for within this time were produced most of his immortal ballads. We say immortal, believing that if all else that he has written shall perish, his finest ballads will carry his name down to a remote posterity.

* The beginning of this decade nearly coincides with the fourth or final period in our classification. upon the consideration of which we shall now enter.

16

"The Tent on the Beach" is mainly a series of ballads; and "Snow-Bound," although not a ballad, is still a narrative poem closely allied to that species of poetry, the difference between a ballad and an idyl being that one is made to be sung and the other to be read: both narrate events as they occur, and leave to the reader all sentiment and reflection.

The finest ballads of Whittier have the power of keeping us in breathless suspense of interest until the *dénouement* or the catastrophe, as the case may be. The popularity of "Maud Muller" is well deserved. What a rich and mellow translucence it has! How it appeals to the universal heart! And yet "The Witch's Daughter" and "Telling the Bees" are more exquisite creations than "Maud Muller": they have a spontaneity, a subtle pathos, a sublimated sweetness of despair that take hold of the very heart-strings, and thus deal with deeper emotions than such light, objective ballads as "Maud Muller" and "Skipper Ireson's Ride." But the surface grace of the two latter have of course made them the more popular, just as the "Scarlet Letter" finds greater favor with most people than does "The House of the Seven Gables," although Hawthorne rightly thought the "Seven Gables" to be his finest and subtlest work.

Mark the Chaucerian freshness of the opening stanzas of "The Witch's Daughter": —

> "It was the pleasant harvest time,
>   When cellar-bins are closely stowed,
>   And garrets bend beneath their load,
>
> And the old swallow-haunted barns —
>   Brown-gabled, long, and full of seams
>   Through which the moted sunlight streams,
>
> And winds blow freshly in, to shake
>   The red plumes of the roosted cocks,
>   And the loose hay-mow's scented locks —
>
> Are filled with summer's ripened stores,
>   Its odorous grass and barley sheaves,
>   From their low scaffolds to their eaves."

A companion ballad to "The Witch's Daughter" is "The Witch of Wenham," a poem almost equal to it in merit, and like it ending happily. These ballads do not

quite attain the almost supernatural simplicity of Wordsworth's "Lucy Gray" and
"We are Seven"; but they possess an
equal interest, excited by the same poetical
qualities. "Telling the Bees," however,
seems to the writer as purely Wordsworthian as anything Wordsworth ever
wrote: —

> " Stay at home, pretty bees, fly not hence !
>   Mistress Mary is dead and gone ! "

How the tears spring to the eyes in reading this immortal little poem!   The bee-
hives ranged in the garden, the sun "tan-
gling his wings of fire in the trees," the
dog whining low, the old man "with his
cane to his chin," — we all know the scene:
its every feature appeals to our sympathies
and associations.

"The Double-headed Snake of Newbury"
is a whimsical story, in which the poet
waxes right merry as he relates how —

> " Far and wide the tale was told,
>   Like a snowball growing while it rolled.
>   The nurse hushed with it the baby's cry ;
>   And it served, in the worthy minister's eye,
>   To paint the primitive serpent by.

Cotton Mather came galloping down
All the way to Newbury town,
With his eyes agog and his ears set wide,
And his marvellous inkhorn at his side;
Stirring the while in the shallow pool
Of his brains for the lore he learned at school,
To garnish the story, with here a streak
Of Latin, and there another of Greek:
And the tales he heard and the notes he took,
Behold! are they not in his Wonder-Book?"

A word about Whittier's "Prophecy of Samuel Sewall." It seems that old Judge Sewall made the prophecies of the Bible his favorite study. One of his ideas was that America was to be the site of the New Jerusalem. Toward the end of his book entitled " Phenomena Quædam Apocalyptica; . . . or . . . a Description of the New Heaven as it makes to those who stand upon the New Earth" (1697), he gives utterance to the triumphant prophecy that forms the subject of Whittier's poem. His language is so quaint that the reader will like to see the passage in Sewall's own words: —

" As long as Plum Island shall faithfully keep the commanded post, notwithstanding all the hectoring words and hard blows of

the proud and boisterous ocean; as long as
any salmon or sturgeon shall swim in the
streams of Merrimac, or any perch or pickerel in Crane Pond; as long as the sea-fowl
shall know the time of their coming, and
not neglect seasonably to visit the places
of their acquaintance; as long as any cattle
shall be fed with the grass growing in
the meadows, which do humbly bow down
themselves before Turkey Hill; as long as
any sheep shall walk upon Old-Town Hills,
and shall from thence pleasantly look down
upon the River Parker, and the fruitful
marshes lying beneath; as long as any free
and harmless doves shall find a white oak
or other tree within the township, to perch,
or feed, or build a careless nest upon, and
shall voluntarily present themselves to per-
form the office of gleaners after barley-har-
vest; as long as Nature shall not grow old
and dote, but shall constantly remember to
give the rows of Indian corn their education by pairs; so long shall Christians be
born there, and being first made meet, shall
from thence be translated to be made par-
takers of the inheritance of the saints in
light."

Moses Coit Tyler, in his "History of American Literature," II., p. 102 (note), says: "Whittier speaks of Newbury as Sewall's 'native town,' but Sewall was born at Horton, England. He also describes Sewall as an 'old man,' propped on his staff of age when he made this prophecy; but Sewall was then forty-five years old."

There are two or three other ballads in which Whittier is said to have made historical blunders. It really does not seem of much importance whether he did or did not get the precise facts in each case. The important point is that he made beautiful ballads. But it will be right to give, in brief, the objections that have been brought against "Skipper Ireson's Ride" and "Barbara Frietchie." "The King's Missive" will be discussed in another place.

Apropos of Skipper Ireson, Mr. John W. Chadwick has spoken as follows in *Harper's Monthly* for July, 1874: —

"In one of the queerest corners of the town [Marblehead], there stands a house

as modest as the Lee house was magnificent. So long as he lived it was the home
of 'Old Flood Oirson,' whose name and
fame have gone farther and fared worse
than any other fact or fancy connected with
his native town.   Plain, honest folk don't
know about poetic license, and I have often
heard the poet's conduct in the matter of
Skipper Ireson's ride characterized with
profane severity. He unwittingly departed
from the truth in various particulars. The
wreck did not, as the ballad recites, contain
any of 'his own town's-people.' Moreover,
four of those it did contain *were* saved by
a whale-boat from Provincetown. It was
off Cape Cod, and not in Chaleur Bay, that
the wreck was deserted; and the desertion
was in this wise: It was in the night that
the wreck was discovered. In the darkness
and the heavy sea it was impossible to give
assistance. When the skipper went below,
he ordered the watch to lie by the wreck
till 'dorning'; but the watch wilfully dis-
obeyed, and afterward, to shield themselves, laid all the blame upon the skipper.
Then came the tarring and feathering. The
women, whose *rôle* in the ballad is so strik-

ing, had nothing to do with it. The vehicle was not a cart, but a dory; and the skipper, instead of being contrite, said, ' I thank you for your ride.' I asked one of the skipper's contemporaries what the effect was on the skipper. ' Cowed him to death,' said he, ' cowed him to death.' He went skipper again the next year, but never afterward. He had been dead only a year or two when Whittier's ballad appeared. His real name was not Floyd, as Whittier supposes, but Benjamin, 'Flood' being one of those nicknames that were not the exception, but the rule, in the old fishing-days. For many years before his death the old man earned a precarious living by dory-fishing in the bay, and selling his daily catch from a wheelbarrow. When old age and blindness overtook him, and his last trip was made, his dory was hauled up into the lane before his house, and there went to rot and ruin. . . . The hoarse refrain of Whittier's ballad is the best-known example of the once famous Marblehead dialect, and it is not a bad one. To what extent this dialect was peculiar to Marblehead it might be difficult to determine. Largely, no doubt, it was inherited from

English ancestors. Its principal delight consisted in pronouncing *o* for *a*, and *a* for *o*. For example, if an old-fashioned Marbleheader wished to say he 'was born in a barn,' he would say, 'I was barn in a born.' The *e* was also turned into *a*, and even into *o*, and the *v* into *w*. 'That vessel's stern' became 'that wessel's starn,' or 'storn.' I remember a schoolboy declaiming from Shakspere, 'Thou little walliant, great in willany.' There was a great deal of shortening. The fine name Crowninshield became Grounsel, and Florence became Flurry, and a Frenchman named Blancpied found himself changed into Blumpy. Endings in *une* and *ing* were alike changed into *in*. Misfortune was misfartin', and fishing was always fishin'. There were words peculiar to the place. One of these was planchment for ceiling. Crim was another, meaning to shudder with cold, and there was an adjective, crimmy. Still another was *clitch*, meaning to stick badly, surely an onomatopoetic word that should be naturalized before it is too late. Some of the swearing, too, was neither by the throne nor footstool, such as 'Dahst my eyes!' and 'Godfrey darmints.' The ancient dialect in all its purity is now seldom used. It crops out here and there sometimes where least expected, and occasionally one meets with some old veteran whose speech has lost none of the ancient savor."

Now for "Barbara Frietchie." The incident of the poem was given to Whittier by the novelist, Mrs. E. D. E. N. Southworth, whose letter we append. The philanthropist, Dorothea Dix, investigated the case in Frederick, and she says that Barbara did wave the flag, etc. An army officer also made affidavit of the truth of the lines. A young Southern soldier has declared that he was present, and that his was one of the shots that hit the flagstaff!

On the other side are Samuel Tyler and Jacob Engelbrecht, the latter an old and greatly respected citizen of Frederick, and living directly opposite Barbara's house. Jacob wrote to the Baltimore *Sun*, saying that Stonewall Jackson's corps marched through another street, and did not approach Dame Frietchie's house at all. Lee's column did pass it, he says; but he, who stood watching at his window, saw no flag whatever at *her* window.

He says that when ten days later General McClellan passed through the town she did exhibit a flag.

Finally, General Jubal Early comes upon the witness stand, and testifies that as the Southern troops passed through Frederick, there were only two cases of waving of Union flags; one of these was by a little girl, about ten years old, who stood on the platform of a house and waved incessantly a little "candy flag," and cried in a dull, monotonous voice: "Hurrah for the Stars and Stripes! Down with the Stars and Bars!" No one molested her. The other case was that of a coarse, slovenly-looking woman, who rushed up to the entrance of an alley and waved a dirty United States flag.

"The Pipes at Lucknow" is a poem full of martial fire and lyric rush, — the subject a capital one for a poet. A little band of English, besieged in a town in the heart of India, and full of despair, hear in the distance the sweetest sound that ever fell upon

their ears, namely, the shrill pibroch of the
MacGregor Clan; and —

> " When the far-off dust-cloud
> To plaided legions grew,
> Full tenderly and blithesomely
> The pipes of rescue blew ! "

Another group of ballads comprises " Cobbler Keezar's Vision," " Amy Wentworth,"
and " The Countess."

In the first of these, old Cobbler Keezar,
of the early Puritan times, by virtue of a
mystic lapstone, sees a vision of our age
of religious tolerance, and wonders greatly
thereat: —

> " Keezar sat on the hillside
> Upon his cobbler's form,
> With a pan of coals on either hand
> To keep his waxed-ends warm.
>
> And there, in the golden weather,
> He stitched and hammered and sung;
> In the brook he moistened his leather,
> In the pewter mug his tongue."

The ballad of " Amy Wentworth " treats
of the same subject as " Among The Hills,"

namely, a superior woman, of the white-handed caste, falling in love with and marrying a broad-shouldered, brown-handed hero, with a right manly heart and brain.

Many and many a poem of Whittier's is spoiled by its too great length, — a thing that is fatal in a lyric. The long prelude to "Amy Wentworth" should have been omitted.

The scene of the lovely poem entitled "The Countess" is laid in Rocks Village, a part of East Haverhill, and lying on the Merrimack, where —

> "The river's steel-blue crescent curves
>   To meet, in ebb and flow,
> The single broken wharf that serves
>   For sloop and gundelow.
>
> With salt sea-scents along its shores
>   The heavy hay-boats crawl,
> The long antennæ of their oars
>   In lazy rise and fall.
>
> Along the gray abutment's wall
>   The idle shad-net dries;
> The toll-man in his cobbler's stall
>   Sits smoking with closed eyes."

Whittier dedicates his poem to his father's

family physician, Elias Weld, of Rocks
Village. The story which forms the subject
of the poem is a romantic one, and exqui-
sitely has our poet embalmed it in verse.
From a sketch by Rebecca I. Davis, of East
Haverhill, the following facts relating to the
personages that figure in the poem have
been culled : —

The Countess was Miss Mary Ingalls,
daughter of Henry and Abigail Ingalls, of
Rocks Village. She was born in 1786,
and is still remembered by a few old inhabitants as a young girl of remarkable beauty.
She was of medium height, had long golden
curls, violet eyes, fair complexion, and rosy
cheeks, and was exceedingly modest and
lovable. It was in the year 1806 that a little
company of French exiles fled from the
Island of Guadaloupe on account of a bloody
rebellion or uprising of the inhabitants.
Among the fugitives were Count Francis de
Vipart and Joseph Rochemont de Poyen.
The company reached Newburyport. The
two gentlemen just mentioned settled at
Rocks Village, and both married there.
Mary Ingalls was only a laborer's daughter,
and of course her marriage with the count

created a sensation in the simple, rustic community. The count was a pleasant, stately man, and a fine violinist. The bridal dress, says Miss Davis, was of a pink satin, with an overdress of white lace; her slippers also were of white satin. The count delighted to lavish upon her the richest apparel, yet nothing spoiled the sweet modesty of her disposition. After one short year of happy married life the lovely wife died. Assiduous attention to a sick mother had brought on consumption. In the village God's-acre her gray tombstone is already covered with moss.

The count returned to his native island overwhelmed with grief. In after years, however, he married again. When he died he was interred in the family burial-place of the De Viparts at Bordeaux. He left several children.

Mr. Stedman, in his fine synthetic survey of American poetry, published in *The Century*, has remarked that most of our early poetry and painting is full of landscape. The loveliest season in America is the autumn, when, as Whittier beautifully says, the woods "wear their robes of praise, the south winds softly sigh," —

> "And sweet, calm days in golden haze
>   Melt down the amber sky."

We have plenty of idyls of autumn color, like Buchanan Read's "Closing Scene," and portions of Longfellow's "Hiawatha." But American winter landscapes are as poetical as those of autumn.* It is probable that

---

* What is the subtle fascination that lurks in such bits of winter poetry as the following, collected by the writer out of his reading?

> "Yesterday the sullen year
>   Saw the snowy whirlwind fly." — *Gray.*

> "All winter drives along the darkened air." — *Thomson.*

> "High-ridged the whirled drift has almost reached
> The powdered keystone of the churchyard porch ;
> Mute hangs the hooded bell ; the tombs lie buried." — *Grahame.*

> "Alas ! alas ! thou snow-smitten wood of
>   Troy, and mountains of Ida." — *Sophocles.*

> "O hard, dull bitterness of cold." — *Whittier.*

> "And in the narrow house o' death
>   Let winter round me rave." — *Burns.*

> "The mesmerizer, Snow,
>   With his hand's first sweep
>   Put the earth to sleep." — *Robert Browning.*

> "And the cakèd snow is shuffled
>   From the plough-boy's heavy shoon." — *Keats.*

17

the scarcity of snow-idyls hitherto is due to the supposed cheerlessness of the snow. But with the rapid multiplication of winter comforts, our nature-worship is cautiously broadening so as to include even the stern beauty of winter. There are already a good many signs of this in literature. We have had, of late, lovely little snow-and-winter vignettes in prose by John Burroughs of New York, and Edith Thomas of Ohio; and there is plenty of room for further study of winter in other regions of the United States. The most delicate bit of realistic winter poetry in literature is Emerson's " Snow-Storm." Mr. Whittier is an ardent admirer of that writer — as what poet is not? — and his own productions show frequent traces of Emersonianisms. He has prefixed to " Snow-Bound " a quotation from the " Snow-Storm," and there can scarcely be a doubt that to the countless obligations we all owe Emerson must be added this: that he inspired the writing of Whittier's finest poem, and the best idyl of American rural life. It is too complex and diffusive fully to equal in artistic purity and plastic proportion the " Cotter's Saturday Night " of Burns; but it is much richer than that poem in felicitous single epithets, which, like little wicket doors, open up to the eye of memory many a long-forgotten picture of early life.

"Snow-Bound" was published in 1860, and was written, Mr. Whittier has said, "to beguile the weariness of a sick-chamber." The poet has obeyed the canon of Lessing, and instead of giving us dead description wholly, has shown us his characters in action, and extended his story over three days and the two intervening nights,—that is to say, the main action covers that time: the whole time mentioned in the poem is a week. It is unnecessary to give here any further account of the idyl than has already been furnished in the account of Whittier's boyhood.

"The Tent on the Beach" is a cluster of ballads. In accordance with a familiar fiction, they are supposed to be sung, or told, by several persons, in this case three, namely, the poet himself, "a lettered magnate" (James T. Fields), and a traveller (Bayard Taylor). All of the poems are readable, and many of them are to be classed among Whittier's best lyrics. "The Wreck of Rivermouth,"

"The Changeling," and "Kallundborg Church" are masterpieces in the line of ballads. In "The Dead Ship of Harpswell" we have the fine phrase, —

"O hundred-harbored Maine!"

Whittier has now become almost a perfect master of verbal melody. Hearken to this: —

"Oho!" she muttered, "ye're brave to-day!
But I hear the little waves laugh and say,
'The broth will be cold that waits at home;
For it's one to go, but another to come!'"

There is a light and piquant humor about some of the interludes of the "Tent on the Beach." The song in the last of these contains a striking and original stanza concerning the ocean: —

"Its waves are kneeling on the strand,
    As kneels the human knee,
Their white locks bowing to the sand,
    The priesthood of the sea!"

"Among the Hills" is a little farm-idyl, or love-idyl, of the New Hampshire mountain land, and bearing some resemblance to Tennyson's "Gardener's Daughter." It is an excellent specimen of the poems of

Whittier that reach the popular heart, and engage its sympathies. In the remotest farm-houses of the land you are almost sure to find among their few books a copy of Whittier's Poems, well-thumbed and soiled with use. The opening description of the prelude to "Among the Hills" could not be surpassed by Bion or Theocritus. In this poem a fresh interest is excited in the reader by the fact that the city woman falls in love with a manly farmer, thus happily reversing the old, old story of the city man wooing and winning the rustic beauty. The farmer accuses the fair city maid of coquetry. She replies:

> "'Nor frock nor tan can hide the man;
> And see you not, my farmer,
> How weak and fond a woman waits
> Behind this silken armor?
>
> 'I love you: on that love alone,
> And not my worth, presuming,
> Will you not trust for summer fruit
> The tree in May-day blooming?'
>
> Alone the hangbird overhead,
> His hair-swung cradle straining,
> Looked down to see love's miracle, —
> The giving that is gaining."

In "Lines on a Fly-Leaf," the author of "Snow-Bound" gives in his hearty adherence to that movement for the elevation of woman, and the securing of her rights as a human being, which is perhaps the most significant and important of the many agitations of this agitated age.

The poem "Miriam," like "The Preacher," is one of those long sermons, or meditations in verse, which Whittier loves to spin out of his mind in solitude. It contains in "Shah Akbar" a fine Oriental ballad.

The narrative poem called "The Pennsylvania Pilgrim," published in 1872, has no striking poetical merit, but is valuable and readable for the pleasant light in which it sets forth the doings of the quaint people of Germantown and the Wissahickon, near Philadelphia, nearly two hundred years ago. It introduces us to the homes and hearts of the little settlements of German Quakers under Francis Daniel Pastorius, the Mystics under the leadership of Magister Johann Kelpius, and the Mennonites under their various leaders. "The Pennsylvania Pilgrim" is a poem for Quakers, for Philadelphians who love their great park and its Wissahickon drives, and for antiquarian historical students. We may regret, if we choose, that the poet has not succeeded in embalming the memory of the Germantown Quakers in such felicitous verse as other poets have sung the virtues and ways of the Puritans, but we cannot deny that he has garnished with the flowers of poetry a dry historical subject, and so earned the gratitude of a goodly number of students and scholars.

In "The King's Missive, and Other Poems," published in 1881, the most notable piece is "The Lost Occasion," a poem on Daniel Webster, finer even than the much-admired "Ichabod," published many years previously. "The Lost Occasion" is pitched in a high, solemn, and majestic strain. It is a superb eulogy, full of magnanimity and generous forgiveness. Listen to a few stanzas: —

> "Thou
> Whom the rich heavens did endow
> With eyes of power and Jove's own brow,
> With all the massive strength that fills
> Thy home-horizon's granite hills,
>
> .   .   .   .

> Whose words, in simplest home-spun clad,
> The Saxon strength of Caedmon had,
>
> .   .   .   .
>
> Sweet with persuasion, eloquent
> In passion, cool in argument,
> Or, ponderous, falling on thy foes
> As fell the Norse god's hammer blows,
>
> .   .   .   .
>
> Too soon for us, too soon for thee,
> Beside thy lonely Northern sea,
> Where long and low the marsh-lands spread,
> Laid wearily down thy august head."

The poem of " The King's Missive " calls for such extended discussion that a brief chapter shall be devoted to it.

CHAPTER IV.

THE KING'S MISSIVE.

" Under the great hill sloping bare
To cove and meadow and Common lot,
In his council chamber and oaken chair,
Sat the worshipful Governor Endicott."

So run the opening lines of the historical poem contributed by Whittier to the first volume of the Memorial History of Boston (1880). While the governor is thus sitting, in comes Clerk Rawson with the unwelcome news that banished Quaker Shattuck, of Salem, has returned from abroad. The choleric governor swears that he will now hew in pieces the pestilent, ranting Quakers. Presently Shattuck is ushered in: "Off with the knave's hat," says the governor. As they strike off his hat he smilingly holds out the Missive, or mandamus, of Charles II. The governor immediately asks him to cover, and humbly removes his own hat. The king's letter commands him to cease persecuting the Quakers. After consultation with the deputy governor, Bellingham, he obeys, and the then imprisoned Quakers file out of jail with words of praise on their lips.

The poem fascinates us, for the incident is dramatic, and focusses in a single picturesque situation all the features of that little historical episode of two hundred years ago, *i. e.*, the persecution of the Quakers by the Puritan Commonwealth of Massachusetts. A brief setting forth of the facts connected with this persecution will not only be full of intrinsic interest, but is indispensable to a right understanding of the Quaker poet's inherited character, as well as to a comprehension of his prose and poetry. One whose ancestors have been persecuted for generations will inherit a loathing of oppression, as Whittier has done. And this hatred of tyranny will be intensified in the case of one who is thoroughly read in the literature of that persecution, and is in quick and intimate sympathy with the victims, as Whittier is.

But first a word more about the " King's Missive." Joseph Besse, in his " Collection of the Sufferings of the People called Quakers " (a sort of " Fox's Book of Martyrs," in two huge antique volumes), says [II., p. 226] that the principal instrument in procuring the royal mandamus (styled by Whittier the King's Missive) was Edward Burroughs,* who went to the king and told him that " There was a Vein of innocent Blood open'd in his Dominions, which if it were not stopt might over-run all. To which the king replied, 'But I will stop that Vein.'" Accordingly, in the autumn of 1661, Samuel Shattuck was selected to bear a letter to America. The London Friends hired Ralph Goldsmith, also a Friend, to convey Shattuck to his destination. They paid him £300 for the service. The ship entered Boston Harbor on a Sunday in the latter part of November, 1661.

" The Townsmen," says Besse, " seeing a

---

* " There is a story," says Dr. George E. Ellis, " that Burroughs got access to the king out of doors, while his Majesty was playing tennis. As Burroughs kept on his hat while accosting the king, the latter gracefully removed his plumed cap and bowed. The Quaker, put to the blush, said, ' Thee need'st not remove thy hat.' ' Oh,' replied the king, ' it is of no consequence, only that when the king and another gentleman are talking together it is usual for one of them to take off his hat.'"

Ship with *English* Colours, soon came on board, and asked for the Captain? *Ralph Goldsmith* told them, *He was the Commander.* They asked, *Whether he had any Letters?* He answered, *Yes.* But withal told them, *He would not deliver them that Day.* So they returned on shore again, and reported, that *There were many* Quakers *come, and that* Samuel Shattock (who they knew had been banished on pain of Death) *was among them.* But they knew nothing of his Errand or Authority. Thus all was kept close, and none of the Ship's Company suffered to go on shore that Day. Next morning *Ralph Goldsmith,* the Commander, with *Samuel Shattock,* the King's Deputy, went on shore, and sending the Boat back to the Ship, they two went directly through the Town to the Governour's House, and knockt at the Door: He sending a Man to know their Business, they sent him Word, that *Their Message was from the King of* England, *and that they would deliver it to none but himself.* Then they were admitted to go in, and the Governour came to them, and commanded *Samuel Shattock's* Hat to be taken off, and having received the

Deputation and the *Mandamus*, he laid off his own Hat; and ordering Shattock's Hat to be given him again, perused the Papers, and then went out to the Deputy-Governour's, bidding the King's Deputy and the Master of the Ship to follow him: Being come to the Deputy-Governour, and having consulted him, he returned to the aforesaid two Persons and said, *We shall obey his Majesty's Command.* After this, the Master of the Ship gave Liberty to his Passengers to come on shore, which they did, and had a religious Meeting with their Friends of the Town, where they returned Praises to God for his Mercy manifested in this wonderful Deliverance."

The persecution, it is true, only ceased for about a year (the next recorded whipping-order bearing date of December 22, 1662). But the Quakers were greatly encouraged by the interposition in their favor.

In an address before the Massachusetts Historical Society, Dr. George E. Ellis, of Boston, read a paper criticising Mr. Whittier's "King's Missive." This address was published in the Proceedings of the Society for March, 1881. In the "Memorial History of Boston " [I., p. 180] he asserts that the Quakers were all "of low rank, of mean breeding, and illiterate."   He says that they courted persecution, and that they were a pestilent brood of ranters, disturbers of the public peace, and dreaded by the leaders of the infant Commonwealth as they would have dreaded the cholera.   He quotes Roger Williams, who wrote of the Quakers that they were " insufferably proud and contentious," and advised a " due and moderate restraint of their incivilities."   Dr. Ellis, it is true, takes the theoretical ground of "the equal folly and culpability of both parties in the tragedy," but seems entirely to nullify this statement by his apparently unbiassed, but really partisan treatment of the subject. When you have finished his paper you perceive that the impression left on your mind is that the really bitter and unrelenting Puritan persecutors were long-suffering, angelic natures, while their victims, the Quakers, were mere gallows' dogs.   His theoretical position is summed up in the following words: —

"The crowning folly or iniquity in the course of the Puritans was in following up their penal inflictions, through banishments, imprisonments, fines, scourgings, and mutilations, to the execution on the gallows of four martyr victims. But what shall we say of the persistency, the exasperating contemptuousness and defiance, the goading, maddening obstinacy, and reproaching invectives of those who drove the magistrates, against their will, to vindicate their own insulted authority, and to stain our annals with innocent blood?"—Memorial History of Boston, I., 1882.

Dr. Ellis is right in holding that some of the Quakers were gadflies of obstinacy, and full of self-righteous pride; but he fails to tell us of the patience, Christian sweetness, and meekness of character of the majority of them; and it is only when we turn to the pages of Fox and Besse that we see the inadequate character of such a picture as that drawn by Dr. Ellis. In the plain, *naïve* annals of Besse, the hard-heartedness and haughty pride of the Puritan magistrates (traits still amply represented in their descendants) are thrown into the most striking relief. They glower over their victims like tigers; they are choked with their passions; they spurn excuses and palliatives; they demand blood.

In the *Boston Daily Advertiser* for March 29, 1881, Mr. Whittier published a long reply to Dr. Ellis, in which he fortified the positions taken by him in his ballad, showing that he did not mean to hold up Charles II. as a consistent friend of toleration, and that there must have been a general jail delivery in consequence of the receipt of the mandamus. He says: —

"The charge that the Quakers who suffered were 'vagabonds' and 'ignorant, low fanatics,' is unfounded in fact. Mary Dyer, who was executed, was a woman of marked respectability. She had been the friend and associate of Sir Henry Vane and the ministers Wheelwright and Cotton. The papers left behind by the three men who were hanged show that they were above the common class of their day in mental power and genuine piety. John Rous, who, in execution of his sentence, had his right ear cut off by the constable in the Boston jail, was of gentlemanly lineage, the son of Colonel Rous of the British army, and himself the betrothed of a high-born and cultivated young English lady. Nicholas Upsall was one of Boston's most worthy and substantial citizens, yet was driven in his age and infirmities, from his home and property, into the wilderness."

Mr. Whittier further remarks: —

" Dr. Ellis has been a very generous, as well as ingenious defender of the Puritan clergy and government, and his labors in this respect have the merit of gratuitous disinterestedness. Had the very worthy and learned gentleman been a resident in the Massachusetts colony in 1560, one of his most guarded doctrinal sermons would have brought down upon him the wrath of clergy and magistracy. His Socinianism would have seemed more wicked than the 'inward light' of the Quakers; and, had he been as ' doggedly obstinate' as Servetus at Geneva (as I do him the justice to think he would have been), he might have hung on the same gallows with the Quakers, or the same shears which clipped the ears of Holder, Rous, and Copeland might have shorn off his own."

Let us look a little more closely at the evidence on both sides.

In the fourth chapter of the seventh book

18

of Cotton Mather's "Magnalia" we have a specimen of Quaker rant. After stating that he is opposed to the capital punishment of Quakers, but advises shaving of the head, or blood-letting, the proud and scornful old doctor concludes as follows: —

"*Reader*, I can foretell what usage I shall find among the *Quakers* for this chapter of our *church-history;* for a worthy man that writes of them has observed, *for pride and hypocrisie, and hellish reviling against the painful ministers of Christ, I know no people can match them.* Yea, prepare, friend *Mather*, to be assaulted with such language as *Fisher* the Quaker, in his pamphlets, does bestow upon such men as Dr. *Owen; thou fiery fighter and green-headed trumpeter; thou hedgehog and grinning dog; thou bastard that tumbled out of the mouth of the Babilonish bawd; thou mole; thou tinker; thou lizzard; thou bell of no metal, but the tone of a kettle; thou wheel-barrow; thou whirlpool; thou whirlegig. O thou firebrand; thou adder and scorpion; thou louse; thou cow-dung; thou moon-calf; thou ragged tatterdemallion; thou Judas; thou livest in philosophy and logick which are of the devil.* And then let *Penn* the Quaker add, Thou gormandizing Priest, one of the abominable tribe; *thou bane of reason, and beast of the earth; thou best to be spared of mankind; thou mountebank priest.* These are the very words, (I wrong them not!) which they vomit out against the best men in the *English* nation, that have been so hardy as to touch their *light within:* but let the *quills* of these *porcupines* fly as fast as they will, I shall not feel them! Yea, every *stone* that these *Kildebrands* throw at me, I will wear as a *pearl.*"

As an offset to this quaint and amusing tirade, and to the charges of Dr. Ellis, one may read the following words of Whittier, and, by striking a general average between all the speakers, get a tolerable approximation to the exact truth. Mr. Whittier says: —

"Nor can it be said that the persecution grew out of the 'intrusion,' 'indecency,' and 'effrontery' of the persecuted.

"It owed its origin to the settled purpose of the ministers and leading men of the colony to permit no difference of opinion on religious matters. They had banished the

Baptists, and whipped at least one of them. They had hunted down Gorton and his adherents; they had imprisoned Dr. Child, an Episcopalian, for petitioning the General Court for toleration. They had driven some of their best citizens out of their jurisdiction, with Ann Hutchinson, and the gifted minister, Wheelwright. Any dissent on the part of their own fellow-citizens was punished as severely as the heresy of strangers.

"The charge of 'indecency' comes with ill-grace from the authorities of the Massachusetts Colony. The first Quakers who arrived in Boston, Ann Austin and Mary Fisher, were arrested on board the ship before landing, their books taken from them and burned by the constable, and they themselves brought before Deputy Governor Bellingham, in the absence of Endicott. This astute magistrate ordered them to be *stripped naked and their bodies to be carefully examined, to see if there was not the Devil's mark on them as witches.* They were then sent to the jail, their cell window was boarded up, and they were left without food or light, until the master of the vessel

that brought them was ordered to take them
to Barbadoes. When Endicott returned, he
thought they had been treated too leniently,
and declared that he would have had them
whipped.

"After this, almost every town in the
province was favored with the spectacle of
aged and young women stripped to the middle, tied to a cart-tail and dragged through
the streets and scourged without mercy by
the constable's whip. It is not strange that
these atrocious proceedings, in two or three
instances, unsettled the minds of the victims.
Lydia Wardwell of Hampton, who, with
her husband, had been reduced to almost
total destitution by persecution, was sum-
moned by the church of which she had been
a member to appear before it to answer to
the charge of non-attendance. She obeyed
the call by appearing in the unclothed condition of the sufferers whom she had seen
under the constable's whip. For this she
was taken to Ipswich and stripped to the
waist, tied to a rough post, which tore her
bosom as she writhed under the lash, and
severely scourged to the satisfaction of a
crowd of lookers-on at the tavern. One,

and only one, other instance is adduced in
the person of Deborah Wilson of Salem.
She had seen her friends and neighbors
scourged naked through the street, among
them her brother, who was banished on pain
of death. She, like all Puritans, had been
educated in the belief of the plenary inspiration of Scripture, and had brooded over
the strange 'signs' and testimonies of the
Hebrew prophets. It seemed to her that
the time had arrived for some similar demon-
stration, and that it was her duty to walk
abroad in the disrobed condition to which
her friends had been subjected, as a sign
and warning to the persecutors. Whatever
of 'indecency' there was in these cases was
directly chargeable upon the atrocious persecution. At the door of the magistrates
and ministers of Massachusetts must be laid
the insanity of the conduct of these unfortunate women.

"But Boston, at least, had no voluntary
Godivas. The only disrobed women in its
streets were made so by Puritan sheriffs and
constables, who dragged them amidst jeer-
ing crowds at the cart-tail, stripped for the
lash, which in one instance laid open with

a ghastly gash the bosom of a young mother!"*

We may conclude this discussion by giving a few instances of. Quaker persecutions, in addition to those mentioned by Mr. Whittier. In England the members of the sect suffered a whole Jeremiad of woes: they were dragged through the streets by the hair of the head, incarcerated in loathsome dungeons, beaten over the head with muskets, pilloried, whipped at the cart's-tail, branded, their tongues bored with red-hot irons, and their property confiscated to the State. One First Day, George Fox went into the "steeple-house" of Tickhill. "I found," he says in his Journal, "the priest and most of the chief of the parish together in the chancel. I went up to them and began to speak; but they immediately fell upon me; the clerk up with his Bible, as I was speaking, and struck me in the face with it, so that my face

* Mr. Whittier stated to a member of the Massachusetts Historical Society that it was his intention "at some time to prepare a full and exhaustive history of the relations of Puritan and Quaker in the seventeenth century." It may be added that the newspaper articles quoted above, with the several replications of their authors, may all be found in the Proceedings of the Massachusetts Historical Society for 1880-81 (see the index of that volume).

gushed out with blood, and I bled exceedingly in the steeple-house. The people cried, 'Let us have him out of the church.' When they had got me out, they beat me exceedingly, threw me down, and threw me over a hedge. They afterwards dragged me through a house into the street, stoning and beating me as they dragged me along; so that I was all over besmeared with blood and dirt. They got my hat from me, which I never had again." Fox was at various times thrust into dungeons filled ankle-deep with ordure, and was shot at, beaten with stones and clubs, etc.

One evening he passed through Cambridge: "When I came into the town, the scholars, hearing of me, were up and exceeding rude. I kept on my horse's back, and rode through them in the Lord's power; but they unhorsed Amor Stoddart before he could get to the inn. When we were in the inn, they were so rude in the courts and in the streets, that the miners, colliers, and carters could never be ruder. The people of the house asked us what we would have for supper. 'Supper!' said I, 'were it not that the Lord's power is over them, these rude scholars look as if they would pluck us in pieces and make a supper of us.' They knew I was so against the trade of preaching, which they were there as apprentices to learn, that they raged as bad as ever Diana's craftsmen did against Paul."

In the declaration made by the Quakers to Charles II. it appears that in New England, up to that time, "thirty Quakers had been whipped; twenty-two had been banished on pain of death if they returned; twenty-five had been banished upon the penalty of being whipped, or having their ears cut, or being branded in the hand if they returned; three had their right ears shorn off by the hangman; one had been branded in the hand with the letter H; many had been imprisoned; many fined; and three had been put to death, and one (William Leddra) was soon after executed."

Besse, in his "Sufferings of the Quakers," states that one William Brand, a man in years, was so brutally whipped by an infuriated jailer, in Salem, that "His Back and Arms were bruised and black, and the Blood hanging as it were in Bags under his Arms, and so into one was his Flesh beaten that the

Sign of a particular Blow could not be seen."
And the surgeon said that " His Flesh would
rot from off his Bones e'er the bruized Parts
would be brought to digest." To all this must
be added the humiliating fact that four persons
were hanged on Boston Common for the
crime of being Quakers.   Their names were
Marmaduke Stephenson, William Robinson,
William Leddra, and Mary Dyer.

CHAPTER V.

POEMS BY GROUPS.

BESIDES "The King's Missive," Whittier has written numerous other Quaker poems, the finest of which are "Cassandra Southwick," "The Old South," and the spirited, ringing ballad of "The Exiles." In the first two of these the poet shows a delicate intuition into the feelings that might have prompted the Quaker women who witnessed for the truth in Boston two hundred years ago.

There is nothing in American literature, unless it be the anti-slavery papers of Thoreau, which equals the sevenfold-heated moral indignation of Whittier's poems on slavery, — a wild melody in them like that of Highland pibrochs; now plaintively and piteously pleading, and now burning with passion, irony, satire, scorn; here glowing with tropical imagery, as in "Toussaint L'Ouverture," and "The Slaves of Martinique," and there rising into lofty moral atmospheres of faith when all seemed dark and hopeless. Every one knows the power of a "cry" (a song like "John Brown's Body," or a pithy sentence or phrase) in any great popular movement. There can be no doubt that Whittier's poems did as much as Garrison's editorials to key up the minds of people to the point required for action against slavery. Some of these anti-slavery pieces still possess great intrinsic beauty and excellence, as, for example, "Toussaint L'Ouverture," "The Farewell," "The Slave Ships," and "The Slaves of Martinique." In these four productions there is little or none of the dreary didacticism of most of the anti-slavery poems, but a simple statement of pathetic, beautiful fact, which is left to make its own impression. Another powerful group of these slavery poems is constituted by the scornful, mock-congratulatory productions, such as "The Hunters of Men," "Clerical Oppressors," "The Yankee Girl," "A Sabbath Scene," "Lines suggested by Reading a State Paper wherein the Higher Law is

Invoked to Sustain the Lower One," and "The Pastoral Letter." * The sentences in these stanzas cut like knives and sting like shot. The poltroon clergy, especially, looks pitiful, most pitiful, in the light of Whittier's noble scorn and contempt.

"Randolph of Roanoke" is a noble tribute to a political enemy by one who admired in him the man. The long poem, "The Panorama," must be considered a failure, poetically speaking. Its showman's pictures and preachings do not get hold of our sympathies very strongly.

The Tyrtaean fire in Whittier was so thoroughly kindled by the anti-slavery conflict that it has never wholly gone out. All through his life his hand has instinctively sought the old war-lyre whenever a voice was to be raised in honor of Freedom. The formal close of the anti-slavery period with him may be said to be marked by "Laus Deo," a triumphant, almost ecstatic shout of joy uttered on hearing the bells ring when the Constitutional Amendment abolishing slavery was passed.

----

* "The Pastoral Letter" was an idiotic manifesto of the clergy of Massachusetts aimed at the Grimké sisters.

Naturally, the war poems of a Quaker—and even of our martial Whittier—could not be equal to his peace poems. Still there are many strong passages in the lyrics written by Whittier during the civil war of 1861–65. At first he counsels that we allow disunion rather than kindle the lurid fires of fratricidal war:—

> "Let us press
> The golden cluster on our brave old flag
> In closer union, and, if numbering less,
> Brighter shall shine the stars which still remain."
>
> *A Word for the Hour.*

So he wrote in January, 1861. But afterward he becomes a pained but sadly approving spectator of the inevitable conflict:—

> "Then Freedom sternly said: 'I shun
> No strife nor pang beneath the sun,
> When human rights are staked and won.
>
> .   .   .   .   .   .
>
> The moor of Marston felt my tread,
> Through Jersey snows the march I led,
> My voice Magenta's charges sped.'"
>
> *The Watchers.*

As a Friend, he and his brethren could not personally engage in war. But they could minister to the sick and dying, and care for the slave.

"THE SLAVE IS OURS!"

he says, —

> " And we may tread the sick-bed floors
>   Where strong men pine,
> And, down the groaning corridors,
> Pour freely from our liberal stores
>   The oil and wine."

Anniversary Poem.

" Barbara Frietchie" is, of course, the best of these war lyrics. The "Song of the Negro Boatmen" was set to music and sung from Maine to California during the war days: —

> " De yam will grow, de cotton blow,
>   We'll hab de rice an' corn;
> O nebber you fear, if nebber you hear
>   De driver blow his horn!"

After "Voices of Freedom," in the complete edition of Whittier's poems, come a cluster of Biblical, or Old Testament poems, — "Palestine," "Ezekiel," "The Wife of Manoah to her Husband," "The Cities of the Plain," "The Crucifixion," and "The Star of Bethlehem." The best of these, perhaps, are "Cities of the Plain," and " Crucifixion,"— the former intense and thrilling in style, and suggesting the " Sennacherib " and " Waterloo " of Byron; the latter a high, solemn chant, and well calculated to touch the religious heart. Whittier has drawn great refreshment and inspiration from the thrice-winnowed wheat and the living-water wells of Old Testament literature.

Allusion has already been made to the hymns of our poet. Hymn-book makers have had in his poems a very quarry to work. The hymn tinkers, too, have not spared Whittier even while he was alive, and many of his sacred lyrics have been " adapted " after the manner of hymn-book makers. Dr. Martineau's " Hymns of Praise " (1874) contains seven of Whittier's religious songs; the " Unitarian Hymn and Tune Book " (1868) also has seven; the Plymouth Collection (1855) has eleven, and Longfellow and Johnson's " Hymns of the Spirit " (1864) has twenty-two.

The Essex minstrel has written quite a number of children's poems, such as " The Robin," " Red Riding Hood," and " King Solomon and the Ants." He has also compiled two books of selections for children, as has already been mentioned.

Like many authors, Whittier has been attracted, in the autumn of his life, to the rich fields of Oriental literature. His Oriental poems show careful and sympathetic study of eastern books. "The Two Rabbis" and "Shah Akbar" are especially fine. The little touch in the former of "the small weeds that the bees bow with their weight" is a very pretty one. In "The King's Missive" we have a few "Oriental Maxims," being paraphrases of translations from the Sanscrit. "The Dead Feast of the Kol-Folk," and "The Khan's Devil," are also included in the same volume.

Mr. Whittier has also made successful studies in Norse literature, for which his beautiful ballads, the "Dole of Jarl Thorkell," "Kallundborg Church," and "King Volmer and Elsie" are vouchers.

19

CHAPTER VI.

PROSE WRITINGS.

IT is to be feared that the greater portion of the prose writings of Whittier will be *caviare* to many readers of this day. He himself almost admits as much in the prefatory note to the second volume of the complete edition of his essays. That many of the papers are entertaining reading, and that they are written often in a light and genial and vivacious style, is true; and, as he himself hints, they will at least be welcomed and indulgently judged by his personal friends and admirers. His prose work was done in a time seething with moral ideas; the air was full of reforms; the voice of duty sounded loud in men's consciences, and the ancestral buckler called —

> " Self-clanging, from the walls
> In the high temple of the soul ! "
>
> *Lowell.*

That particular era is now passed. The great secular heart is now in its diastole, or relaxation. Hence it is that the philanthropic themes discussed by Mr. Whittier thirty years ago (and most of his essays are of a philanthropic character) possess but a languid interest for the present reading public. The artistic essays, however, are charming, and possess permanent interest. Let us except from these the long productions, "Margaret Smith's Journal" and "My Summer with Dr. Singletary." Some have thought these to be the best papers in the collection. But to many they must appear frigid and old-fashioned in the extreme. They seem aimless and sprawling, mere *esquisses*, tentative work in a field in which the author was doubtful of his powers. They would ordinarily be classed under the head of Sunday-school literature. It has been suggested that the idea of "Margaret Smith's Journal" might have been derived from the "Diary of Lady Willoughby," which appeared about the same time. "The Journal" is a reproduction of the antique in style and atmosphere, and is said to be very successful as far as that goes.   But certainly the iteration of the archaism, " did do," " did write," etc., gets to be very wearisome.   The " Journal " purports to be written by a niece of Edward Rawson, Secretary of Massachusetts from 1650–1686.   The scene is laid in Newbury, where Rawson settled about 1636.   We have pleasant pictures of the colonial life of the day, of the Quakers and Indians and Puritans, and, on the whole, the sketch is well worth reading by historical students.

"Old Portraits and Modern Sketches" consists chiefly of newspaper articles on modern reformers.   They were originally contributed to the *National Era*.   The portraits drawn are those of John Bunyan, Thomas Ellwood, James Nayler, Andrew Marvell, John Roberts, Samuel Hopkins, Richard Baxter, — and, among Americans, William Leggett and Nathaniel Peabody Rogers, — both anti-slavery reformers and journalists; and, lastly, Robert Dinsmore, the rustic Scotch-American poet of Haverhill.   The last three papers mentioned are the best.

The second volume of Mr. Whittier's prose writings bears the title " Literary

Recreations and Miscellanies," and consists of various reviews, thumb-nail essays, and indigenous folk-and-nature studies, made in the region of the Merrimack. These last are of most interest, and indicate the field which Mr. Whittier would have cultivated with most success. In the reviews of the volume the newspapery tone and journalist diction are rather unpleasantly conspicuous. As a critic, our poet is not very successful, because he is too earnest a partisan, too merciless and undistinguishing in his invective or too generous in his praise. For example, what he says about Carlyle, in reviewing that author's infamous "Discourse on the Negro Question," is true as far as it goes. But of the elementary literary canon, that the prime function of the critic is to put himself in the place of the one he is criticising,— of this law Mr. Whittier has not, practically, the faintest notion. He considers everything from the point of view of the Quaker or of the reformer.

Numerous specimens of Mr. Whittier's prose have already been given in various parts of this volume, but for the sake of illustration we may add two more. For an example of his serious style take the following from "Scottish Reformers": "He who undertakes to tread the pathway of reform — who, smitten with the love of truth and justice, or, indignant in view of wrong and insolent oppression, is rashly inclined to throw himself at once into that great conflict which the Persian seer not untruly represented as a war between light and darkness — would do well to count the cost in the outset. If he can live for Truth alone, and, cut off from the general sympathy, regard her service as its own 'exceeding great reward'; if he can bear to be counted a fanatic and crazy visionary; if, in all good nature, he is ready to receive from the very objects of his solicitude abuse and obloquy in return for disinterested and self-sacrificing efforts for their welfare; if, with his purest motives misunderstood and his best actions perverted and distorted into crimes, he can still hold on his way and patiently abide the hour when 'the whirligig of Time shall bring about its revenges'; if, on the whole, he is prepared to be looked upon as a sort of moral outlaw or social heretic under good society's interdict of food and fire; and if he is well assured that he can, through all this, preserve his cheerfulness and faith in man, — let him gird up his loins and go forward in God's name. He is fitted for his vocation; he has watched all night by his armor. . . . Great is the consciousness of right. Sweet is the answer of a good conscience. He who pays his whole-hearted homage to truth and duty, — who swears his life-long fealty on their altars, and rises up a Nazarite consecrated to their service, — is not without his solace and enjoyment when, to the eyes of others, he seems the most lonely and miserable. He breathes an atmosphere which the multitude know not of; 'a serene heaven which they cannot discern rests over him, glorious in its purity and stillness.'"

For a specimen of our author's vein of pleasantry take the following bit of satire on "The Training": "What's now in the wind? Sounds of distant music float in at my window on this still October air. Hurrying drum-beat, shrill fife-tones, wailing bugle-notes, and, by way of accompaniment, hurrahs from the urchins on the crowded sidewalks. Here come the citizen-soldiers, each martial foot beating up the mud of yesterday's storm with the slow, regular, up-and-down movement of an old-fashioned churn-dasher. Keeping time with the feet below, some threescore of plumed heads bob solemnly beneath me. Slant sunshine glitters on poli shed gun-barrels and tinselled uniform. Gravely and soberly they pass on, as if duly impressed with a sense of the deep responsibility of their position as self-constituted defenders of the world's last hope, — the United States of America, and possibly Texas. They look out with honest, citizen faces under their leathern vizors (their ferocity being mostly the work of the tailor and tinker), and, I doubt not, are at this moment as innocent of bloodthirstiness as yonder worthy tiller of the Tewksbury Hills, who sits quietly in his wagon dispensing apples and turnips without so much as giving a glance at the procession. Probably there is not one of them who would hesitate to divide his last tobacco-quid with his worst enemy. Social, kind-hearted, psalm-singing, sermon-hearing, Sabbath-keeping Christians; and yet, if we look at the fact of the matter, these very men have been out the whole afternoon of this beautiful day, under God's holy sunshine, as busily at work as Satan himself could wish in learning how to butcher their fellow-creatures, and acquire the true scientific method of impaling a forlorn Mexican on a bayonet, or of sinking a leaden missile in the brain of some unfortunate Briton, urged within its range by the double incentive of sixpence per day in his pocket and the cat-o'-nine tails on his back!"

Part III.

Twilight and Evening Bell.

CHAPTER I.

TWILIGHT AND EVENING BELL.

THE passing away from earth of John Greenleaf Whittier occurred on September 7, 1892, at four-thirty A. M., at Hampton Falls, N. H., in the very heart of the region he has immortalized by his ballads. The hour was just as the reddening east was mingling its light with that of the full harvest moon. Around his bedside were numerous relatives and friends. He fell asleep in an unconscious state, after an illness of a week. Let us now go back and, taking up the thread of the narrative where it was dropped on page 152, run over the incidents that have intervened in the decade since 1882 in the life of this pleasant singer — this plain Quaker farmer, who drew such soul-thrilling strains from his home-made rustic flute as to concentrate upon himself the attention of the whole world.

In 1883 (January 7) died, in Boston, Whittier's brother, Matthew Franklin Whittier, whose daughter Elizabeth, before her marriage to Samuel T. Pickard, was housekeeper for a number of years for her uncle, the poet, at Amesbury. "Frank," as his associates called him, obtained, it is said, his position in the Boston Custom House through the influence of his brother. Says a friend (Mr. Charles O. Stickney) : —

"Frank was not a poet, and being of a practical turn of mind, had the good sense not to attempt the impossible ; but he was a man of intellect, an omnivorous reader, was well posted, and, though inclined to seclusion and taciturnity, was nevertheless genial and companionable ; his conversation spiced with his quiet, quaint humor, which bubbled up in some happy *mot*, neat fun, or well-turned bit of satire which raised a laugh, but left no sting behind." His quaint, humorous dialect articles, over the signature "Ethan Spike," are said to have given Nasby and Artemus Ward their cue. They were chiefly contributed to the Portland *Transcript*, the Boston *Carpet Bag*, and New York *Vanity Fair*. They all purported to emanate from "Hornby," a "smart town" in Maine — "a veritable down-east wonderland, whose wide-awake citizens were up to the times and ready to settle any great question of the day at 'a special town meetin'.'"   Mr. Spike was as intense in his anti-slavery views as his brother Greenleaf. Specimens of his work may be found in the Portland *Transcript*, January 10, 1846, the *Carpet Bag*, October 14, 1850, and November, 1851.

In 1884 Whittier's seventy-seventh birth-day was observed at Oak Knoll, when the genial old bachelor received with courtesy and hospitality all who called.   Gifts of flowers poured in to serve as foil to the two huge birthday cakes from relatives.

An editorial writer in one of Boston's chief dailies thus describes a visit to Mr. Whittier, made in 1884:—

" Mr. Whittier met us at the door of the pleasant house at Oak Knoll.   He came out on the piazza, and shook us each by the hand, and said, ' I am glad to see thee.'   He concerned himself about our rubbers and waterproofs in the hall-way, and said that we were kind to come.   I had taken a great fit of shyness on seeing him, and was surprised to hear my friend speaking to him in the same quiet tone that she had used when alone with me. I listened, and reveled in silence as the old poet and the young artist spoke together. He led us into the parlor, and they talked of a landscape on the wall, of pictures, and of a portrait.

" Presently he said: ' It is a little cold here. Shall we go into my room?' He led the way to the bright library where most of his days are now spent. Mr. Whittier happened to glance from the window as we stood for a moment speaking with him : he saw our cab waiting for us on the drive. The rain had begun again.   Then a wonderful thing befell.

" He forbade us to go away within the quarter hour; he forbade us to go for three hours. He went out and sent the cabman away, then he took us into the library. We sat down in front of the cheery open fire, and Mr. Whittier talked with us. He spoke of the claims of young people on life, it was different from any talk I had heard ; in the face of my poets, I used to think that all good people believed that life is our creditor and hard taskmaster."

On October 24, 1884, a portrait of Whittier was presented by Charles F. Coffin, of Lynn, Mass., a devoted friend and admirer of his, to the Friends' School of Providence, R. I. It was painted by Edgar Parker, of Boston, and represents Whittier sitting in an arm-chair in an attitude of peaceful thought.

It is hung in Alumni Hall, between busts of Elizabeth Fry and John Bright, and is considered to be a worthy memorial of the poet. Letters on this occasion were read from James Russell Lowell, Dr. Holmes, E. P. Whipple, John Bright, George William Curtis, Boyle O'Reilly, Matthew Arnold, and others. From Mr. Whipple's letter the following is an extract: —

"I have had the privilege of knowing him intimately for many years, and of doing all I could through the press to point out his exceptional and original merits as a writer. My admiration of his genius and character has increased with every new volume he has published and every new manifestation of that essential gentleness which lies at the root of his nature, even when some of his poems suggest the warrior rather than the Quaker. One thing is certain: that the

20

reader feels that the writer possesses that peculiar attribute of humanity which we instinctively call by the high name of soul; and, whether he storms into the souls of others or glides into them, his hot invectives equally with his soft persuasions mark him as a man; a man, too, of might; a man whose force is blended with his insight, and who can win or woo his way into hostile or recipient minds by innate strength or delicacy of nature."

In 1885 the poet's birthday was again quietly celebrated at Oak Knoll, and in the afternoon Mr. Whittier's portrait was unveiled before a large audience in the Town Hall of Haverhill.

In September, 1885, occurred a most interesting festival — the reunion of the graduates of the old Haverhill Academy, for whom the poet cherished to the end of his life an earnest and outspoken affection. It was here that Whittier got all the scholastic education he ever had outside of the district school; the reunion was thoroughly enjoyed therefore by him, although it was in his honor. For his health was pretty good, and he was in fine spirits. An interesting letter was received from the aged Miss Arethusa Hall, a preceptress in the Academy when Whittier attended it. Among others, Dr. Holmes wrote : " The class of 1829 [Harvard] has a bright record; but how much brighter it would have been if we could have read upon the triennial and quinquennial catalogues: Johannes Greenleaf Whittier, A. B., A. M., LL. D., etc! But what, after all, can all the degrees of all the colleges do for him whose soul has been kindled by that 'ae spark of Nature's fire,' which Burns caught from her torch on the banks of Ayr, and Whittier among the mists that rise from the Merrimack ? "

Mr. Whittier presented photographs of himself with his autograph to his schoolmates, promised to think over the sitting for an oil portrait, and entered with zest into any bit of mirthfulness that sparkled out during the evening, although, as will be seen from the following description of a representative of the Boston *Advertiser*, he could scarcely understand the situation : —

" In the company was one man who seemed neither to accept nor to comprehend the situation. That man was John G. Whittier.

His face and demeanor that day would have afforded study for a psychologist. That it was fifty-seven years since he entered Haverhill Academy he remembered with a certain sweet melancholy. That everybody was vying with everybody else in making love to him he could not help observing. But what it was all about, and why people should persist in talking of him when he wanted other, more congenial topics to be uppermost — these questions evidently puzzled him. A countenance on which was a look of shyness, of surprise, of perplexity; withal, a countenance irradiated by reciprocal affection and pleasure in seeing others pleased — if any one of the present artists could have caught and delineated those features, the painter would have been destined to share the immortality of the poet. On such a subject the temptation to indulge in reminiscence is strong. But space will permit me to mention only two or three characteristic incidents. A gifted vocalist had just sung a composition prepared for that day; and Mr. Whittier, turning to her, said, ' Friend, I wish that I could write a song for thee to sing.' An elocutionist of note read aloud one of the author's poems. He listened eagerly, as if it was wholly new to him; and a little mist gathered in those deep, dreamy eyes at the lines beginning, ·

> ' I mourn no more my vanished years,'

but there was an answering gleam at the words,

> ' The windows of my soul I throw
> Wide open to the sun.'

" Two circumstances made that one of the few red-letter days in the memory of the present writer. I had known in Kansas a lady who belonged to that band of Haverhill Academy pupils whose boast and joy it was to have studied and played with the Quaker poet. On mentioning this lady's name, I found myself instantly accepted as her proxy. For some minutes Mr. Whittier seemed to have no other interest than to learn all possible particulars of her and send to her all possible expressions of regard.

" The other circumstance was the result of my connection with the *Advertiser*. Taking me into one corner of the room, he asked me to sit beside him on the sofa. Then, drawing from his pocket the manuscript of the poem which he had written for that occasion and on portions of which the ink was not yet dry, the author, in a manner irresistibly winning, seemed to take his humble brother of the pen-craft into confidence, explaining the motive for various lines and passing on to speak of those boyhood days which the poem and the occasion recalled."

December 17 again came round in 1886, and found Whittier receiving friends, presents, and congratulatory telegrams at Oak Knoll. Wendell Phillips, for example, sent him a handsome cane, and some one else sent a great frosted cake and a basket that strained its sides to hold the gift of fruit it contained.

In December, 1887, it occurred to a young lady journalist on the staff of the Boston *Advertiser* (Miss Minna C. Smith) that it would be a good idea to have a " Whittier number " of that journal. The thought was a fertile one and was put into execution in great haste, but with eminent success. Poems were contributed by Walt Whitman,

Dr. Holmes, James Jeffrey Roche, Hezekiah Butterworth, Herbert D. Ward, Minot J. Savage, Margaret Sidney (Mrs. D. Lothrop), Elizabeth Stuart Phelps, and others, and there was a great array of letters from other writers and eminent persons. Edward Everett Hale told the story of Whittier's Kansas " Emigrants' Song," how it was sung *en route* and in the West by brave pioneers of New England. James Parton, of Newburyport, Whittier's Amesbury neighbor, wrote that Whittier was carrying his burthen of eighty years "with considerable ease and constant cheerfulness." He continued : —

" I am sometimes asked, ' Is the poet Whittier really a Quaker or only one by inheritance ? ' He is really a Quaker. He wears, it is true, a silk hat of the kind familiarly called the stove-pipe, which gleams in the brilliant sun of winter, and seems to indicate at once the man of Boston and the man of the world. But it is not the broad-brimmed hat that makes the Quaker. The poet does actually keep a Quaker coat for Sundays and other dress occasions, which coat was made by a firm of Orthodox Friends in Philadelphia, the metropolitan city of the gentle sect. He also uses the *thee* and *thou* in conversation, although without attaching the least importance to these trifles. But he is also a Friend from heartfelt conviction. A few miles from his home is one of the smallest meeting-houses in New England, standing alone in a land of farms and fields. It is painted white, and looks a little like a small schoolhouse. This edifice will seat perhaps forty persons, but the usual congregation numbers about fourteen, who on winter Sundays dwindle often to seven and sometimes to three. This is the meeting-house which the poet Whittier attends whenever he is at home, unless prevented by the weather.

"What an extraordinary thing is this! The poet who has most deeply felt and most beautifully expressed the sentiment and soul of New England is a member of the sect to which New England was so intolerant and so cruel! When the essential New England has ceased to exist, it will live again, and live long, in Whittier's poems; and he a Quaker! Was there ever before a revenge so complete and so sublime?"

Mr. Charles M. Thompson sent for this octogenarian birthday a fine poetical stanza:—

> "A thousand stars swim on through time,
> Unknown and unregarded in the skies.
> But one, kings followed ; one, thy rhyme,
> Led on a land of kings in liberty's emprise!"

Mr. James H. Carleton knew Whittier in connection with a circle of intellectual and social people that centred around the family of Judge Pitman in the years just preceding the rise of the abolition movement. " The Pitmans were neighbors of mine," said Mr. Carleton, " and I (I hardly know why) was admitted to the meetings of the people who gathered there. They were the leaders in everything that was progressive. They have since become widely scattered.

" I remember Mr. Whittier as a leader of these leaders. These people formed to a large extent his social world at that time. It was the one place at which Mr. Whittier threw off his natural reserve and took his proper place. He was a good conversation-alist on occasion, and when he spoke he was worth listening to. I remember him as intensely interested in whatever subject occupied the attention of the circle. He was never the first to begin a discussion, but rather bided his time for an especial opportunity."

Mr. George C. How wrote of Mr. Whittier's friendliness, his cordiality, and his unassuming manner: " In the few delightful days I spent in his company in the White Mountain region, I saw no signs of formality or reserve. He told me, under the trees, many stories of his life and of his earliest successes. He impresses you strongly as a true and generous friend to everything and every man he believes good and honest. He does not like to be lionized, and refused to be introduced to a man whose only claim to his friendship was that he had read all his works. When, however, Mr. Whittier learned that this same man was an ardent admirer of the poet Hayne, a chord of sympathy was struck that made them firm friends during this stranger's stay."

At Oak Knoll the winter day was clear and sunshiny, if cold, and warm hearts within laughed the season to scorn. The ladies of Boston, at the suggestion of Mrs. D. Lothrop, sent up a most unique and exquisite gift; eighty beautiful roses edged a large basket fringed with fern-sprays, that held an open book of white roses, across whose face lay a pen of violets, and on the wide satin book-mark was inscribed the closing stanza of " My Triumph." The Essex Club of Boston presented a large album ; fruit and flowers flanked a mighty birthday cake in the dining-room. Mr. Charles F. Coffin, of Lynn, sent a large overflowing basket of fruit, arranged under his personal supervision, " every fruit in its season," of exquisite colors and shapes, to express his affection for his life-long friend, the poet.

The new town of Whittier, in California, sent an advance copy of the first issue of the town's newspaper ; the Governor of the Commonwealth, as the winter afternoon quickly declined, cut and distributed to the guests slices of the birthday cake, while all through the day Whittier passed to and fro from room to room, conversing with young and old, and hospitable to all.

Whittier himself is reported as saying on his eightieth birthday : " When a man is eighty years old, it is time to give up active mental work. Oh! I am able to go about these grounds pretty well. I have never attempted to imitate Gladstone and chop down trees, but I like to split wood."

This was James Russell Lowell's verse
for Mr. Whittier on his eightieth birthday : —

> " How fair a pearl chain, eighty strong,
> Lustrous and hallowed every one
> With saintly thoughts and sacred song,
> As 'twere the rosary of a nun ! "

The excitement and nervous exhaustion
attendant upon these birthday occasions, it
always took Mr. Whittier three or four weeks
fully to recover from.   Hence in 1889 (and
partly on account of the recent death of a beloved cousin), the poet announced, through
the press, that he should have to ask his
friends to spare him any public reception.
However, December 17 was observed as
" Whittier Day " very generally throughout
the country, as it had been in 1887, in
accordance with the custom that has grown
up of celebrating the birthdays of eminent
men in the schools, and introducing into
their courses of supplementary reading selected portions of the writings of each.
Among the gifts received at Oak Knoll was
a painting of a golden vase by Mr. Herman
Marcus, of New York City, to whom the
poet had appeared in a dream, bearing in his

hand an elegant portfolio of red morocco, containing a picture of a vase of Grecian design, richly ornamented, and inscribed with the legend, " May in the smallest part thy sorrows lie concealed and all the rest be filled with joy overflowing." The portfolio and the picture on its page are a close realization of what the donor saw in his dream.

Speaking of visitors, Col. Higginson tells two incidents in point. He says two nice little boys called one day on Whittier, saying that they had recently called on Longfellow, and, as he had died soon after, they thought it best to call at once on Mr. Whittier. One of the poet's housekeepers once asked him in severe tones whether all " these people " came on business or whether they were relatives. When told that neither was the case, she said she did not see what they came for then. " Neither did I," said Whittier, with laughing eye.

In December, 1890, Mr. Whittier, who had gone down to Amesbury to vote, had been taken ill there, and hardly expected to be able to get back to Oak Knoll by the seventeenth. He did arrive, however, on a sunny day. Many of his friends spared him visits, merely leaving their cards or sending remembrances.   His mail was very large, as usual on this day.

In the summer of 1891 Mr. Whittier's health was so feeble that he was obliged to abandon his daily walks, except about the grounds at Oak Knoll.   Driving was too fatiguing for him, and his hearing had grown so bad that he could converse only with difficulty.

In Whittier's poem," The Red River Voyageur," there is a beautiful allusion to the " bells of the Roman mission," now the Archepiscopate of St. Boniface.   Archbishop Tache was reminded by Lieut.-Gov. Schultz that December 17, 1891, was the eighty-fourth birthday of the poet, the suggestion being made that the anniversary should be greeted by a joy-peal from the tower of the Cathedral of St. Boniface, in Winnipeg, Manitoba.   His Grace cordially concurred, and the graceful tribute was rendered at midnight with the last stroke of the clock ushering the natal day. Mr. Whittier, having been informed of the incident by United States Consul Taylor, wrote to the Archbishop: " I have reached an age when literary success and manifestations of popular favor have ceased to satisfy one upon whom the solemnity of life's sunset is resting; but such a delicate and beautiful tribute has deeply moved me. I shall never forget it. I shall hear the bells of St. Boniface sounding across the continent, and awakening a feeling of gratitude for thy generous act."

Our poet's eighty-fourth birthday (1891), and alas! his last on earth, was delightfully observed at the home of the Cartlands, his cousins, in Newburyport, with whom he was spending the winter. Mr. Joseph Cartland is himself a Quaker, and his white hair and genial cheery temperament are quite of the old régime. He and his wife were teachers in the Friends' School at Providence, R. I. Their fine old mansion on High Street is the identical one built and lived in by Judge Livermore, father of the shrewish saint and devotee of "Snow-Bound." It may be stated, too, that it was to succeed one of the Cartlands in the editorial chair of the *Pennsylvania Freeman* that Whittier went to Philadelphia in 1838. In this house is kept the old maple-wood desk, made by Joseph Whittier, grandfather of the poet, who, by the way, " wrote on it his first poem."

The desk is about one hundred and eighty years old now. On the back are carved the initials " J. W., 1786," in large letters. The wood has been smoothed down a little and a coat of shellac applied. On the back of the drawers are memoranda in chalk and pencil made by Greenleaf's father. On December 17, 1891, the old piece of furniture was covered with hundreds of congratulatory letters which would have made the old farmer Quaker, its builder, rub his eyes in astonishment, could he have seen them.

"As he walks slowly down the broad stairs of the Cartland's at Newburyport," says one who saw him on his birthday, " there is much to suggest his years, it is true, yet no signs of unusual feebleness. He is erect for a man of eighty-four; his early litheness has not degenerated into the hopeless leanness of an ill-nourished and un-cared-for old age; his step does not drag after his body as if unwilling to carry the burden longer; his head is not lowered, awaiting the smite of Time."

Another thus describes Whittier in 1891 : " In personal appearance he is remarkable. Tall, and as straight as one of the young pines in his favorite grove, it seems impossible that he is at the end of fourscore years. The crown of his head is bald, and his hair is glossy silver; but his great black eyes are as clear, bright and piercing as if he were in the prime of life. He walks with the deliberation and dignity of age, but without a suggestion of physical feebleness, and while he remains standing his head is as finely poised as a soldier's. The straightness of his figure is the more noticeable on account of his Quaker dress, the coat of which fits him as neatly and closely as if it were the conventional 'swallow-tail.' When seated and listening, his head drops slightly forward and aside — a pose which seems peculiar to poetic natures the world over. He is a most appreciative reader of other men's books and poems, and talks admirably of all good writings except his own, of which he can scarcely be persuaded to speak, even to his dearest intimates."

Mr. S. T. Pickard, and Mr. and Mrs. Cartland received the guests in the wide hall of the old-fashioned hospitable Quaker home; and the poet himself wandered here and there about the room, so said the Boston

Advertiser, " greeting every guest informally
and pleasantly, from the old and tried com-
rades of anti-slavery's earliest days to the
little girl in cream-white dress and wide hat,
his little friend Margaret Lothrop, who had
to stand on tip-toe to greet the bowed head
with her childish kiss ; and whose small hand
he held closely as he kept her by his side."

A pleasant note was received from Phillips
Brooks : —

" DEAR MR. WHITTIER:

" I have no right save that which love and
gratitude and reverence may give, to say how
devoutly I thank God that you have lived,
that you are living, and that you will always
live. May his peace be with you more and
more.

" Affectionately your friend,

" PHILLIPS BROOKS."

The first guests to arrive were a deputation
of fifty from Haverhill, members of the
Whittier Club of that town. Whittier made
them a little speech, saying it was evident
that sometimes a prophet was honored in
his own country.

The house was filled with cut flowers—in the window-seats, on the tables, in the poet's bedroom, up-stairs — all gifts from friends. The Whittier Club of Haverhill brought eighty-four roses. There was a basket of English violets from Mr. and Mrs. D. Lothrop. Mr. C. F. Coffin, of Lynn, sent, as usual, his generous basket of fruit. From Mr. E. C. Stedman came a painting " High Tide, Hampton Meadows," by Carroll D. Brown. And some kindly old soul sent a half-dozen pairs of socks — the spirit that prompted the gift as deeply appreciated as that of others. Other gifts were : an oil painting of a scene at York Harbor, painted by J. L. Smith, of Boston, the frame carved by A. G. Smith; a ruler of various inlaid woods from California, the gift of pupils of the workshop at West Point, Calaveras County, who wrote a letter, saying that they would devote the birthday to reading and speaking selections from his works; a paper-cutter made from the wood of Fort Loudon, of Winchester, Penn., and sent by the ladies of that place; a hand-painted tray from artist Florence Cammett of Amesbury; a late photograph of Dr. Holmes, " with his hat in his hand, and his most man-of-the-world air;" a souvenir spoon of Independence Hall from W. H. and S. B. Swazey, of Newburyport; a picture of the old Mission at Santa Barbara, done on native olive-wood, from Professor John Murray, of California; a handsome footstool from Elizabeth Cavazza, of Portland, Me.; photogravures of scenes about the Whittier homestead in Haverhill; a transparency ("Snow-Bound") from Austin P. Nichols; eighty-four roses from the girls of Lasell Seminary near Boston, and a wreath of evergreens from Mrs. Annie Fields.

Among the messages was one from a little Indian maiden whom Whittier had befriended: "Your young Mohawk friend asks for you to-day the Great Spirit's blessing"— signed, E. Pauline Johnson; a letter came from Abby Hutchinson, of the Hutchinson singers.

Among those present were, Mrs. Alice Freeman Palmer, Sarah Orne Jewett, "Margaret Sidney," Mrs. James T. Fields, Mrs. William Claflin, Harriet McEwen Kimball, T. E. Burnham, Mayor of Haverhill, and others.

Among the company, conspicuous by those natural gifts that make one a centre for intellectual and genial comradeship, was Mr. D. Lothrop — the eminent publisher — (since passed away, mourned by all) who probably has done more than any other man of present times to create a new literature for children and young people, all achieved when it cost to do it, and that consumed years of patient, persistent struggling, till his splendid success was won.

Mr. Whittier writes to his widow, " Thy husband and Mr. Coffin " (the old-time friend referred to), " were the life of my birthday reception, and now both are gone before me." (Mr. Coffin died the week after the birthday.)

Again, to quote one of the many extracts of Mr. Whittier's letters concerning Mr. Lothrop: " Let me sit in the circle of thy mourning, for I too have lost in him a friend."

There was much to draw the two men together; both sprang from New England ancestry, sturdy as the granite hills of their native State ; each possessed the same indomitable will, where a question of right was involved, and the same breadth of charity for all, of whatsoever creed or divergence of opinion.

Mr. Whittier partook of but little food in the dining-room, nibbling a bit here and there, and refusing firmly all offers of tea or coffee. His eyes, every one noticed, flamed with old-time lustre, whenever he was interested.

Letters of congratulation were received from Robert C. Winthrop, Celia Thaxter, Julia Ward Howe, Harriet Prescott Spofford, Andrew P. Peabody, Rose Terry Cooke (who has since died), George W. Cable, T. W. Higginson, Charles Eliot Norton, and others.

Donald G. Mitchell wrote that above Whittier's literary art he admired the broad and cheery humanities of the man.

For the eighty-fourth birthday the Boston *Advertiser* printed a superb illustrated Whittier number, as did also the Boston *Journal*. For the latter Dr. Holmes contributed the following letter:

MY DEAR WHITTIER: — I congratulate you on having climbed another glacier and crossed another crevasse in your ascent of the white summit which already begins to see the morning twilight of the coming century. A life so well filled as yours has been cannot be too long for your fellowmen and women. In their affections you are secure, whether you are with them here or near them in some higher life than theirs. I hope your years have not become a burden, so that you are tired of living. At our age we must live chiefly in the past. Happy is he who has a past like yours to look back upon.

It is one of the felicitous incidents — I will not say accidents — of my life that the lapse of time has brought us very near together, so that I frequently find myself honored by seeing my name mentioned in near connection with your own. We are lonely, very lonely, in these last years. The image which I have used before this in writing to you recurs once more to my thought. We were on deck together as we began the voyage of life two generations ago. A whole generation passed, and the succeeding one found us in the cabin, with a goodly company of coevals. Then the craft which held us began going to pieces, until a few of us were left on the raft pieced together of its fragments. And now the raft has at last parted, and you and I are left clinging to the solitary spar, which is all that still remains afloat of the sunken vessel.

I have just been looking over the headstones in Mr. Griswold's cemetery, entitled "The Poets and Poetry of America." In that venerable receptacle, just completing its half-century of existence — for the date of the edition before me is 1842 — I find the names of John Greenleaf Whittier and Oliver Wendell Holmes next each other, in their due order, as they should be. All around are the names of the dead — too often of forgotten dead. Three which I see there are still among those of the living. Mr. John Osborn Sargent, who makes Horace his own by faithful study and ours by scholarly translation ; Isaac McLellan, who was writing in 1830, and whose last work is dated 1886 ; and Christopher P. Cranch, whose poetical gift has too rarely found expression.

Of these many dead you are the most venerated, revered and beloved survivor; of these few living the most honored representative. Long may it be before you leave a world where your influence has been so beneficent, where your example has been such inspiration, where you are so truly loved, and where your presence is a perpetual benediction.

Always affectionately yours,

Oliver Wendell Holmes.

Following is one of two stanzas sent to the Poet of Freedom by his friend " Margaret Sidney," and which, says the *Advertiser*, with one other tribute, was the only one of the innumerable letters and poems sent him that he read in its entirety that day, owing to his failing eyesight :

> " To be near the heart of Christ
>   Was his creed ;
> White as truth the life
>   That all men may read ;
> Strengthful of soul,
>   Yet lowly in meekness ;
> Dreading no hate of men,
>   Scorning all weakness,
> He sounded the warning note,
>   When it cost to be brave and true ;
> Sang freedom for the slave,
>   Then almost death to do.
> ' Unbind every shackle,
> Loosen each chain,
> Bid every slave go free ! ' "

Mr. F. B. Sanborn wrote some interesting autobiographical reminiscences for the *Ad-*

vertiser. He stated: " I can scarcely remember when I did not read Whittier and Holmes. Their verses were eagerly caught up and reprinted by all the newspapers, and I knew them by heart before I ever saw a volume of them. Whittier, indeed, was almost my neighbor, living only eight miles away across the Merrimack, and sometimes coming for silent worship or to hear Mrs. Edward Gove speak in the Quaker meeting-house at Seabrook, only three miles from the farm of my ancestors. But I did not know this then; I never went there to see him. He is a distant cousin of mine, both of us tracing descent, through his daughters, from that stout and ungovernable old Puritan minister, Stephen Bachiler, who planted the old town of Hampton, in whose wide limits I was born, and which extended almost to Amesbury."

Another scholarly writer in the same paper wrote instructively of Whittier in the Massachusetts Legislature. The Legislature of 1835 he describes as a notable one in the quality of its members and in the work accomplished. An extra session was held in the autumn. The Speaker of the House was Judge Julius Rockwell of Pittsfield, with whom Whittier had already formed a personal acquaintance through Judge Rockwell's contributions to the *New England Review.* Among the Suffolk County representatives were such names as Frothingham, Brooks, Otis, Sturgis, Peabody, and Hon. Robert C. Winthrop, also Col. J. B. Fay, the first mayor of Chelsea. It is not remembered that Whittier made any set speech, but he nevertheless did so much and such arduous work as to make himself ill before the session was half over. Dr. Bowditch, he often recalled with amusement, told him that, if he followed implicitly the rules he laid down for him, he might live to see his fiftieth birthday; otherwise, not.

Perhaps no one man has been more frequently interviewed concerning the policy of party politics than John G. Whittier. With gifted qualities of heart and mind, was added wisdom, prudence and sagacity, in all that related to governmental affairs. The late Henry Wilson once said of him, " I can rely more safely upon the advice of Whittier than upon any other man in America."

In the early movements of the Republican party he was acknowledged to be the power behind the throne. Sumner, wise and learned, could trust to the advice of Whittier. His correspondence with such men as Giddings, Chase, Sumner, Wilson, John P. Hale, Upham and other celebrities, upon national topics, is known to a few of his friends. They contain sentiments which prove him as wise in statesmanship as he is eloquent in verse.

How well and faithfully he labored is best expressed in his words:

" I am not insensible to literary reputation; I love, perhaps too well, the love and praise of my fellowmen; but I set a higher value on my name as appended to the Anti-Slavery Declaration of 1833, than on the title page of any book."

On the subject of the abolishment of capital punishment, Whittier's vote is found recorded in the affirmative, as might have been expected. He has said that one of the pleasantest years of his life was that passed during the session of the Legislature in 1835.

One of the chief reasons why Whittier went seven miles from his Amesbury home last summer was to " escape pilgrims " (as he

called them).   One Sunday after meeting at
Amesbury he said to his life-long friend,
Miss Gove, " Abby, has thee a spare room
up at thy house ? "   She responded in the
affirmative, and he went to her home in
Hampton Falls for the latter part of the
summer.   It was here he penned his last
poem — the verses " To Oliver Wendell
Holmes : "

> " The gift is thine the weary world to make
> More cheerful for thy sake,
> Soothing the ears its Miserere pains
> With the old Hellenic strains."

In a letter to one of the editors of the
Critic (August 29, 1892), Dr. Holmes wrote,
concerning his birthday :

" I have received two poems in advance,
and our dear friend Whittier, whose heart is
a cornucopia of blessings for his fellow-creatures, has remembered me in the pages of
the *Atlantic*, where we have found ourselves
side by side for so many years.   Long may
the sands of his life keep running, for they
come from the bed of Pactolus."

The news of his friend's death was received by Dr. Holmes in Beverly, just as he

was coming in from a drive along the shore. It was a heavy blow, coming as it did just upon the death of Lowell, Thomas Parsons, and George William Curtis. He remarked that his acquaintance with Whittier dated from the year of the founding of the *Atlantic Monthly*. He had frequently visited him at Oak Knoll. He was there last year, and the two old fellows walked and talked among the trees and had a good time together. When the Doctor was leaving, his friend loaded him down with fruit. It was on one of these recent visits that Dr. Holmes with characteristic keenness of perception, discovered the beautiful symmetry of the grand Norway spruce in front of the mansion on the wide sweep of lawn, and he laughingly named it "The Poet's Pagoda," and this name it has kept ever since.

To return to "Elmfield," as the old Gove mansion is called. The old-fashioned house, with its upper balconies, heavy chimneys, and rich collection of historical relics, stands on a hill not far from the falls which gave the name to the village — Hampton Falls. The sight from Whittier's window commanded a little balcony, with a view of the distant blue sea. One day after another passed quietly away, he rising at seven, going across through a pine grove to the adjoining tavern for his breakfast, getting the mail at the little post-office, reading the papers, looking at the distant sails on the sea through a glass, conversing with friends or walking in the neighboring orchard, with its paths and rustic seats. The region is that where his Bachiler and Hussey ancestors both lived, as Mr. F. B. Sanborn tells us (Boston *Advertiser*, September 8, 1892). Daniel Webster's Bachiler ancestors also lived on a farm, a mile and a half from the Gove mansion; namely, where now stands the villa of Warren Brown. As Mr. Sanborn truthfully says, Whittier has been the local poet of this whole region of Essex and adjoining counties. " No poet of New England," he continues, " has lived so close to the actual habits of the people, in the present and the past centuries, as did Whittier; and his poems of locality will become as much a feature of New England literature as are those of Burns and Scott in their native country. This fidelity to homely fact and profound sentiment have made Whittier more than any other the patrial and religious poet of New Hampshire and Eastern Massachusetts. He has done in verse what Hawthorne did in prose. It was only the accident or accomplishment of verse which separated these two poets, and made one of them our most graceful and romantic prose-writer, while the other became our most spiritual and literal poet."

The truth of these statements comes home to me with force since I made a week's itinerary through this Whittier ballad land a year ago, and saw how every mile of coast land was celebrated in storied verse by Whittier.

On Wednesday, August 31, Mr. Whittier was taken ill. The malady was acute diarrhea, which by the Saturday following developed a new and alarming symptom, a remarkable irregularity of the heart's action, accompanied by partial paralysis of the left side, arms, and vocal organs. He remained conscious until Tuesday at three P. M., when the symptoms became markedly worse. He was surrounded by ministering relatives and friends, who gave him every loving attention, but all were powerless to stay the hand of death.

When urged to take the nourishment prescribed by his physicians, he said: " I want water from Abby's (Miss Gove) nice well," and as it was given, remarked with a bright smile, " That's good — nothing better." Soon after, as his forehead was being bathed, he said, " That is all that can be done." ·To his attending physicians, Drs. Douglass and Howe, and nurse, he said: " I am worn out — thee have done what thee could — I thank thee." And as the end drew near the dying poet recognized his niece from Portland, and remarked in faltering words, " Love — to — the — world." These were his last words. He died at four-thirty on the morning of the seventh. At seven o'clock on Friday evening the silent form of the poet was brought to Amesbury, accompanied by Mr. and Mrs. S. T. Pickard, and Mr. and Mrs. Cartland.

On Saturday morning business was entirely suspended in Amesbury. The selectmen issued the following proclamation : —

" To the Citizens of Amesbury : — Our town has been saddened by the death of its great poet and one of its noblest and best-loved citizens. We feel that our country at large, and the civilized world, mourns with us the death of the poet and liberty-loving philanthropist, John G. Whittier.

"Sharing the sadness which must come to the wise and good everywhere, we, the people of Amesbury, mourn the loss

22   THE GOVE HOUSE, HAMPTON FALLS, N. H., IN WHICH WHITTIER DIED.

of a friend and neighbor endeared to us by his lovable qualities and the purity of his daily life in our midst.

"We revered him for his greatness, and loved him for
himself. Always identified with every good work in Amesbury, sustaining the right and defending the oppressed, his
life for more than half a century has been to us a daily
sermon.

"If it be true that

'The heart speaketh most when the life move,'

we can only add that such a life, with its fullness of years and
its crown of blessings, is a rich legacy to the community."

At ten o'clock the public was admitted to
the house, passing in a continuous line (as
at the funeral of dear old Walt Whitman,
his brother-poet of Democracy, a few months
before in Camden) through the humble little
parlor of the Amesbury home. It was originally intended to hold the services in the
Friends' meeting-house near by; but the
dense fog clearing up and the bright sun
coming out — as one beautifully said, "the
mystery of death typified by the shifting and
elusive shadows of the fog, and the glory
and hopefulness of the resurrection by the
bright rays of the sun" — it was decided to
let the body rest in the house, and hold
memorial services in the quiet garden in the

rear of the house. The funeral arrangements were in charge of William Lloyd Garrison, Jr., S. T. Pickard and Judge G. W. Cate, the tenant of the house. The atmosphere was one of peace and restfulness, and the simplicity of the life of the Friends was seen in all the arrangements. In the quaint parlor of the homestead lay all that was mortal of the poet, on whose face was an expression of supreme peace; his form was encircled by a delicate fringe of trailing fern. A most beautiful wreath from Dr. Oliver Wendell Holmes — eighty-four white roses, fringed with carnations and maidenhair ferns, one for each year of the poet's life, — was laid around the name-plate on the coffin. It was a touching tribute by the last one of that remarkable galaxy of poets that marked such a distinguished era in our American literature. Two crossed palms, with the Japan lilies Whittier loved so well, encircled by a broad white satin ribbon, were from Mrs. Daniel Lothrop. The fronds of the long palms encircled the face of the dead poet as it looked out from the large engraving between the windows of the parlor. Upon the end of the ribbon was delicately painted

six lines from Whittier's " Andrew Rykman's
Prayer : "

> " Some sweet morning yet in God's
> Dim æonian periods,
> Joyful I shall wake to see
> Those I love who rest in Thee,
> And to them in Thee allied
> Shall my soul be satisfied."

Upon the accompanying card was this:
" In memory of my husband's dear friend.
This verse of ' Andrew Rykman's Prayer '
was consolation in the hour of death to both
him who wrote it, and to him who loved it.
— Mrs. Daniel Lothrop."

Another exquisite floral offering came
with these lines :

> " I know not where His islands lift
>   Their fronded palms in air ;
> I only know I cannot drift
>   Beyond His love and care."

On the back of the card were the words
" Oak Knoll."

The alcove behind the casket was filled
with floral tributes. Here was a large St.
Andrew's cross of exquisite white roses

upon a bed of ivy, from a very near and dear friend of Mr. Whittier's at Lexington, whose name is withheld. There was a ladder of hydrangeas, gladioli, carnations and snow-balls from Mrs. Albert Clarke of Amesbury, an ivy wreath from Sarah Orne Jewett, a sheaf of wheat from Mrs. Lizzie Cheney and the Misses Coffin of Lynn, a broken shaft of white carnations from Mr. and Mrs. J. Henry Hall of Amesbury. A massive wreath of Whittier's own much-loved pine tassels was hung above the portrait of his sister Elizabeth, the tribute of Mrs. Joseph A. Purington; the heavy green was relieved by a spray of bright, contrasting goldenrod. Mrs. Samuel Rowell, Jr., sent a basket of white roses and maidenhair. There was a beautiful spray of the passion flower from L. Keleher, Hotel Winthrop, Boston, and an hour-glass of white carnations from Mr. J. R. Fogg. Many touching little clusters of flowers came from the children; and his neighbors sent a beautiful wreath of fringed gentian — Whittier's favorite flower. This came from the far Pacific Slope: "Lay one flower for me upon the bier of the beloved friend who rests. No purer soul ever passed from earth to Heaven, or bore with it greater love and blessing than does his. — Ina D. Coolbrith, Oakland, Cal."

In the garden, and overlooked by the windows of the study where Mr. Whittier wrote and thought for so many years, was gathered to pay the last tributes of love and reverence to the dead poet, a large and notable assemblage: Gen. O. O. Howard, E. C. Stedman, Mrs. Alice Freeman Palmer, Mrs. Elizabeth Stuart Phelps-Ward, Gail Hamilton, Lucy Larcom, Edna Dean Proctor, Horace E. Scudder, T. W. Higginson, ex-Governor Claflin, Parker Pillsbury, Francis H. Underwood, Edward L. Pierce, Robert S. Rantoul, Mrs. C. A. Dall, "Margaret Sidney," Harriet Prescott Spofford, Mrs. Endicott, Wm. Lloyd Garrison, Jr., Frank J. Garrison, etc

And the sight was one never to be forgotten. Under the soft September sky, blue and cloudless, in the shade of pear and apple trees which Whittier himself had planted and tended and loved, were his relatives, friends, neighbors and men and women whose names are known wherever the English language is spoken.

It scarcely seemed like a funeral, so unaffectedly natural and sincere was every
spoken word and every act. And the entire
absence of formality and stiffness deprived
the occasion of that artificial gloom which is
so often characteristic of funerals.

Perhaps, too, the subtle influence of the
balmy air and the beauties of the place
helped to lift the pall that must have hung
over many a heart. It was as if the friends
of some dearly beloved man, who was going
on a journey, had gathered to bid him God-
speed — not as if they had come to bid him
farewell.

A hollow square was formed around a low
platform, and near by was a table with a
Bible upon it. Gentians, one of Whittier's
favorite flowers, and goldenrod formed the
only floral ornaments. Back of the seats
stood a dense crowd that must have num-
bered thousands, almost filling the garden.
Children climbed the trees and looked with
open-eyed wonder on the scene. On an
apple bough, his naked legs dangling in the
air almost over the head of Edmund Clarence
Stedman, was an urchin who might have inspired the " Barefoot Boy; " faces peered.

from many a tree, from the vine-clad arbor
and from the window of a neighboring barn,
down upon the crowd.

The poet's relatives, and members of the
Society of Friends from various places, occupied the seats forming the hollow square, an
easy-chair being reserved for Oliver Wendell
Holmes, but he was unable to be present.

The Friends gave the exercises their
peculiar complexion; first one and then
another rising to eulogize their friend as the
" Spirit moved them." Verses of Whittier
were recited by " that lovely Quaker lady,"
Mrs. Gertrude Cartland, and by Mrs. James
H. Chace. Mr. E. C. Stedman was the last
speaker.

He spoke of the personal loss he felt
in the poet's death. " To know him was a
consecration, to have his sympathy a benediction. His passing away was not so much
a death as a translation. He is gone, and
has not left his mantle! How could he?
Why should he? No one can overestimate
his artless art, his power, vigor and effect
in his polemic efforts. No one put so much
heart or so much religion into his writings.
He was one of the great trio of New Eng-

land poets, of whom there is only one now left. They are the vanishers of whom he spoke. He was a believer in the inward life, as a poet should be. He will be his own successor, and belongs to our time as well as to that earlier time to which he is linked by his work. We may say of him that the chariot swung low and he was translated, dividing the waters of truth, beauty, and religion with his mantle. The last time I spoke at a memorial service was at Bayard Taylor's funeral. Taylor was Whittier's friend, and like Whittier he had a firm belief in immortality."

It is to Mr. Stedman that Whittier dedicated in a few choice lines his latest volume of verse, " At Sundown," which the poet, as if prescient of his coming death, had had privately printed and circulated among a few friends a year before his fatal illness.

The most picturesque and striking figure at Whittier's funeral was that of the venerable John W. Hutchinson, whose long gray hair fell over a broad white Rembrandt collar. He and his sister, Abby Hutchinson Patton, were life-long friends of Whittier; and their voices in the song they sang —

"Close his eyes, his work is done"—were, "like the echoes of sweet bells from the far-away time of their youth, when they and Whittier were one in endeavor."

And then the long procession was formed. In the family lot, in the Friends' section of the Union Cemetery, where are buried his father, mother, sisters and brother, John Greenleaf Whittier was laid to rest.

The Boston *Journal*, in writing of Whittier's obsequies, gathered up this tender reminiscence : —

"We recall the incident of some ten years since, when Mr. Daniel Lothrop, the late publisher, while visiting in California, used Whittier's poem, 'Andrew Rykman's Prayer' to comfort the bereaved. Mr. Lothrop had, as it were, been brought up on Mr. Whittier's poems, there being in many ways a great similarity of tastes and characteristics between them. Of late years there was a strong friendship. The clergyman of a prominent Oakland church had died suddenly in the pulpit some few weeks before, and at the large memorial meeting Mr. Lothrop was asked without warning by the chairman to recite this poem, as he had heard him repeat a few lines from it during a consecration meeting. Mr. Lothrop ascended the platform and gave the poem entire. There was a profound hush throughout the vast assembly, like that following the instant when the beloved pastor had suddenly fallen before their eyes. Many were in tears, all agreeing that Whittier's strong, uplifting words comforted them more than anything else that had been said. Rev. Dr. Gordon, in the address at Mr. Lothrop's funeral in the Old South Church, appropriately recited this poem for the late publisher, who on his death-bed used this poem, as he had in health and strength."

James G. Blaine telegraphed that he had "long regarded Whittier with affectionate veneration," and over the wire came from Frederick Douglas the words, " Emancipated millions will hold his memory sacred." Speaking of Mr. Blaine, a writer, " S. F. M.," in the Boston *Journal*, December 18, 1891, tells of Mr. Blaine's presenting his, " S. F. M.'s," brother with a morocco-bound copy of the beautiful Mussey edition, and of Mr. Blaine's reading and re-reading aloud, one Sunday at their house in Charlestown, Mass., the poem " Among the. Hills," which had then just been issued.

Memorial services on the afternoon of the funeral were held in Danvers, Haverhill, Salem, Mass., and Vassalboro, Maine. The old Whittier grange at the cross roads in Haverhill was draped in mourning. The present owner of the birthplace is Mr. George E. Elliott, a retired wealthy gentleman of Haverhill ; and it is hoped that at no distant day he may be induced to sell it to the town of Haverhill, who would sacredly keep this cherished spot marking the nativity of her distinguished son, so that all lovers of John G. Whittier's poetry may have an opportunity to see his early home.

The day after the funeral between seventeen and eighteen hundred people visited the grave. And, as in the case of Walt Whitman's grave, each one wanted a leaf or flower as a memento, so that it was necessary in both cases to have the place of sepulture guarded by special watchmen, in order that anything green be left.

The funeral of the poet was conducted as he himself wished. For in his will he wrote, " It is my wish that my funeral may be conducted in the plain and quiet way of the Society of Friends, with which I am connected not only by birthright, but also by a settled conviction of the truth of its principles and the importance of its testimonies." Mr. Whittier, by the way, in his will requests all who have letters of his to refrain from publishing them unless with the consent of his literary executor, Mr. S. T. Pickard.

So beautifully ended a most beautiful life — beautiful because just and heroic in the defense of justice. As says of him James Herbert Morse : —

> " Such was the man --- no more than simple man,
>   Plain Quaker, with the Norman-Saxon glow ;
> But seeing beauty so, and justice so,
>   We love to think him the American."

And as Lowell says : —

> " Peaceful by birthright as a virgin lake,
>   The lily's anchorage, which no eyes behold
> Save those of stars, yet for thy brother's sake
>   That lay in bonds thou blew'st a blast as bold
> As that wherewith the heart of Roland brake,
>   Far heard through Pyrenean valleys cold !"

The lines strong and resonant, of Stedman's " Ad Vatem," addressed to Whittier

while living, might well have been uttered
over his bier :—

> " Whittier, the land that loves thee, she whose child
> Thou art, and whose uplifted hands thou long
> Hast staid with song availing like a prayer —
> She feels a sudden pang who gave thee birth,
> And gave to thee the lineaments supreme
> Of her own freedom, that she could not make
> Thy tissues all immortal, or, if to change,
> To bloom through years coeval with her own ;
> So that no touch of age nor frost of time
> Should wither thee, nor furrow thy dear face,
> Nor fleck thy hair with silver. Ay, she feels
> A double pang that thee, with each new year
> Glad youth may not revisit, like the spring
> That routs her northern winter and anew
> Melts off the hoar snow from her puissant hills."

Many pleasant anecdotes of the Quaker
poet appeared shortly after his death. Col.
T. W. Higginson, writing of the Amesbury
home, said of Whittier's mother :—

" On one point only this blameless soul
seemed to have a shadow of solicitude, this
being the new wonder of Spiritualism just
dawning on the world. I never went to the
house that there did not come from the gentle lady very soon a placid inquiry from behind her knitting needles, ' Has thee any
further information to give in regard to the

spiritual communications, as they call them ?'
But if I attempted to treat seriously a matter
which then, as now, puzzled most inquirers
by its perplexing details, there would come
some keen thrust from Elizabeth Whittier
which would throw all serious solution
further off than ever.

"She was indeed a brilliant person, unsurpassed in my memory for the light cavalry
charges of wit; as unlike her mother and
brother as if she had been born into a different race. Instead of his regular features,
she had a wild, bird-like look, with prominent nose and large liquid dark eyes, whose
expression vibrated every instant between
melting softness and impetuous wit. There
was nothing about her that was not sweet
and kindly, but you were constantly taxed to
keep up with her sallies and hold your own;
while her graver brother listened with delighted admiration and rubbed his hands
over bits of merry sarcasm which were
utterly alien to his own vein. His manifold
visitors were touched off in living colors; two
plump and rosy Western girls among them,
who had lately descended upon the household beaming with eagerness to see the poet.

" They had announced themselves as the Cary sisters, who had lately sent him their joint poems — verses, it will be remembered, crowded with deaths and melodious dirges that seemed ludicrously inconsistent with the blooming faces at the door. Mrs. Whittier met them rather guardedly and explained that her son was out. ' But we will come in and wait for him,' they smilingly replied. ' But he is in Boston, and may not be home for a week,' said the prudent mother. ' No matter,' they said, in the true spirit of Western hospitality ; ' we can stay till he returns.' There was no resource but to admit them ; and happily the poet came back next day, and there ensued a life-long friendship, in which the mother fully shared."

And another reminiscence appeared in the press, touching the poet's residence in Boston.

" When Mrs. Celia Thaxter was boarding at the little English-like inn on the sunny slope of Beacon Hill called Hotel Winthrop, Mr. Whittier went there one day to see her. Mrs. Thaxter liked the quiet place, with its ivied window and its glimpse of the strong, short, green-draped tower of St. John the

23

Evangelist's, and she praised it to her old friend. That was some time in 1881, and in November of that year he joined his Oak Knoll cousins, Mrs. Woodman and her daughter and the Misses Johnson, at the Winthrop. The ladies of the family came in September, but Mr. Whittier did not join them until November. He said that he did not want to lose his vote in Amesbury.

It was a winter full of pleasure to the poet. He was then not too feeble to go out evenings, and he spent many pleasant hours with friends like the Claflins and others. But the hours in the parlor of the hotel make the place historic, and give it a special interest and meaning for his future biographer. Mr. Whittier had room fourteen (the number of a sonnet's lines, twice seven, with luck for a poet), and the fire-escape made a little balcony for him on a corner toward St. John's. The landlord had a door cut through the thick old wall to the rooms adjoining, and these were the rooms of Mrs. Woodman and the rest. It is old Boston decidedly in that quarter. The brick of the houses is mellow old red, and there is nothing newfangled anywhere about. Mr. Whittier said he preferred coming here rather than to one of the big hotels, because there he was "overwhelmed with the service," and here it seemed "more like Amesbury," where people "are neighborly and drop in without knocking." He had "always been used to waiting upon himself," and he "liked being in a place where they would let him."

It was his custom, mornings, to come down into the little reception-room on the street floor, and "sitting right in that chair where you're sitting," as the writer was told, he "used to read his letters and throw all the papers in a pile on the floor and go off and leave them." That little room was a great place of congregation for "the family," as the boarders who were there with Mr. Whittier liked to call themselves.

The poet would sit on the sofa with a favored one on each side of him and the rest in a group about, "often on footstools or on the floor, as like as not," while he "told stories of war times." Gen. Stevens was there during one of the poet's long stays; he had been a classmate of Gen. Lee and of Jefferson Davis at West Point, and he and the abolition poet discussed these men and their times from the broader view of later days.

"Once a friend, a lady who had some property in Virginia, wrote Mr. Whittier of having named a street in a new town for him, and of having set aside a portion of ground in his name. He replied with thanks, saying that he had that week received news of no less than three towns or streets being named for him with a gift of town lots, adding, ' If this sort of thing goes on much longer, I shall be land poor.'

" During the winters he was at the Winthrop, Mr. Whittier's favorite way of getting about was in a herdic. They were ' not pretty,' but they ' knew the way to places.' Politicans used to go there to see him and try to get him to banquets. But his life-long avoidance of politics in the minor sense made him easily resist their wiles. ' I have seen Mr. —— (a well-known name) come here and just about go down on his knees to get Mr. Whittier to speak or even to come to a banquet,' says the landlord (who is, by the way, an old-time character worthy of a novelist's pen), ' but Mr. Whittier would just sit here — right in that chair you're in — and kind of smile to himself as if to say, "Oh! your talk don't amount to anything." Well, once Mr.——— came here and staid and staid a-talking and persuading, and gave Mr. Whittier an earache if ever a man had one. But he didn't make anything by it, although he finally had to take a bed and stay all night.' "

Mr. Charles Brainard visited Whittier soon after the publication of "Snow-Bound." Finding his house painted and improved, he remarked to him, "It is evident that poetry has ceased to be a drug in the market."

"The next morning Mr. Whittier's answer came. It was in the winter, and, as the poet went up to the fire to warm his boots preparatory to putting them on, he said, 'Thee will have to excuse me, for I must go down to the office of the Collector.' Then, with a humorous gleam in his eye, he added, 'Since "Snow-Bound" was published, I have risen to the dignity of an income tax.' "

To an Englishman who visited him not long before his death, Mr. Whittier expressed his surprise that his guest should know so much of his poetry by heart. "I wonder," he said, "thou shouldst burden thy memory with all that rhyme. It is not well to have too much of it: better get rid of it as soon as possible. Why, I can't remember any of it. I once went to hear a wonderful orator, and he wound up his speech with a poetical quotation, and I clapped with all my might. Some one touched me on the shoulder, and said. 'Do you know who wrote that?' I said, 'No, I don't; but it's good.' It seems I had written it myself. The fault is I have written far too much."

Here is a story illustrating Whittier's kind-heartedness: A young lady, a neighbor, was asked to take tea at his house. " He had no servant at the moment, and, with the assistance of his guest, prepared the simple meal with his own hand. She contributed to the press for her support, and prepared a minute account of the affair, of which Mr. Whittier chanced to be advised, and sent off a remonstrance post haste. But when the young author pleaded the real need of the money which the little story was to bring her, and the harmlessness to its subject of its effective details, the former reason (for the latter would never have overcome his abhorrence of what he must have felt a

. vivisection) actually prevailed, and he permitted the publication with a benignant forbearance."

The Hon. Nathan Crosby, LL. D., writes in the Essex Institute Collections for 1880.

" James F. Otis, nephew of the Hon. H. G. Otis, while reading law in my office, found in some newspaper a piece of poetry which he said he was told had been written by a shoemaker boy in Haverhill, and he wished to go and find him. Upon his return he told me he found the young man by the name of Whittier at work in his shoe shop, and, making himself known to him, they spent the day together in wandering over the hills on the shore of the Merrimack, and in conversation upon literary matters. The next year he became an editor. Mr. Whittier is not only a poet, but is himself a poem."

Mr. Whittier, when interviewed some time ago as to his favorite works, replied: "Oh! really, I have none. Much that I have written I wish was as deep in the Red Sea as Pharaoh's chariot wheels. Much of the bread cast on the waters I wish had never returned. It is not fair to revive writings composed in the shadow of conditions that make every acceptable work impossible. In my early life I was not favored with good opportunities. Limited chances for education and a lack of books always stood in my way. When I began to write I had seen nothing, and virtually knew nothing of the world. Of course, things written then could not be worth much. In my father's house there were not a dozen books, and they were of a severe type. The only one that approached poetry was a rhymed history of King David, written by a contemporary of George Fox, the Quaker. There was one poor novel in the family. It belonged to an aunt. This I secured one day, but when I had read it about half through I was discovered and it was taken away from me."

This was about the time when Judge Pickering, of Salem, and a party of ladies called at the farmhouse to see him. "He was then an awkward boy of seventeen — as he used to tell the story — and was just then under the barn, looking for eggs. Hearing his name called, he came up with his hat full and found himself suddenly in the presence of people more elegant in appearance than any he had ever met. In telling the story, he added naïvely, ' They came to see the Quaker poet — and they saw him!' This must have been about the year 1824."

Mr. T. W. Ball (in the Boston *Journal,* Dec. 18, 1891, weekly edition), the journalist, wrote of his sole interview in 1848 with Whittier, in a little editorial den at the junction of Spring Lane and Water Street with Devonshire Street (the building recently torn down), where Henry Wilson was then editing the Free-Soil paper (owned by him as well). " I was busy," says Mr. Ball, " getting up some local items one morning, when a gentleman of staid appearance, with a beaming countenance, a broad-brimmed fur hat — the old-fashioned fur hat, so different from the silk tile — and a brownish coat of formal cut, entered the room, and, after the usual courtesies of salutation, fell into a close chat with the ' Natick cobbler,' by which popular title the future Vice-President was then known. It was the summer season, and Wilson was resplendent in a brown linen coat and a flaming red-checked velvet waistcoat, which was much affected in those days. As the conversation between the two waxed interesting, I noticed that the visitor unbuttoned his vest for comfort, and possessed himself of an exchange paper which he converted into a fan.   The interview closed, and the visitor, buttoning up his vest and donning his hat, turned to depart, when for the first time he appeared to take notice of my presence.   With a rapid glance at Wilson, he said, ' Henry, who is thy young friend ? '

" ' Oh, that's William, my local reporter,' was the reply.   ' Here, William, this is Mr. Whittier, the Quaker poet, that you have heard about ; shake hands with him.'   I timidly extended my hand, and the great man not only grasped it with a cordial grasp, but, patting me on the head with his other hand, said, ' My young friend, thee has chosen a noble calling.' "

Mr. Whittier, in speaking of Longfellow's works a few years ago, said, " ' Evangeline ' is a favorite with me.   I think it is one of the most beautiful of poems.   Longfellow had an easy life and superior advantages of association and education, and so did Emerson. It was widely different with me, and I am very thankful for the kind esteem that people

have given my writings. Before 'Evangeline' was written I had hunted up the history
of the banishment of the Acadians, and had
intended to write upon it myself, but I put it
off, and Hawthorne got hold of the story and
gave it to Longfellow. I am very glad he
did, for he was just the one to write it. If I
had attempted it I should have spoiled the
artistic effect of the poem by my indignation
at the treatment of the exiles by the Colonial
Government, who had a very hard lot after
coming to this country. Families were separated and scattered about, only a few of
them being permitted to remain in any
given locality. The children were bound
out to the families in the localities in which
they resided, and I wrote a poem upon finding in the records of Haverhill the indenture
that bound an Acadian girl as a servant in
one of the families in that neighborhood.
Gathering the story of her death, I wrote
' Marguerite.' "

In addition to what has been stated in
this volume and elsewhere by me on the
Barbara Frietchie ballad, are to be finally
appended a few words, suggested by the one
who sent the raw material of the ballad to

Whittier, namely, Mrs. E. D. E. N. South-worth, who, soon after the poet's death, at her pretty home in Georgetown, D. C., recalled the circumstances as they occurred back in 1863. It seems that the story was told her by a neighbor of hers who was also a relative of Barbara — Mr. C. S. Ramsburg. Mrs. Southworth's son, who was present, remarked, " What a grand subject for a poem by Whittier, mother!"

She thereupon sat down, and with tears in her eyes, wrote the incident out and sent it to Amesbury. Mr. Whittier replied as follows : —

" AMESBURY, 9mo. 8, 1863.

" MY DEAR MRS. SOUTHWORTH:— I heartily thank thee for thy very kind letter and its inclosed " message." It ought to have fallen into better hands, but I have just written out a little ballad of " Barbara Frietchie," which will appear in the next *Atlantic.* If it is good for anything thee deserves all the credit of it.

" With best wishes for thy health and happiness, I am most truly thy friend,

" JOHN G. WHITTIER."

It is said that Mr. Whittier expressed regret for having made a bonfire of nearly all the letters he had received from his correspondents for over half a century. It is to be hoped that his literary executor will be liberal-minded in allowing the publication of the most interesting of Whittier's own letters, for he put a good bit of his sister Elizabeth's wit and vivacity into his letters; and scarcely a day passed that one or more of these was not written, overflowing with kindly words and good humor, though these, it is true, could give no hint of that lambent gleam of the marvelous eyes, nor of that sudden compression of the upper lip with which he repressed a smile when he had flashed out a bit of humor.

Whittier was not only quick in repartee, but quick and lithe in all his movements, and quick in his mental processes. His friend, Judge G. W. Cate, says he latterly read books very rapidly by inspection, turning the leaves and seizing the contents by intuition. The poet's imagination, continues Judge Cate, was wonderful. Years ago he may have read an accurate description of some remote place — Malta,

Jerusalem, or some smaller town in the far East. He would then converse at any time as readily about such a place as if he had been there. It was this vivid remembrance of places, Whittier himself said, which made him not care so much to visit them in person. He was never a traveler, not having been farther from home than Philadelphia (half a century ago), and Washington somewhat later. He said that he should like to be in California or Florida for a winter, but the getting there appalled him, and so he sat contentedly in his Northern study, with its bright open fire, finding in its crumbling embers a compensatory dream of the *Morgenland* with its palms, mirages and luxuriant blossomry. He followed with deep interest the toils and adventures of his friend Greely in the arctic regions, and rejoiced with all his neighbors when word came of his rescue. And at another time he said he "would rather shake hands with Stanley than with any other man in the world just then."

The sincerest mourners at Whittier's funeral were women. One of the peculiarities of his life was the devotion and loving care given to him by noble women — sisters, mother, nieces, cousins and such poet friends as Lucy Larcom, Mrs. Spofford, Rose Terry Cooke, Sarah Orne Jewett, Celia Thaxter, Elizabeth Stuart Phelps and Mrs. Annie Fields. He was always an ardent defender of woman suffrage, and such advocates of that noble cause as Adelaide A. Claflin publicly expressed their sorrow on the death of their coadjutor and friend.

He was not only liberal in politics, but also in religion, and while remaining from choice in the creedless church of his fathers, yet he had sympathies that allied him with the broad humanitarian movements of the times in religion. There was no shred of bigotry in his nature. Who ever heard of a persecuting Quaker? It is they who have always patiently suffered persecution. Whittier, indeed, belonged with the advance guard of the Friends, in spirit at least, and he said in a letter written shortly before his death, " For years I have been desirous of a movement for uniting all Christians, with no other creed or pledge than a simple recognition of Christ as our leader."

The Whittier Club of Haverhill, an organization the poet had thoroughly enjoyed, not only because it represented the feeling of his native town toward him, but also from the constant attentions paid him by it, held a memorial service in Haverhill, October 7. It was a rare day of tribute and thanksgiving, and all who participated in it felt grateful for the honor allowed them. It was just a month from the day when the loved poet and former citizen passed from earth. Mr. George E. Elliott, the owner of Whittier's birthplace, very generously allowed the club to hold its meeting in the old homestead, and he furthered in every way their well-conceived plan by which the several rooms presented an appearance as near as possible to that of the poet's boyhood. The partition in the old kitchen, that had been put up of late years, was taken down, disclosing the array of ancient cupboards and queer little window; there was the kettle hanging on the crane in the wide fireplace, along whose hearth one almost expected to see "the apples sputtering in a row," as of yore. There were the iron fire-dogs and the antiquated chairs, the wainscoting untouched by the hand of Time, save to grow mellower of tint, and there was " the sagging beam," the uneven floor and the quaint staircase, all. just as Whittier, the boy, saw and touched and lived amongst, all those impressible years of his life.

It was a notable company gathered in that old homestead that beautiful October day — bidden there by the Whittier Club — not large in numbers, as the invitations were of necessity limited to the capacity of the old homestead. But they were mostly the poet's dear friends who came to do honor to his name. There was Lucy Larcom, William Lloyd Garrison, Jr., Mrs. Ednah D. Cheney and " Margaret Sidney " (Mrs. D. Lothrop); there was Charles Carleton Coffin and Mr. and Mrs. Frank Garrison and Miss Sparhawk, whose father, Dr. Thomas Sparhawk of Amesbury, was one of the poet's life-long friends. There was the dear Quaker presence of Mrs. Purington, Mr. Whittier's cousin, and the members of his family at Oak Knoll, Mrs. Woodman, her daughter, Miss Phebe, and the Misses Johnson; there was Mr. S. T. Pickard of Portland, Maine, who married the poet's niece Lizzie, and who is Mr. Whittier's literary executor.

And there were other relatives and friends and Haverhill citizens thronging the house, and listening outside the little many-paned windows to catch the echoes of the words being uttered within.

The day was all that one could desire who looked for sympathy in Nature toward this her favorite child who has so interpreted her woods and fields, her autumn skies and the trembling line of river and coast. The old kitchen was filled with chairs, and on them, and crowded in the doorways and peeping in the windows, were the interested and reverent listeners. Mr. Charles Howe, the president of the club, presided with great grace and dignity; with rare tact culling from the large amount of what waited to be read and said, just such choice extracts and bits of reminiscence as would best serve the purpose of the hour. Selections from " Snow-Bound " were read by a member of the club in that room where " Snow-Bound " was lived, if one may so express it. And to the listeners there came a vision of wintry fields and whirling storm ; of the little knot of friends drawn close to the friendly comforting fire on the hearth ; in the midst the thoughtful sensitive boy who was to awaken the love and veneration of future generations all over his country.

There were reminiscences of a visit to his birthplace paid by the poet some ten years since with Mr. S. T. Pickard, who told to the assembled company many amusing stories related by Mr. Whittier on that occasion. There was the quaint staircase down which the poet, when a baby, wrapped in a blanket, was rolled by his sister only two years older, who probably thought it the greatest kindness in the world to thus project her infant brother into space. There was the queer old cupboard where Mr. Whittier when a boy was dragged by his jacket collar by a tramp who had forcibly entered the house; and there he was compelled to stand while the unwelcome visitor searched high and low for any chance jug or bottle that would yield another supply to his already over-weighted condition. Seizing a jug from a dark corner, he ejected the cork without a glance at the contents, and took a long deep draught of whale oil used for filling lamps. The embryo poet took advantage of the confused spluttering that ensued, to make good his escape. Mr. Will Carleton recited with dramatic vigor " Barbara Frietchie," till the walls and rafters rang. Lucy Larcom read from the poet's writings, and Mr. William Lloyd Garrison, Jr. recited an original poem. A young English lady, who was visiting friends of Mr. Whittier's, read by request Tennyson's " Crossing the Bar," the Poet Laureate's death having just occurred.

There were reminiscences by Dr. Fiske of Newburyport, who told several characteristic stories connected with Joshua Coffin, the " Yankee Schoolmaster," and life-long friend of the poet; and Charles Carleton Coffin, the historian, gave the account of his capture of the big key of the last slave prison in Richmond, and of his giving it to Mr. Whittier who returned it to him a year or so ago. At the close of his remarks, Mr. Carleton hung the key on the nail above the fireplace where, in Whittier's boyhood, the big bull's-eye watch used to hang. Fitting place was it for the silent symbol of agony and shame to the slave brother; and all who witnessed it hanging there, felt the heart beat to a newer and a keener sense of the debt we owe to him whose songs (as one who gave a reminiscence that day told us) influenced Abraham Lincoln to project the Emancipation Proclamation upon the American people. The beautiful poem of Mr. Whittier's, " My Psalm," was rendered with deep feeling by Mrs. Julia Houston West for whom, several years ago, the verses had been set to music. And to bring to a fitting close these memorial exercises, the assembled company of relatives and friends rose and sang one stanza of of " Auld Lang Syne."

www.ingramcontent.com/pod-product-compliance
Lightning Source LLC
Chambersburg PA
CBHW021722110726
47902CB00005B/1306